Ajay Singh was born in India i̶... of his life. He now resides in Hong Kong where he is a staff writer with *Asiaweek* magazine. He was formerly with the *Associated Press* and the *Asian Wall Street Journal*. He has also been a tea planter and a chicken farmer. This is his first novel.

Give 'Em Hell, Hari

Ajay Singh

Library of Congress Catalog Card Number: 97–069088

A complete catalogue record for this book can be
obtained from the British Library on request

First published in 1998 by Serpent's Tail,
4 Blackstock Mews, London N4
website: www.serpentstail.com

Phototypeset in Plantin by Intype London Ltd.
Printed in Great Britain by Mackays of Chatham

10 9 8 7 6 5 4 3 2 1

To the Speaths, especially Tony, Ritsu, Ryu and Sho

I stop to correct my balance. I tilt my head and find a sky that is cloudless and perfectly blue. A breeze rustles my shirt and then my hair. I push it from my eyes. I lower my gaze to the horizon: an expanse of cultivated land stretching in all directions. The land that is India, with glints of a river winding through. My eyes continue downward to a mass of whitewashed houses, alleys and temples with tapered towers. My hands rise in a pranam. *I nod. And this brings my gaze down another notch. I had nearly forgotten them: a sea of humanity garbed in white and orange, swaying and gesturing and mouthing words in a kind of mass pantomime. They're gesturing at me. What are they saying? And why to me?*

Then I look directly down. Below me is stone, four centuries old and blackened by the elements. It curves away from my shoes.

I don't know why I'm here, all alone, forty feet above the massed crowds. Minutes ago I was of them, or at least with them. Never have I seen so many people. They are separate – I see faces, expressions – but obviously together in spirit. And then comes the sound: the vacuum that has filled my brain clears and I am engulfed in the roar of people with a message.

I crouch forward, palms on my knees. A man in the crowd catches my eye. He is waving a triangular red flag on a pole and, like countless others, wears a saffron headband with the emblazoned words Jai Shri Ram. *Our eyes lock. He gives a frenzied cry and hurls the flag like a javelin. It lands on the stone with a clatter. The crowd cheers. I pick it up. I hoist the flag in the air. A great cheer rises. I wave the flag – wave it in wide arcs with both my hands. The cheering reaches a crescendo. I am brimming with excitement of a kind I can't understand.*

The crowd looks at me expectantly. I poke the flag in the sky and shout: 'Jai Shri Ram.'

The crowd roars: 'Jai Shri Ram.'

I yell 'Jai Shri Ram' *several times and each time the crowds respond with a deafening roar.*

I feel a rush of joy.

Then I see them: a separate group of white-skinned people with cameras and notebooks, wearing fishing vests, dark glasses and hats. I'm surprised I hadn't noticed them before. Memories spin in my head, building, until they threaten to take me over.

There's an Indian in the group – a single non-white person. He waves at me. I hear him shout: 'Hari!'

I lean forward. The crowd noise makes it hard to understand.

'Hari,' he shouts. 'What are you doing up there, Hari?'

Suddenly, looking at those white faces squinting up at me with derision, everything becomes clear. I know why I feel the way I do. I know why I am where I am: on top of a 16th century mosque. I feel a shudder beneath my shoes: the sensation of imminent destruction. And it makes me happy. I lean forward and call: 'I belong here!'

Oh lord, oh lord: it has been such a weird and twisting road that brought me to the top of this dome. Who would think it could have started with a letter written nearly a decade ago? A letter to the editor, yet?

Part One

The Editor
The Times of India

Dear Sir,

I, the humble undersigned, submit to your esteemed newspaper that the current high price of onions in the market is cutting the pocket of the common man.

Since the past two months onion price has sky-rocketed. As everybody is knowing, onions are fundamentally connected to Indian diet and any increase in onion price is adversely affecting well-being of the whole country.

Hitherto, my neighbour's wife was using at least five onions (medium size) for daily cooking. Presently India is having population of 685 million people. Therefore, at the rate of five people per family, about 68 million kilos of onions are being cooked daily in India.

But after the price rise, my neighbour's wife is making do with only one onion daily. Extrapolating this figure to typical Indian family, national onion consumption today is merely 13.7 million kilos per day. This is making the poor and middle-class people feel weak and amenable to illnesses because according to our ancient system of medicine onions are the preventive factor in more than 80 diseases, like tuberculosis, gout and impotence.

Sir, currently another serious problem is plaguing the nation. I am referring to the low price of potatoes.

Last year the Government boosted potato prices to such an extent that all the farmers planted potatoes. Naturally, the prices hit rock bottom. One poor farmer in my village has already committed suicide over the low potato price – and, who knows, high price of onions as well!

I think Central Government should get on war footing immediately.

Please to oblige me with a clipping of this letter, or a full copy of your newspaper, issue date when it appears.

Respectfully yours,

Hari Rana

The Editor
The Times of India

Respected Sir,

In spite of daily perusal of your esteemed newspaper I am not finding my letter dated January 12, 1983 published in it. Perhaps your screening committee is not agreeing with my views. However, it is not for me to reason why!

Sir, a topic that may be more interesting than onion or potato prices is the important subject of WORLD GOVERN-MENT. I hope you will be kind enough to air my views on this matter for urgent publication.

Abraham Lincoln (1809–1865), the President of the United States of America, said long ago: 'The legitimate object of government is to do for a community of people whatever they need to have done, but cannot do at all in their separate and individual capacities.'

Sir, much water has flowed down the Mississippi River since those great words issued forth. In the President Lincoln era, individual governments in many countries worked hard for their respective people's welfare. But they also wasted energy by fighting each other and trying to consolidate their empires. In fact, in those bygone days, the British Empire was so big that the sun never setted there.

Today, in post-President Lincoln era, the whole world is becoming closer. This is the historical background.

President Lincoln correctly said that the job of a government is to do for the people what they are unable to do 'in their separate and individual capacities'. Sir, in today's changed world equation there should be a WORLD GOVERNMENT, which is the only body capable of doing for humanity what various governments can never do in their separate and individual capacities. If President Lincoln was indeed with us today, he would have surely agreed with my humble view.

Sir, needles to say, the modalities will have to be figured, i.e., how the WORLD GOVERNMENT will be run, who will vote it in and where it will be headquartered – a very important factor for employment opportunities in the said lucky country. Beyond that, the whole thing is anybody's guess.

WORLD GOVERNMENT – The Last Hope of Mankind Everywhere.

Most humbly and respectfully yours,
Hari Rana

The Editor
The Times of India

Dear Editor,

Truth is a bitter tablet. Is that why *The Times* has failed to print my missives (Onion and Potato Prices, January 12, 1983; and WORLD GOVERNMENT, January 19, 1983)?

No offence intended here, but how can you say you are the upholder of Free Speech? The motto of your newspaper is 'Let Truth Prevail'. Are stupid advertisements and good-for-nothing speeches of politicians 'Truth'?

The Times has been a family member since before my birth. My father (winner of Sahitya Kala Akademi award) used to proudly proclaim that it is not simply a newspaper but a national institution. However, he was probably referring to pre-independence period, when the British opposed us tooth and nail (and vice-versa) but defended throughout our right to Free Speech.

Today, Free Speech has become a scarce commodity. *The Times* is only diluting its credibility by bending backwards in the face of political thrusting and censoring of bold ideas.

Sir, your refusal to publish my letters has constrained me to change the views I inherited from my father. And with them, my newspaper.

Yours etc.

Hari Rana

The Times of India
Day of Shame

Sir,

The date February 18, 1983 will go down in Indian history as a date of national shame. On that day, our paramilitary troops killed more than 2,000 innocent people in the far-flung village of Nellie in Assam. Yes, 2,000, my fellow countrymen, not 200 as the government has said.

The real story of Nellie is unknown. Practically nobody has survived to tell the tale. When my colleagues in the international press reached the site of the massacre they saw endless rows of blood-soaked bodies – men and women of every age, some of them having tiny babies – lying in fields, on dusty village roads, the highway. There were bodies all around and policemen threatening to shoot any witnesses. And yes, vultures, lots of vultures.

It was a scene that would have certainly broken the heart of our first Prime Minister, Pandit Jawaharlal Nehru. It seems that the incident has not affected in the least his daughter, Indira Gandhi, the iron-fisted tyrant who makes Timur and Nadir Shah look like monks and who ordered the merciless killings.

Why did Nellie meet this cruel fate? Because the people of Assam wanted justice against decades of exploitation by New Delhi. Because Assam wanted to put an end to the rape and plunder of its natural wealth at the hands of the Central Government. Because the Assamese are a minority, and these days nobody cares for minorities, which in Nehru's era were the very essence of India's grand diversity.

Today it is Nellie, tomorrow it could be Punjab, Kerala, Gujarat, or even the Hindi heartland of Uttar Pradesh where the holy rivers Ganga and Jamuna originate. The message behind Nellie is clear: Don't defy the powers that be. But the powers that be forget one thing: Bullets can

kill people but they cannot silence the mind of this great
vibrating nation.
Hari Rana
New Delhi

Hari Rana
Union News International
Claridges Hotel
New Delhi 110 003
February 27, 1983

Mr Jeevan Shinde
President, Indian Letter Writers' Association (Regd.)
A 2/32 Greenfields
Mahakali Caves Road
Andheri East
Bombay 400 094

Dear Mr Shinde,

It was a great honour for me to be the favoured recipient of your kind and encouraging letter dated the 22nd instant, inviting me to join the Indian Letter Writers' Association (Regd.) of which you are the honourable president.

I am very happy to know that you appreciated my letter on the Nellie killings, and that you found it to be the 'most noteworthy of more than three dozen letters' written on the topic and reviewed by your organisation. I agree with your assessment 110 per cent that the Nellie incident is 'unrivalled in the history of Independent India'. Let us hope that this is not the beginning of the end for national unity and diversity.

I am very interested in your organisation, as described in the brochure you kindly enclosed. In my view, 'Letters to the Editor' are not only the pulse of the nation but they give a more true picture of the country than the news pages which are mostly full of boring political speeches. I look forward to someday attending the annual ceremony in which awards are awarded to recipients in such categories as 'Most Promising Letter Writer of The Year' etc.

Regarding my background, I started writing letters to the

editor only a few months back but to no avail for a long time. The Nellie letter was my first publication – truly a red-letter day for me.

I am not a professional journalist as you conjectured. But for the last four years I am working in the Communications Department of Union News International (UNI) bureau in New Delhi. As you might be knowing, UNI is a top American international news agency with world-wide offices.

I am very interested to know from you that I 'appear to be a budding letter writer'. To be very frank, it is the first time I am hearing the word 'budding'. You know, the British are saying 'pudding' and the Americans are saying 'kidding' but until now I never heard 'budding'. According to Oxford Advanced Learner's Dictionary the meaning is 'beginning to develop well'. Indeed, that is a great compliment for me and I thank you sincerely.

I have not got any favourite letter writing topics as such, but I am basically interested in issues related to the welfare of the common man. I am not knowing what is the term for such topics at ILWA but at UNI we are calling such topics 'human interest stories'. I think such stories are very important for development of any country and the moulding of its national character. I admit to being interested at one time in the concept of World Government but recently I have been re-evaluating the notion. I mentioned it to one of my former colleagues at UNI, one Mr Daniel Pressberger, a most jolly and fat man with red hair and grey teeth who was inseparable from his pipe. He said India was the only place where he had heard of such an idea, and Mr Pressberger is a very world-travelled man. He then asked me whether Indians would be running this so-called World Government and he and certain other Americans in the bureau got a good laugh at the idea. Would you be knowing: Is World Government an Indian concept?

I am sure that by joining ILWA I will not only become a better letter writer but also contribute to the daunting task of nation and character building. I hope that through sheer dint of hard work, and some prodding by veteran letter writers like yourself, I will quickly turn from being a 'budding' to a 'bidding' writer: bidding for the 'New Comers' Award for the Best Letter'!

Please find enclosed herewith a bank draft for the sum of Rs 100–00 towards life membership of Indian Letter Writers' Association. I will appreciate it if you could send me by post a copy of the ILWA guidelines for better letter writing at your very earliest. Also, if possible, please advise names of some top letter writers and their favourite publications so that one can anticipate their letters for personal learning and development.

Thanking you in anticipation.

Yours truly,

Hari Rana

Col. Narendra Pai
Lancer's Lodge
P.O. Urulikanchan
Dist. Pune 412 202

Dear Col. Pai,

Sir, thank you indeed for your most kind words of congratulation, dated February 22, 1983 regarding my letter about the Nellie incident. It is indeed honourable to receive a letter from a senior citizen of your high position and stature.

Sir, allow me to introduce my good self. I am a 25 years old man hailing from a modest rural background. My father was a school teacher. He was the eldest son of a marginal farmer who discouraged education in the family. But my father used to run away from home every morning and walk five kilometres to the nearest school. Five km going and five km coming. My grandfather used to say to him: 'Manohar, what is the use of education? It does not increase the yield of wheat.' But my father turned a deaf ear.

After school, my father completed his BA and MA and fortunately got a job as a school teacher in Government Boys Senior Secondary School, Timarpur. From his village, he was the first person to migrate to Delhi. He wanted to give the best education to his younger three brothers and almost all his salary went for their higher education. He was a man of very fine character and high principles. Service Before Self was his motto in life. Today, by God's grace and my father's hard work, all three of my uncles are second class government gazetted officers.

It is solely due to my father that myself and my elder brother are well settled. Both of us received a sound education, although in Hindi medium because our father could not afford the high fees of public schools. But we learned some English in school and moreover, our father also taught us English at home. Every night he would read English books to us for one hour. I read *David Copperfield* and *The Count of Monte Cristo* when I was in class eight only.

My elder brother is a government veterinary surgeon in Haryana. As you know, Haryana is a progressive but also a very corrupt state. He is not like other government doctors in charge of the district hospitals who have to be bribed in order to attend to sick village cattle. Even then they are afraid to treat aggressive buffaloes and cows. On the contrary, my brother never takes bribes and is fearless in his duty. My father was very proud of him.

As for me, my father wanted me to become an engineer. But I was weak in Maths. So while I was doing my B.Sc. (in evening college) I managed to get a job in the technical section of Press Trust of India (PTI). After three years service at PTI I joined Union News International, the world-wide American news agency.

I am in charge of the smooth functioning of office telephones, telex and all the printers connected to the various news wires. It is a 24-hour job and I am at call night and day, like soldiers. The job might become easier when computers, which are expected soon in our bureau, arrive. But who knows? (I wonder if computers are necessary in a country with so much excess manpower.) My job also involves going with the reporters into the 'country' – that is, remote areas devoid of any communication facilities. I type the stories dictated by the reporters and then take them to the nearest town and send them via telex to our bureau in New Delhi. From there the news is sent to the UNI head office in New York. Sometimes the deadline is so tight that we have to file straight to New York. Once the news reaches New York it is transmitted worldwide to more than 1,500 subscribers – mostly newspapers but also various government and UN offices.

Sir, to tell you the honest truth, my ambition in life is to be a writer. I would like to write the stories for UNI, not type them and carry them to the telex office. I feel writing is my role in life. That is why I am being frustrated in my current job and began writing letters to the editor. I believed this would be good journalistic experience for me and good for my use of English also. Also, I thought that after one year, if I was having a portfolio of say 52 letters, that is one per week, on an impressive variety of subjects, showing much sophistication and general knowledge, I could take these letters to the bureau chief, a woman named Ellen Newcomb and, when she is least expecting it, say, 'Sir. I'd like to show you something.' And she would look up at me and say, 'Hari, *well*, I had no idea you could write so wonderfully.' And then I would get out of the communications room – which is the gloomiest and least ventilated room in the bureau, with the exception of the dark-room – and get a reporter's job. Thus my letter writing.

Nonetheless, UNI is very professional unlike our local news agencies that are always committing blunders in both form and content. Often, they are flashing the wrong news. Unfortunately, most Indian organisations are like that – they are lethargic, content with the status quo and don't want to improve even an inch. But they are living in fool's paradise because this is not the 12th century when you can get away with anything.

Sir, you might be agreeing with me that the future of India is doomed unless there is urgent self-analysis on a national scale. Mahatma Gandhi said necessity is the mother of invention. But the question of invention doesn't arise, I say, unless one realises what the necessity is in the first place. Our government is having no sound policies and all the wrong priorities. One of my bosses at UNI used to say, 'The world is passing India by every second – even as I say this.' Whenever he said this, I always wanted to look over my shoulder, half-expecting to see the world passing us by.

Sir, don't you think we have to wake up from our sleep if we want to advance in the world? Years ago, Nehru said that we had a tryst with destiny. Today's leaders are having trysts only with black market racketeers, fixers and most of them with high-class call girls. In the process, the country is going to the dogs.

Sir, you are much older than me and surely knowing the facts of life better. The need of the hour is to discuss, discuss, and self-introspect. That is why I am proud to be a letter writer, helping to push forward this national introspection.

We are all, especially youths, needing the guidance of our elders. I therefore hope and pray that our correspondence will continue to flourish.

Thanking you once again for your graciousness.

Yours truly,

Hari Rana

The Times of India
Amazing Feats

Sir:

Last month, one Mr P. Dorairaj, a lawyer known for his spearheading of the rights of exploited rubber planters in Tamil Nadu, sprang a surprise on the whole world when he entered the hollowed pages of the Guinness Book of World Records by giving the longest after-dinner speech in the history of humanity.

The speech which took place in Madurai and lasted 40 hours (non-stop without water), is unique in the oratorical anals of the 20th century and a welcome sign that Indians are finally rubbing shoulders with foreigners in the art of holding forth. The amazing feat of Mr Dorairaj is an outstanding example for all those in India and abroad still suffering from blinkered eyesight and colonial hangover.

Mr Dorairaj defeated the previous record holder – one Reverend Henry Whitehead, who in a tavern in London in 1874 spoke for only three hours and probably on subject of God. Mr Whitehead's victims were unsuspecting, according to the Guinness Book, and were possibly forced to lend their ears as was often done by the clergy in those days. Also, it may be that the whole group was under the influence of alcohols, given the venue. That was undoubtedly not the case in Mr Dorairaj's case.

With this achievement, Mr Dorairaj has willy-nilly jumped on to the bandwagon of such luminaries as:

– Swami Vivekananda who in late 19th century held forth fearlessly to the World Congress of Religions in Chicago on the concept of zero for fully 24 hours.

– Krishna Menon, our erstwhile foreign spokesman whose bombastic verbal punches made life hell for everybody at the United Nations, except himself, of course.

– Jawaharlal Nehru, whose every speech on national unity

and communal virus was like a long burst of machine-gun fire.

India is urgently needing exactly such voices as Mr Dorairaj to be heard in the current day's highly competitive and cut-throat international sphere.

Hari Rana
New Delhi

The Times of India
Abused Servants

Sir:

Every second day one is reading in the newspapers about the spate of murders and robberies committed by domestic servants. But the newspapers are not giving the full picture why these murders are taking place.

I first became interested in the topic of servants when I met Bhawani, a young servant from Garhwal Hills who worked near my office. Bhawani had a very good nature and he was full of respect for others. That is why I was shocked when he asked me one day if I thought he was mad. I said, of course not. He told me that his mistress, a high society lady, always told him that he was mad, regardless of his good work. 'At first I didn't believe her,' said Bhawani. 'But after two years of hearing it every day, I do.' Bhawani finally quit after five years. I ran into him recently and found a totally different person: bitter, cynical and full of contempt for the upper classes. A good soul was destroyed.

According to mental health experts, when a servant kills his employer it is usually because he is treated badly or humiliated. In one recent case, police found a murdered couple in their bedroom. It transpired that the couple was done to death by their servant because they refused to pay him his salary for more than one year. Even the police opined that the couple had asked for it.

Another case: A single man hired a servant and started calling him 'asshole' instead of his real name, which was Gandharva. The servant – a simple young man from East U.P. – took offence, but his employer persisted. He would call the servant to the dining table in front of guests and ask him his name, forcing the helpless servant to say, 'Asshole'. The guests would get a good laugh at the poor fellow's expense. All this went on for several months. One day, after much wining and dining, the employer was found slumped in his chair at the dinner table. He had been poisoned by the servant.

Servants have a sense of dignity and self respect. It is as simple as that.

Hari Rana
New Delhi

The Times of India
Dog Menace

Dear Sir:

The other day, a tragic incident occurred in my colony. My neighbour, Mr Nanda, an elderly chartered accountant of repute, was returning home from his office and was just about to walk up to his first-floor apartment when a big dog hiding under the stairs jumped up at his throat all of a sudden. Mr Nanda had an aversion to dogs, never having kept one of the canines as a pet. As a result, when the dog leaped up at him, Mr Nanda suffered a heart failure and died on the spot.

Later on, it was discovered that the dog was a street dog who had taken refuge under the stairs because of the hot weather outside. Normally street dogs are not aggressive by nature, but exceptions are always there. Unfortunately, Mr Nanda was the victim of such an exception.

After this tragic incident, various suggestions were mooted by our community members on the street-dog problem. Some people proposed that all street dogs should be shot down, but others objected to it because of the noise factor and also because the bullets might hit innocent people, especially if the police is given the job. Some people suggested poisoning, but objections were raised that it is too cruel. Mr Nanda's widow said that dogs should have their teeth pulled, rendering them harmless and unthreatening to potential victims like her late husband. The meeting ended minus a consensus.

The issue is a burning one and deserves more attention than it is currently getting in the press. Do readers have suggestions?

Hari Rana
New Delhi

The Times of India
Inspirational Reading

Sir:

Close on the heels of Mr P. Dorairaj's entry into the Guinness Book of World Records for the longest after-dinner speech comes this gem: another Indian, incidentally also from Tamil Nadu, has broken the Guinness record for non-stop clapping.

Mr V. Jeyaraman clapped continuously for a total of 58 hours and nine minutes, according to the Guinness Book of World Records.

The Guinness Book of World Records is must reading for all Indians because it sharpens one's educational, recreational and motivational faculties. The spiritually inclined can pursue records of religious nature, like non-stop hymn singing, etc. As the book is dear by Indian standards, I request the government to provide copies of the book to public libraries in every state. Alternatively, and since many Indians grace its pages, perhaps the Guinness office in London will be kind enough to provide the said copies.

Hari Rana
New Delhi

The Times of India
Bigger Menace: Rats or Dogs?

Sir:

This is in reply to the letter of Mr Naresh Rattanani regarding the rat menace in Bombay. Mr Rattanani finds it ridiculous that some people are complaining about street dogs in Delhi when the entire Bombay is being infested with giant rats that are scaring away even the dogs and cats.

No doubt Mr Rattanani is having a point that rats are scrambling all over the metropolis and scaring the citizens, especially in the night. But nobody has heard of rats causing heart failure. Just because a particular animal species is predominant in a city does not mean that it is more important than other man-animal issues. For example, what about cockroaches? These creeping, crawling creatures are everywhere, including five-star hotels and NASA space shuttles. The important question is not how many animals there are in a given area, but how many heart beats we are missing when we see them!

Rats and cockroaches will always be there whether we like it or not. But something can be done about street dogs. So far, veterinary doctors and municipal authorities are divided on the issue of how to handle street dogs in Delhi. Meanwhile, the family of Mr Nanda, cut down in his prime by a street dog and other dog-fearing citizens of this city are eagerly awaiting a suitable solution to the problem. Keep writing with your suggestions.

Hari Rana
New Delhi

The Times of India
Indians Make Guinness

Sir:

Not many people can walk for ten steps with a milk bottle on their heads. So when a young man walks 65 kilometres – that is 40 miles! – with a full pint milk bottle on his bare head, what does it mean?

Some people will say that he has a loose screw in his skull. Others will worry about the returnable milk bottle. Not many will appreciate the ambition and the guts and the determination that goes into the act, not to speak of the body balance and co-ordination. Such people, needless to say, will never be in the exalted position to break an international Guinness record!

Mr Milind Deshmukh, from Pune, is a hero not so much because long-distance milk-bottle balancing got him into Guinness Book of World Records, but because the very future of India depends on people like him. The fact is that these people throw caution to the winds and embrace life with a sense of ambition and purpose. They refuse to follow their lazy peers who drink endless cups of tea, smoke cigarettes and gossip all day long. (Excepting, of course, Mr Dhananjay Kulkarni, also of Pune, who is challenging the records for both tea drinking – 91 cups in one minute – and simultaneous smoking of 35 ciga-rettes, non-filter Charminars no less.)

India already finds extensive mention in the Guinness book. We have the world's lengthiest railway platform, the highest petrol station, the tree with the largest canopy and the world's oldest prime minister (81 years old when sworn in), who is still going strong thanks to wonders of auto-urine therapy. Mr Morarji Desai: not one Indian leader has impressed the world like you have.

We need to concentrate on the human achievement records like backward running, longest sitting on flag-poles, rolling up temple steps, longest hair, longest fingernails and even the longest marriage, all of which India already holds. This will show the world that India is not a country to be ignored. It's a country of grit, nails, hair and determination.

Hari Rana
New Delhi

Col. Narendra Pai
Lancer's Lodge
P.O. Urulikanchan
Dist. Pune 412 202

Dear Col. Pai,
Strange are the ways of fate. Ever since our correspondence
began I have been nurturing a desire to own a typewriter so
that I can write to you neatly in my spare time at home. Well,
Sir, the other day my wish came true. There was an old Corona
lying unused for so many years at the office, and our bureau
chief finally decided to sell it off to members of the staff. It
was very cheap – 300 rupees only – and everybody wanted it,
in particular the senior reporter, a highly arrogant and selfish
man from Bengal. So a lottery was held. I won it, much to
the chagrin of my Bengali friend. He didn't talk to me for
several days or even look in my direction. Of course, his
behaviour changed when he had some important work which
needed my help.

Now you won't have to read all those long letters in my
untidy handwriting. The typewriter will also help me in
becoming a more productive writer. I can type my letters to
the editor as well as articles and short stories for publication.

(Steady progress on the Guinness front. I have to date
published 63 letters. I have also communicated with Guinness
telling them of my intention. No response as of yet!)

The assassination of Mrs Gandhi by her own Sikh bodyguards was a big shock, although I have to say that she had
put her head on a platter the moment she sent the army to
storm the Golden Temple. When you play with fire you get
burned. Besides, who has come out unscathed in a fight with
the Sikhs? Not the British, not the Mughals before them, and
certainly not Mrs G.

I can understand the circumstances of her death. But

what I can't understand are the revenge killings of some 20,000 innocent Sikhs, aided and abetted by Mrs Gandhi's Congress Party. It was the most savage and revolting behaviour I have ever seen in my life.

Indeed, the killings of Sikhs makes me want to disown India and run away to some other country. But where can a poor Indian go? He is unwanted everywhere, and not for the wrong reasons either – cunning, deceit, dishonesty have become universal Indian trademarks. The Indian ship has been leaking for a long time and the leaks have started giving way to gaping holes. How long will it be before the ship founders and sinks is anyone's guess.

As it happens, I was a witness to the first victim of the nation-wide massacre of Sikhs. It happened just outside the All India Institute of Medical Sciences, where Mrs Gandhi was taken for treatment. (She was dead before she reached there – who could survive twenty bullets?) It was around five in the evening and I was returning home early that day. A crowd had collected outside the hospital. Suddenly, a mob of about fifty people marched from its gates, shouting slogans in praise of Mrs Gandhi. They spotted a Sikh motorcyclist stopped for a red light. The mob surrounded the Sikh. Someone unscrewed the cap of his gas tank. Another man yanked off his turban. They dipped the turban in the gas tank – all five yards of it – and draped it, soaked with petrol, around the helpless fellow's body. He pleaded with folded hands: 'Please, why are you killing me? What have I done?' Somebody shouted back, 'You killed our leader!' The mob screamed: 'Kill the bastard.' A traffic policeman stood nearby, watching the scene; in the hospital, barely twenty metres away, scores of armed policemen stood on guard. None came to the Sikh's rescue. Then somebody struck a match-stick and lit the cloth.

He burned to death without uttering a sound. I found myself trembling, unable to move. I was angry, but I suppose my anger was born out of cowardice, for I had done nothing to try and stop the mob from murdering the Sikh. When I recovered from my paralysis the mob had moved on. The murdered Sikh's body lay in the middle of the road, wrapped in sputtering flames. Nobody went near it. I ran to the cops at the hospital gate and asked them to do something. But they just shrugged. One of them said flatly: 'The Sikhs will have to bear the brunt of their mistake.'

I will never forget this incident, Col. Pai, as long as I live.

An incident also occurred at our bureau causing tremendous turmoil and turbulence, uncannily timed to coincide with the tragedy of the nation. It has made me wonder if the fates of individuals and nations are sometimes connected. It all began last Tuesday, when I arrived at the bureau to get the communications equipment ready for the day ahead. I was the second person to arrive: our bureau chief, Ellen, a stern middle-aged American divorcee, had already come in. I could see, from the newsroom, the light shining under her office door.

I went to the communications room, turned on the lights and arranged my desk. Then I went to the newsroom to change the ribbons in the teleprinters: the first job of the day. On the newsroom bulletin board was a message that immediately caught my attention. It was from New York.

RE OVERNITER ON RALLY FILED AT 1532 GMT:

PLS ADVISE WHAT IS FIRST WAR OF INDEPEN-DENCE. DONT RECALL SEEING TERM IN PAST STORIES.

DO U MEAN INDEPENDENCE FROM BRITAIN? DIDN'T THAT HAPPEN IN 1947 STED 1857?

THANKS AND REGARDS, BRUBECK, NY INTL DESK.

The words 'first war of independence' were underlined in

green, Ellen's favourite colour. Beneath the message, in her minuscule handwriting, was a single word: *Correction?*

A little bit about the UNI bureau. It is located in a row of connected suites in the Claridges Hotel, a somewhat dilapidated colonial-style building located in one of the poshest neighbourhoods of New Delhi. The bureau is on the second floor. To get to it, you have to walk through a winding corridor with musty carpets and doors with large brass knobs. The inside of the hotel is maze-like and our bureau is far from the lift or stairs. Finding it can be difficult. Often, we hear visitors shouting, 'UNI, UNI, are you there?'

I was still changing the ribbons when the Bengali walked in. He is the senior-most correspondent, a bulky, bespectacled man of 42 with a head of shaggy, prematurely white hair and a drooping white moustache. He has the biggest bags I've ever seen under a pair of human eyes – so big they're almost suitcases. Perched on the bags like little huts on mountain peaks are the Bengali's most irredeemable feature: a pair of glinting, cobra-like eyes.

The Bengali is a Brahmin and casteist to the core. He is forever bragging about his superior background. He was born and raised in Calcutta and remains happiest when his feet touch its pavement and his nostrils breathe the fetid Calcutta air. He claims to have descended from a family of poets, theatre actors and freedom fighters. His father was a publisher of Bengali and Oriya literature, and according to the Bengali, was a 'widely travelled' man, which meant that he had been to every district of Bengal, Orissa and Bihar at least six times and perhaps to England once. There was a story of his said visit to England, which the Bengali never tired of retelling. When he went to the British Deputy High Commission in Calcutta to get his visa, an official asked him to furnish proof of his financial status. 'My father was furious,' the Bengali related. 'He pointed to the *dhoti* he was wearing and said to the official: "This cloth is six yards long, but I can cover your whole country with it." ' The meaning of this reply was lost on us in the bureau, I have to admit. But the Bengali claimed the Britisher was so impressed by his father's answer that he immediately granted the visa and invited him to tea the following weekend.

On that fateful morning, the Bengali said 'Hi' without looking at me – as he always did – and shuffled towards his desk in a corner of the newsroom. He dumped his dirty leather sling bag on the floor, took off his ancient leather jacket, and began to unwrap a soot-smelling, soot-coloured and soot-stained muffler that he wore around his neck for the long scooter ride to the office.

After shedding these ten kilos of clothing, the Bloody Brahmin turned to me, squinted through his smudged spectacles and said in his booming voice: 'And *so*?' He always said that when he came into the bureau. That's all: 'And *so*?' Most newsmen ask a question when they enter a newsroom: 'Anything happening?' 'Anything going on?' 'Everything under control?' Only the Bengali says, 'And *so*?'

Then he turned away, expecting me to have no news of value. I said: 'Dada.' He turned. 'There's a message from New York.' I pointed to the bulletin board. He scowled and said 'New York!' as if it was the most preposterous city in the world. He marched to the kitchen. I heard him say ' . . . tea.' (The Bengali never did any work without tea.) I shrugged – let him lose five precious minutes.

He shuffled back from the kitchen with a glass of hot water with a tea bag in it. He pulled a clipboard from above the teleprinters and read the night log – the record of news stories written by the reporter on duty the night before.

'Kumar didn't do the Dalai Lama's speech. Ha! I don't know what's happening to this bureau. Ever since *she* came.' He gestured at the bureau chief's door.

Then the Bengali turned to the bulletin board, his hands in the pockets of his grease-stained trousers and his feet two feet apart. He scanned the old notices pinned to the board. Finally, he spotted the message from New York. He tilted his head a little sideways and stared hard. It was his custom to read every message at least five times – twice to understand the subject, twice to mentally formulate his reply, and once to see if the message said anything insulting about India or the Indian staff at UNI.

For, Col. Pai, the Bloody Bengali is a scoundrel in the way most self-styled patriots are: he professes undying love for his country largely to stir up trouble. In the Bengali's case, he thinks that he can remain top dog in the bureau as long as everyone else is fighting or licking their wounds. He takes every opportunity to point out the failure of patriotism in other Indian staffers, especially when they write stories critical of the Indian government. His special ploy is to drive a wedge between the Indian correspondents and the American staff. When an Indian correspondent gets chummy with a white colleague, the Bengali quickly spreads the word that he is 'licking the foreigner's arse'. (When the Bengali himself humours the bureau chief or news editor he has a quick defence: 'You idiot,' he says. 'I was making a fool of the Whiteman.')

As a result, the Bengali is the undisputed leader of the Indian staff. His name is Ashit Chatterjee but in his presence everybody (except the office peon) calls him Dada, or elder brother. Dada is appropriate: he is exactly like a bullying elder brother.

The Bengali was breathing heavily. His face had turned red and his eyes were narrow slits. These were signs – to use the Bengali's own words – that his 'mercury was climbing'. After what seemed like an eternity, he turned around. He walked to his corner and sat. He finished his tea in a large gulp. Then he leaned back in his chair and stared at the blank wall in front of his desk, lips moving silently.

When Arun arrived the Bengali was still looking at the wall. Arun read the night log and then strolled to the bulletin board. The Bengali swivelled slightly in his chair. Arun started stroking the tips of his thin moustache while biting his lower lip – a habit that signalled his insecurity. At 27, Arun is the youngest of the three Indian correspondents. But unlike the Bengali Brahmin, Arun is the son of a low-caste *tabla* player from Nagpur – a fact that the Bengali brings up frequently, causing great shame and embarrassment to Arun.

Arun strode nervously to his desk and immersed himself in a newspaper. He sat in an opposite corner from the Bengali's. The two had positioned their desks so that they worked with their backs to each other, although they had different reasons for doing so. The Bengali faced the wall strictly to avoid the sight of a white person's face, which he said he couldn't tolerate without warning. Skittish Arun, on the other hand, didn't want to be surprised by any human face of any skin colour.

The last reporter to come in was Gopalacharya, whose arrival is normally signalled by a series of painful coughs from the hotel corridor. On most days, this sound of lethal choking elicits some joke in the newsroom. But there was no comment on that day. When Gopalacharya entered, a filterless cigarette burning in his hand, the Bengali was still staring at the wall like a monkey meditating. Arun was flipping through the newspaper, biting his lips and fingering his moustache.

Gopalacharya laid his metallic briefcase on his desk, which was in the newsroom's third corner. Gopalacharya didn't face the wall while working. He was positioned so that he could see the entire newsroom and, in particular, the door to Ellen's office, which was in Gopalacharya's direct line of vision.

Gopalacharya sauntered to the bulletin board, puffing hard at his cigarette and producing a loud hiss. (He never touched the cigarette to his lips: he held it upright with the knuckles of his first two fingers; then he made a tight fist and inhaled deeply by sucking at the space between his thumb and first finger.) He ran a finger over the bulletin board and made a low whistling sound every time he encountered an old message. When his finger came to the message from New York, the whistle died away. His eyes bulged like a toad's and his middle-aged, overweight frame rocked slightly back and forth. He took a couple of quick, short drags from his cigarette and darted to his desk. He reached into one of the book shelves and yanked out an Encyclopaedia Britannica. He flopped into his chair, lit a fresh cigarette and frantically leafed through the encyclopaedia.

I knew from past incidents that such a silence in the newsroom was a lull before a mighty storm. The Bloody Bengali was plotting big shenanigans – tilting his huge head at odd angles as he stared at the wall – and feverishly imagining the various ways he could use the message on the bulletin board to wreak havoc. Arun was quiet, hiding behind the newspaper, because he had spotted trouble on the horizon and was terrified he'd be a part of it. Gopalacharya was riffling through encyclopaedias and, at one point, had two cigarettes burning simultaneously – because Gopalacharya had written the story that prompted the message from New York.

Suddenly, the Bengali leaned forward in his chair and fed a piece of paper into his typewriter. He began typing furiously.

At the stroke of 10, the door opened to admit P.K. Gupta, the bureau accountant. P.K. was a rotund, balding man who loved his drinks and was never short of a laugh. The saying in the office was that P.K. Gupta didn't have a vindictive bone in his body. (Or any other bone, according to the Bengali, including a backbone.) P.K. greeted me with a jolly giggle and went to his cubicle where he turned on a transistor radio – P.K. was a radio fiend – and listened to the 10 o'clock news from All India Radio. 'I must have been a radio journalist in my last birth,' he often said. After P.K. came Matthew, my subordinate in the communications department. He immediately went to the communications room where, I knew, he would take his seat by the telex machine and wait for work, hands in his lap, which was Matthew's characteristically passive pose.

The Bengali ripped the sheet of paper out of the typewriter, crumpled it up and tossed it into the wastepaper basket. He was feeding a second sheet into his typewriter when Sam Scott, the bureau's Number Two, appeared in the doorway wearing a baseball cap. Sam was a tall, mustachioed man and a bit of a blunderhead. We called him Daanav, which means, literally, monster.

'Morning all.' He waved his hand. There was no response.

'How's it going?' More silence. The reporters seldom returned Sam's greetings, which clearly troubled Sam. In fact, virtually everything troubled Sam. Before he came to India, Sam had suffered a depressive reaction – a psychological disorder in which the patient becomes melancholy and loses touch with reality, especially with regard to his circumstances. (We looked it up one evening in the bureau's well-thumbed Collier's.) Ever since his illness, Sam had been on drugs, which dulled his senses and slowed his thinking. (This we heard from the UNI doctor.) His memory for names and places was obviously affected. With the exception of the prime minister, Sam couldn't remember the name of a single prominent Indian. He couldn't even get the names of the bureau staff right after two years. He had tried, as I discovered one day when looking for something in his desk. In the top drawer, he had pasted a piece of paper with this written on it:

News Room:

Ashit – Specs, bushy mustache, sloppy eater
Gopalacharya – Smoker, flat ass
Arun – Worried
Prasana Pratap Kumar – Night shift

Dark Room:

Salim Khan – Good looking, fishing vest

Communications:

Hari Rana – Talker
Matthew – Guy at telex machine

General Staff:

P.K. Gupta, Accounts – Giggle
Bhoop Singh, Driver – Pronounce as 'Ba-hoop'
Omi Chand, Peon – Big ears, dandruff. Constantly serving tea

I made a quick, surreptitious Xerox of Sam's list and passed it around the newsroom. Gopalacharya smoothed the seat of his pants and coughed with embarrassment. P.K. giggled. When the Bengali read it, he was livid. 'What do these fucking *goras* know about table manners? You don't need manners to eat hamburgers.'

Sam sat at his desk, which was midway between the Bengali's corner and Arun's hideout. 'Man, oh man,' he muttered. Sam usually said that when he was exasperated about something and he almost always said it on Monday mornings. He pawed through heaps of paper scattered on his desk like a scavenger rummaging through garbage. He moaned: 'Man, oh maaan, oh *maaaan!*' This expression usually signified that Sam had lost something, or was tired, or had forgotten to eat a meal or two. 'Where's that number?' He frequently lost telephone numbers. He scribbled them on pieces of paper; then the pieces of paper joined the other millions of papers on his desk, which was never tidied. 'Oh *man*,' he said in a concluding tone. He abandoned the search and cradled the side of his head against the palm of his hand.

The Bengali continued hammering at his typewriter, pausing every once in a while to study his invisible war map on the wall, or to consult the dictionary. (His spelling was notoriously weak.) Arun's face was still hidden behind the newspaper. Gopalacharya was flipping through what must have been his sixteenth reference book in a frantic search for an answer to the message from New York. All this while, the door to Ellen's office remained shut. The only sign that she was inside were muted, short rings of her private telephone line.

I finished my work and, gathering the used ribbons, started to leave the newsroom. The Bengali suddenly stood up with a violent push of his chair and barked: 'Arun, Gopalacharya, *idhar aana*.' Arun and Gopalacharya jumped to their feet and trotted behind the Bengali to the kitchen, a small room adjacent to the newsroom and directly opposite the entrance to the bureau. Omi Chand, the office peon, stiffened to attention. It was a habit from his days in the army. The Bengali gave a perfunctory nod, ushered the others into the kitchen and shut the door.

'Morning *sa'hb*,' said Omi Chand.

'Good morning, Omi Chand,' I said.

'What is happening, Rana *Sa'hb*?' He pointed to the closed kitchen door.

'It's a very exciting morning, Omi Chand. Very exciting, indeed.'

'Something happening with the white *sa'hbs*, Rana *Sa'hb*?'

'Yes Omi Chand. Exactly.'

Omi Chand's story was a poignant one. Like many villagers, young Omi Chand had found the lure of the Indian army irresistible. He grew up in the deserts of Rajasthan with dreams of firing rifles and cannons for his country. With his angular, six-foot frame – not to mention his proud Rajasthan moustache and flinty desert eyes – he had no trouble being accepted by the army and joined the highly decorated Kumaon infantry regiment. Omi Chand had long nursed a desire to own a gun; guns were considered objects of valour and pride in Rajasthan. His wish soon came true. He was allowed to buy a shotgun from the army at a subsidised price. And every year, when he went home on two months leave, he proudly took the shotgun with him.

One night, while he was on vacation in his village, there was a robbery. A group of armed men broke into the house of the village money-lender. Omi Chand challenged the robbers with his shotgun. There was a shoot-out. Omi Chand killed two robbers.

The next day he was arrested for murder. It turned out the robbers were part of a big state-wide gang that was well connected with the police. The police testified in court that the robbers were friends of the money-lender, not burglars. The money-lender was pressured to say the same thing. Omi Chand was convicted, discharged from the army, tried and sentenced to ten years in prison. He was the only son of old parents. When his prison term ended, Omi Chand went to his village and found his parents near starvation. Their land had been repossessed – by the same money-lender their son had tried to defend.

Omi Chand's only possession was his military uniform. He went to the nearest town and put his uniform on auction in the town square. There were no takers on the first day of the auction. But the matter was reported in the local newspapers and the next day a big crowd gathered. Omi Chand's uniform sold for two thousand rupees, which was enough money for the family until he found a job. But Omi Chand was never the same man again.

I mention Omi Chand, Col. Pai, because as a former army officer I thought you might find it interesting how some soldiers do indeed fade away. Did you know anyone in the army who met with a similar fate? It is sad to see a good man's life being shattered because of our corrupt and callous system. But now I must get on with my story.

The door to the kitchen suddenly flew open. The Bengali stuck his head out.

'Hari,' he barked.

'Yes Dada.'

'Call everyone here. To the kitchen.'

'The kitchen?'

He nodded. 'Everyone, Hari, except them.'

In other words, all the Indians. I thought to myself: The crusty cauldron of office politics has been put on the fire and

soon the brew will indeed be boiling. But I knew the Bloody
Bengali couldn't stir it alone – not for long anyway. He needed
our support. Too many cooks, in this case, would only make
the broth more fiery.

Soon we were all gathered in the kitchen. P.K. had been
rubbing his hands in the hallway in eager expectation, but his
smile faded when he saw the scene before him. The Bengali
was standing in the centre of the room, legs wide apart, hands
on his hips, looking like an Indian version of John Wayne. (If
you can imagine John Wayne in chappals.) Instead of a gun
he wielded a pencil, which he held in the air like an angry
primary school teacher. Gopalacharya was standing on the
Bengali's right, his flat buttocks pressed against the wall. A
cigarette protruded from the knuckles of his clenched fist and
he sucked at it like a baby. Arun was bent over the kitchen
counter scribbling on a sheet of copy paper with a red pen.
The Bengali cleared his throat.

'Brothers, something very important has come up.' He eyed
everybody carefully, looking for signs of enthusiasm. Except
for Omi Chand, who stood at attention in the doorway, nobody
met the Bengali's gaze. 'The matter is important not only on
a professional level, but also for our children, our society and
the future of the country . . .'

The Bengali was a superb angler. His bait always came with
plenty of hooks – some sharp, some blunt – but no matter
which hook you bit, you bloodied yourself. I looked around:
everyone's mouth was tightly shut.

'You all have seen the message from New York on the
bulletin board this morning.' He pointed towards Gopalacharya. 'Yesterday Gopalacharya wrote a story. In it, he
mentioned our First War of Independence.'

Omi Chand took a step forward, eyes shining.

'You all know about the First War of Independence. It was
in 1857. We fought against the British. Many sacrifices were
made by our freedom fighters, especially those from the Delhi-
Agra-Aligarh-Meerut belt of North India plus, of course,

Lucknow. My forefathers were in undivided Bengal at that time so they could not be directly involved in the war, although they lent it intellectual support – in the true Bengali tradition. I am sure that *your* ancestors played honourable roles too.' He looked at Omi Chand and me.

Omi Chand started to say something but was cut short by the Bengali.

'New York is telling us that the First War of Independence is a figment of our imagination! They say it was not a war but a mutiny!'

Gopalacharya interrupted. 'No, Dada, they are not saying that. They're only asking what the First War of Independence was.'

'Ha!' roared the Bengali. 'The whole world knows what the First War of Independence was – except *New York*? Grow up, Gopalacharya. It is understood that when New York questions the term "First War of Independence", New York is telling us to use the colonial termology.'

'Terminology,' said Gopalacharya.

'Whatever! We are not Englishmen and it is not our language.'

'What *is* the colonial terminology?' asked Arun.

The Bengali shot back: 'The British historians call it the Sepoy Mutiny or the Indian Mutiny. But our historians reject both the terms. After all, what is meant by sepoy? It means *sipahi* in Hindi – a good for nothing idiot soldier who doesn't know his arse from his face. We are still having them in India, thanks to the bloody British.'

Omi Chand took a kind of stagger backwards.

I interrupted: 'Maybe Indian Mutiny is UNI style, Dada.' I had been studying the UNI stylebook, in case I might be called on to help the reporters on a story.

'I'm glad you brought that up, Hari. Since you joined UNI, you have been burying your head in the Whiteman's arse too much. No wonder you can't hear the *gora* saying insulting things about Indians. When the Whiteman's god created the universe – they say it took him seven days, ha! what a slow god – he made the *gora* the master of the world and the Indian its permanent sweeper.'

Omi Chand, whose duties included sweeping the bureau, now took a step forward. His face was dark with anger. The Bengali quickly changed the topic. 'You all must have seen the movie, *Junoon*?'

P.K. nodded vigorously.

'It was based on the 1857 war. A classic. Now suppose I change the title of *Junoon* to say, *Choti si Baat. A small matter.* How would you feel?'

'It's a wicked thing to do,' said P.K., rotating a finger in the air. 'Whoever does it should be punished.'

'Exactly!' The Bengali pivoted in a semi-circle and looked at everyone assembled. 'Whoever does it should be punished. Now suppose that "whoever" is New York. Suppose New York asks you – he switched to a falsetto – "But what do you meeeen by *Junoon*? What is first war of indeepennn-dennce?" ' His eyes narrowed and hatred showed on his face. He bellowed: 'Will not your Indian blood boil?'

Normally, a shout from the Bengali was loud enough to jolt the deaf. I pried open the kitchen door and, scurrying through the hallway, peeped into the newsroom. Ellen's door was still shut. Sam, who had a voice as loud as the Bengali's, was talking over the telephone and hadn't heard a thing.

'Now,' continued the Bengali, 'I will read out a letter I have written to Ellen. After I have finished, I want you all to sign it so that we can hand it over to her without wasting any further time. Arun? Are you finished?'

'I changed some spellings.' Arun timidly handed him the paper. It was criss-crossed with corrections in red ink. Half the lines had been struck out.

The Bengali's eyes bulged. 'Spellings?'

'I made it a bit more diplomatic.' Arun shuffled his feet.

The Bengali scanned the sheet. 'You crossed out the demand that our salaries be paid in dollars. And that we get free trips to New York, with foreign exchange allowances. I think now is the best time to remind the old bitch about those promises.'

Arun said, 'The language was very harsh, Dada.'

'Besides they are long-standing demands,' said Gopalacharya. 'They don't have to be mentioned in this letter.'

'Have you been called to New York recently, Gopalacharya?'

'Well, no.'

'Are you getting paid in greenbacks, Arun?'

Arun hung his head.

'Well,' said the Bengali, 'I believe in striking when the iron is hot. Anyway.' He tautened the paper. 'Here it is.'

Dear Ellen:

When rag-tags of the East India Company fought Bengali soldiers in 1757, Western historians called it the Battle of Plassey. Exactly a hundred years later, when another group of Indian soldiers fought the East India Company, Western historians called it the Indian Mutiny, or Sepoy Mutiny.

Evident here is a double standard. The first historical episode is called a 'battle'; the second a 'mutiny'. This also is the issue at the heart of the message received from New York last night, which you have pinned to the bulletin board with a demand for a correction.

The question is: correction employing what criteria? We realise that as a news agency UNI is more Western than Indian in character. Nevertheless, in the interest of fairness and accuracy – not to mention cultural sensitivity – it is our suggestion that we should consider both the Western and Indian perspectives on matters pertaining to historical events. In other words, have a debate on the issue.

Yours sincerely,

Ashit Chatterjee

Bala Gopalacharya

Arun Sahu

Supported by:
P.K. Gupta
Hari Rana
Matthew Kalarkal
Salim Khan

With:
Omi Chand, Witness.

The Bengali shot a glance at Arun. 'What's this business about a debate?'

'I thought it was a nice way to conclude,' replied Arun.

'What about *my* ending?'

'Dada, we can't really ask her to pack her bags and leave.'

'There's a freeze on relocations,' said P.K. 'Company-wide.'

'Anyway, I hope everybody is satisfied with the letter, although the language is too weak to have any impact on the *budiya*. She will get a good laugh, I tell you. My father used to say, "If you want to rip someone's arse you have to strike full force, not softly." It's also more fun that way.' The Bengali smoothed the letter on the counter top and prepared to affix his signature.

'I think we should discuss the issue in greater depth,' said Gopalacharya, extinguishing his cigarette.

'Before we sign,' said Arun.

'It will prepare us in case Ellen invites us to a debate,' said Gopalacharya.

'Fine,' said the Bengali, straightening. He clicked his ball point pen and placed it in his shirt pocket. 'If that's how you want to handle it.' He strode to the kitchen door and wheeled around. 'But remember one thing, gentlemen. You're dealing with a bitch with a dry cunt who hasn't been fucked for three years. She gets sexual satisfaction out of arguing with men. The more you argue, the more she will get aroused. And then someone will have to make her come.' He walked out, leaving the door ajar. P.K. broke out into a cackle, like a child who had heard his first dirty joke.

You had to give it to the Bengali. He started a war and then by hook or crook, by cajoling or joking, he got everybody involved in it. We could hear the rat-a-tat of his typewriter.

'Let's get out of this stinking kitchen,' said Gopalacharya.

We moved to the communications room. Matthew brought in extra chairs and Omi Chand provided tea. Everyone was waiting for Gopalacharya to speak. He was a history major and enjoyed a reputation for being a balanced journalist. After taking a few meditative sucks on his cigarette, he stood and addressed us with the air of a college professor.

'Friends, this whole problem began with my story. Frankly, I wish I hadn't used the term "First War of Independence". After all, you can call a rose by any name, but it still remains a rose.'

Omi Chand looked at me confusedly.

'However, as we all know, matters have a way of getting out of hand here. And whether we like it or not, we are stuck with another cowboys-versus-Indians situation, thanks to our freedom fighter from Bengal.'

Gopalacharya leaned against the telex machine. 'The issue is tricky. Was the battle of 1857 a spontaneous, short-lived outburst of violence limited to a small region – in other words, a mutiny – or was it an expression of some larger nationalistic impulse?'

Arun scratched his head. 'Can I say something?' Everyone looked at him. 'I don't want to take sides, of course, but I do think 1857 was an outburst of national fervour against British policies.' He turned to Gopalacharya. 'Isn't it correct that the British tried to convert Indians, including the so-called mutinous sepoys?'

Matthew, who was the only Christian in the bureau, shifted nervously in his chair.

Gopalacharya thought for a moment. 'Yes, the servants of the East India Company tried to disrupt the religious loyalties of Indian soldiers. British army officers carried the order book in one hand and the bible in the other, according to a renowned British historian.'

Matthew turned away from Gopalacharya.

'But,' he continued, 'the attempts at conversion weren't the only contributing factor in the battle of 1857. The British pursued a policy of annexation, which annoyed Indian princes and the landed gentry. They destroyed local commerce and industry to make way for British goods, which robbed millions of their jobs. They introduced unpopular changes in land revenue.' Gopalacharya extricated his hand from his trouser pocket. 'Many historians, including foreign ones, agree that prior to the battle of 1857, the situation across the country was an explosive one.' He paused, studying our faces. 'And in that sense, it *could* be said that the battle of 1857 was our first war of independence.'

A relieved murmur rippled through the room.

'*But*,' said Gopalacharya, 'on the *other* hand, if we consider the fact that the actual revolt against the British occurred in small pockets of India, and the fact that it was quickly suppressed' – his voice fell – 'it can be argued that the whole episode was a piddly mutiny and not a war.'

There was pin-drop silence. Omi Chand looked sick. P.K.'s eyes were blinking rapidly. Matthew was nervously rubbing his palms on his thighs.

'Any comments?' said Gopalacharya. 'Hari?'

I cleared my throat. 'Just because there was a battle doesn't prove that the popular mood in the country was one of independence from British control.'

'What do you mean?' asked Arun.

'Well, there was virtually no law and order in the country before the British arrived. History tells us that looters and murderers ruled the roost and the worst of them were our own kings. If the people wanted independence it was from the tyranny of their own people – tax officials and gangs of highway robbers – not from the British.'

Omi Chand leaped up from his chair. '*Sa'hb*, I was a small boy during the British times but I still remember that the ladies could walk with jewellery in the night.'

P.K. chuckled. Omi Chand silenced him with an annoyed look. He continued: 'Yes *sa'hb*, nobody had the guts to steal in those days. The district police chief used to camp regularly in the villages and ask the people about their problems. If any crime was committed he made sure that the culprit was caught and punished. *Sa'hb*, I tell you, people were afraid of the British. There was justice. Today, the police is the biggest enemy of the people – worse than the *goondas* themselves. There is no law and order and there is no justice.'

Gopalacharya looked at his watch. 'We don't have much time. Dada will be coming in any moment.'

Everyone leaned in their chairs towards the doorway. P.K. cupped his ear. There was the sound of sporadic typing from the newsroom.

'Have you all decided,' asked Gopalacharya, 'whether to sign the letter or not?'

Omi Chand rose. '*Sa'hb*, I am not going to sign.'

'Why? What's the matter?'

Omi Chand's chest heaved and the veins in his neck stood out. 'Because of what Ashit *Sa'hb* said about soldiers and sweepers.'

'Omi Chand,' said Gopalacharya weakly. 'I'm sure there was nothing personal in what Ashit *Sa'hb* said.'

'No, *sa'hb*,' snapped Omi Chand. 'He is always making fun of poor people. I may be poor but I am from a good caste.'

'Just then the door opened and the Bengali bounded in. He had an excited look on his face. In his hand was a sheet of paper.

'I've written a letter to Mr Sanyal, joint director, Press Information Bureau,' he announced. 'He's a Bengali. I invited him for dinner once and he was very impressed.' Without waiting for a reaction, the Bengali started reading:

Dear Mr Sanyal:

As you are already aware, foreign news organisations indulge in all manner of subversive propaganda aimed at disrupting the unity and integrity of India. On any given day, UNI and other foreign news organisations write at least one if not more stories that portray India as the world's most oppressive, violent and backward country tottering on the brink of disaster.

Recently, however, an alarming incident took place in the UNI bureau that crossed all bounds of decency and intellectual justification. As patriotic Indians we are constrained to bring the matter to your attention for urgent action.

On the night of October 29, one of our Indian reporters wrote a story in which he mentioned India's 'First War of Independence'. The editors in New York questioned the usage of the term. Our bureau chief, Ellen Newcomb suggested that a correction was in order, which clearly meant that she did not acknowledge 'First War of Independence' and wanted the term changed to 'Indian Mutiny' or 'Sepoy Mutiny'. This is tantamount to asking us to toe the Western line.

To date, no Indian scholar has accepted the Western view – at least not publicly – that the war of 1857 was only a mutiny. And the stand of the government of India on the issue is too well known to repeat here.

It goes without saying that the whole affair is part of a larger neo-colonialist plot to undermine the already eroded confidence of the people of India, sow seeds of dissension, and prevent India from being a world leader. There is ample evidence to prove this and some of our right-of-the-centre newspapers are doing a commendable job in exposing the evil imperialist designs. As we do not wish to make this letter too long, we cite three examples to back our argument:

– Long ago, Western imperialists masquerading as historians advanced the dangerous theory of the Aryan Invasion of India, according to which the fair-skinned Aryans destroyed the culture of the dark-skinned Dravidians and pushed them to the south. The theory resulted in the movement for Tamil independence from the Indian union.

– Maps in foreign publications routinely depict a third of Jammu-Kashmir, which is an inalienable part of India, as a part of Pakistan.

– Foreign historians deny that there was ever a 'Golden Age of India' when quite clearly there was such an age during the rule of the Guptas from 319 to 415 B.C.

Sir, it is high time hostile foreign agents were stopped from flaunting their imperialist version of history on our soil. Foreign correspondents and/or news organisations that persist in their racist and anti-Third World coverage should be summarily expelled.
Yours sincerely,
Staff of UNI, New Delhi

P.S.: In case you need them, Ms Newcomb's details are as follows: US citizen, passport no. Z6573914, visa no. 62 SOI DLI, issued Jan. 25, 1982.

The Bengali waved the paper. 'Are you boys ready to sign?'
'But Dada,' said Gopalacharya, 'you didn't tell us there would be a second letter.'
'To the government,' said P.K. looking alarmed.
'We're just debating the first letter,' said Gopalacharya.
'One letter, two letter – what's the bloody difference?'
'If Ellen comes to know we complained to the government . . .'
'What?' said the Bengali in a challenging tone. 'What will bloody happen?'

'We'll get royally screwed,' said Gopalacharya.

'Screwed? By that hag?'

'Seriously, Dada, this is no joke. We can't sign that letter. As it is we're having problems with the first letter.'

'What problems?'

'Well . . . for one,' said Gopalacharya, 'Omi Chand doesn't want to sign.'

The Bengali avoided the glance of Omi Chand who was standing by the door with his arms folded and looking very angry. 'This is why I don't like debates,' said the Bengali. 'It creates disunity.'

Omi Chand thrust his head forward like a dog about to snap. 'It's not the debate,' he growled. 'It's you and your casteist behaviour.'

'*My* casteist behaviour?' The Bengali laughed. 'Caste is a part of our culture. It belongs as much to you as to me.'

'That suits you because you are sitting at a higher level.'

'So what? These days anybody can spit at anybody regardless of caste.'

'When a lower-caste person spits from below the spit lands on his own face.' Omi Chand stormed out of the room.

'Let the bugger go to hell,' muttered the Bengali. 'Bloody washerman! Wants to be a high caste, does he?'

'He's not a washerman,' said P.K. 'He's a milkman. They're a rugged caste, Dada.'

'Ha! I've seen thirty-six people like him. He can't even harm my pubic hair.'

The door opened suddenly and everyone turned. The Bengali looked at the floor.

'Good morning.' It was Salim, the bureau photographer, with his requisite pair of cameras hanging over a fawn-coloured fishing vest. 'The police cordoned off the Chinese Embassy: the Tibetans couldn't get through.'

'Fucking Tibetans,' said the Bengali. 'Why don't they go back to their yaks.'

'Excuse me.' Salim tugged at the shoulder strap of one of

his cameras. 'I have to develop some pictures.' He made his way to the darkroom, which surprised no one: Salim was a quiet individual who always stayed away from office politics.

'Everybody, listen.' The Bengali waved his right index finger, a teacher admonishing unruly students. 'I don't want our cause to suffer because of one recalcitruant washerman.'

'Dada,' said P.K.

'Milkman.'

'And the word is recalcitrant,' said Gopalacharya.

'I propose we have the vote tomorrow morning.' The Bengali looked at each of us one by one. 'If the majority is for signing the letters, then *everybody* must sign. Including the milkman. And the Muslim too.' He was breathing heavily. 'If the majority is against signing, then – well, so be it.' The suggestion was that something drastic would probably happen in that eventuality, like a mass self-immolation, with the Bengali pouring the kerosene on each of us – and only water on himself.

'Dada.' Arun stood up. 'In order to avoid ugly scenes like the one today . . .'

'What ugly scenes?'

' . . . I propose . . .'

'I want to know what you mean by ugly scenes!'

'Dada,' said Gopalacharya in a gentle tone. 'Let him continue.'

'It's just that I think . . . I think . . . we should have a secret ballot.'

'I agree,' said Gopalacharya.

The Bengali was caught off guard.

'Hear! Hear!' P.K. banged the telex machine. Matthew nodded enthusiastically.

'So it's agreed,' said Gopalacharya in a rush. 'Secret ballot at 10 a.m. tomorrow. The majority carries the vote: whether to sign the letters or not.'

'Okay,' said the Bengali threateningly. 'Fine. I already know who's with me and who's not.' He gave Arun an accusing look.

'Excuse me, but . . .' P.K. looked around for a clock. 'Isn't it lunch-time?'

'Before we adjourn,' said the Bengali, 'I have to comment that no one enjoys being accused of being ugly. By his own colleague.'

I couldn't help myself. 'We could vote on that tomorrow, too.'

There was a knock on the door and Sam poked his head in. 'Hi guys. Having a party?'

'Sam, we're plotting the demise of Uncle Sam,' the Bengali joked. 'Want to join us?'

Sam broke out into a loud cackle. 'Yeah. Maybe I do.'

The rest of the day passed without incident. Before he left for an evening press conference, the Bengali came into my office.

'Hari,' he said, 'I want you to do me a favour – as a younger brother.'

I held my breath.

'We *have* to win tomorrow's vote, Hari.' His tone was at once urgent and begging. 'Of all the people in the bureau, I trust you the most, Hari.'

I looked him straight in the eye. 'I think you understand things. About our country. Its blood-drenched past. This country is finished, Hari, if we can't work together as brothers. The British began the destruction of our country with their divide-and-rule policy. The Americans are continuing it now. The only way we can fight back is by pulling together. Now, on the topic of tomorrow's vote. I'm worried about Salim. You know how he stays apart, Hari. He doesn't eat lunch with us – well, no one would eat his food anyway – and he spends all his days in the darkroom. I'm afraid he's not going to vote for us. But he's our only Muslim brother in the bureau and, Hari, it's kind of like Kashmir. I mean, Salim's vote shows that everyone, Hindu and Muslim, is together on this issue. And also I think we're one vote shy of a majority. So Hari, we must get his vote and . . .' – the Bengali put a heavy hand on my shoulder – 'I want *you* to do it. Go to Salim's house tonight.' He looked at me with a kind of sincerity that always surprised me. Either the Bengali wasn't such a bad man or he was an excellent actor. 'I want you to persuade Salim to vote for us. And when the two of you come in tomorrow morning, arm-in-arm, to vote in tandem against that dry-cunted American whore, I tell you, Hari, it will be a proud day for a united India in which all men are truly brothers.'

I was trapped. If I refused to help, the Bengali would hurl all manner of accusations. So I capitulated. 'Okay, Dada, I'll do it. We have to pull together in this country. I've said as much in letters to . . .'

'That's it.' The Bengali slapped me on the back. 'And Hari: get that damned Christian boy of yours in line too. Do his ballot for him, Hari, I'm not sure he understands issues of national importance.' He swung the dirty leather bag over his shoulder. 'I'll come back after the press conference to get Kumar's vote. After that I'll be at the Press Club for a drink.' He tucked his crumpled shirt in his trousers. 'Call me if you have any problems.' He left, giving me a wink and a thumbs up sign.

The vote did look close: the Bengali could probably count on my vote and Gopalacharya's. Voting against him was Omi Chand and, judging by his call for a secret ballot, Arun. P.K. was imponderable now that he was protected by the secret ballot, and Kumar, the night shift reporter, was notoriously independent in his actions. The Bengali did need the Muslim vote as personified by Salim. And I was the vote canvasser.

I left the bureau at 7 p.m. and walked down to the hotel car park. A nearly full moon was in the sky. As I was about to start my motorscooter I noticed a piece of paper taped to the speedometer. It was a Xeroxed letter from the Bengali and it was addressed to the Indian staff at UNI.

Comrades, tomorrow is a crucial day for India.

If a majority decides to sign my letters, it will be a victory for this fractured land.

However, if a majority opposes the letters, it will forebode a tragedy in every sense. We will suffer great humiliation by being forced to accept the perversion of our glorious history by the West. While the defeat will definitely defile every ounce of our sacred soil and every drop of water in the holy Ganga, New York will be singing 'The Star Spangled Banner', adding grave injury to gross insult.

All I can say in the backdrop of this dark scenario is that tomorrow's vote will tell whether we are a band of fearless patriots or just a bunch of weak-kneed, scrounging washermen and milkmen. A wise man once said, comrades: 'Never be haughty to the humble and humble to the haughty.' I think the meaning is clear.

Jai Hind!

Ashit

I put the letter in my coat pocket and rode away from the bureau. The chill in the air felt good on my face. I took several deep breaths to clear my head. For I had decided to go straight to Salim's house. He had left the bureau early, saying he'd be at home in case anything came up.

Salim lived in Press Enclave, a prestigious journalist ghetto. His wife was a reporter for a leading Bombay magazine. The gossip in the bureau was that they made quite a packet.

Two boys with hockey sticks guided me to his building. I climbed a flight of steps, took one last deep breath, and rang the bell.

Salim jerked the door open and pumped my hand vigorously.

'I'm sorry to barge in . . .'

'Oh no, Hari.' He put an arm around my shoulder and led me into the living room. 'Tell me, what brings you to my home? Let me call my wife.' Salim ran up a wooden staircase at the end of the room. 'I'll just be a minute.'

Salim's flat was modern. On one wall was the skin of a tiger with a massive head and a lifelike snarl. Hanging next to the tiger was a long musket. On the main wall was a massive black-and-white canvas showing a forest of ghostly trees. Under the painting was a stereo system replete with tape deck, turntable and spools, playing violin music. Beside it – to my utter amazement – was a small bar with a wooden liquor cabinet built into the wall. I had never seen a bar in a house before. I thought they existed only in hotels. And here was one in the house of a Muslim.

I sat on a leather couch that sank under my weight. I heard the sound of footsteps on the stairs. I tried to get up but couldn't: the couch had caught me like quicksand. I made it on the third attempt, or rather, I *more* than made it, springing up with such force that I was propelled into the centre of the room like a boxer who had failed to connect a powerful punch.

'Uh, hello.' I smoothed my jacket.

'Are you all right, Hari?'

'I'm fine.'

'Meet Farah, Hari.' Salim gestured towards a young woman with large smiling eyes. She was dressed in a saree. 'My other half.'

I folded my hands and bowed slightly.

'Farah, this is Hari Rana, my colleague at UNI.'

She extended a dainty hand.

'Come. What would you like, Hari? Name your poison.'

I said I'd like some rum with warm water.

'Warm?'

'Yes.'

'Farah, Hari's a little cold-blooded so he'll have rum with warm water. Come Hari, sit.'

I avoided the leather couch and chose a cane chair. 'Who shot that?'

'My father.' Salim's eyes brightened. 'He was a crack shot. He killed seven tigers.'

'Seven *tigers*.'

Farah approached with drinks, cheese and roasted peanuts. She said, 'Cheers!'

Salim and I raised our glasses. I pointed to the canvas on the wall. 'And who painted that?'

'Farah.' Salim smiled at her. 'She's the artist in the house.'

'And you? Aren't *you* an artist? I mean, Farah paints. You take pictures.'

Salim gave me a look that suggested he'd heard that line before. 'News photography is hardly art.'

'That's nonsense, Salim,' said Farah. She got up to flip the record.

'Do you like music, Hari?' asked Salim.

'I do, but I prefer Indian classical music to Western. Speaking of things Western and Indian' – I leaned forward in my chair – 'Salim, there's a very important matter.'

'Please to state it. I'm at your command.'

'Did you happen to read the message from New York on the bulletin board today?'

Salim nodded.

'Well . . .' I looked at Farah. 'Sorry,' I said. 'Work.'

She waved casually.

I reached into my jacket pocket and removed carbon copies of the letters to Ellen and the Press Information Bureau. 'Someone is very upset.'

'Ashit sent you here.'

'Yes. He wants everyone to sign these and he thought your signature was crucial because . . .'

'This *is* a democracy, you know.'

'He has agreed to a vote – a secret vote. It'll be held tomorrow morning at ten.' I handed Salim the letters. 'We have agreed that if he wins a majority, everyone in the bureau will sign.'

'*If* he loses?'

'There will be constant war. Every day. With everyone.'

'We don't have much of a choice, do we?'

'Salim.' I cleared my throat. 'I must tell you I'm not here to influence your vote.'

'I know, Hari.' Salim chuckled. 'I'm glad you came, Hari. *We're* glad.' He looked at Farah. 'It's a wonderful evening. Excuse me a second while I read these and in the meantime . . .' He held out his glass and Farah took it. She looked at me. I drained my glass and gave it to her. Salim leaned back and started reading the letters.

I flipped through a magazine with my second drink. Farah disappeared into the kitchen and I heard cooking sounds. Soon, Salim was sitting with his hands folded in his lap, a thoughtful expression on his face.

'Well?'

He gave a deep sigh. 'The first letter isn't so bad.' He handed me the papers. 'It's the second one I'm worried about. It's absolute idiocy to write to the government about this.'

'You mean you are willing to sign the first letter but not the second?'

'I didn't say that, Hari. I meant that the letter to Ellen is balanced.'

'Arun edited it.'

'The one to the government is outrageous. It's sneaky and unprofessional and could land us all in serious trouble. What do you think?'

'As far as I'm concerned, even breathing the same air as the Bengali is not without danger. But please don't tell him. He would eat me alive.'

'If he did, we'd have a man-eater in the bureau.'

'And then you'd get your chance to shoot a Bengal tiger.' I laughed. 'But you'd better be as good a shot as your father.'

'You bet. There's nothing more dangerous than a wounded man-eater.'

It was getting late. I was feeling drunk and it was a long ride back to my place. 'Salim.' I got up. 'I must go.'

'All right, Hari. Tomorrow's a difficult day.'

'Thank you for your hospitality.'

'You're welcome, Hari.' Salim put his arm around my shoulder and escorted me to the door. 'Come any time.'

'What should I tell the Bengali, Salim? He's bound to ask what happened.'

'Ummm . . .' Salim shrugged. 'Say anything. It makes no difference with him anyway: heads he wins, tails we lose.'

'He'll want to know if you're on his side or not.'

'Tell him the Jats have a mind of their own.'

'The Jats? You're not a Jat.'

'I was.' He smiled devilishly. 'Or rather, my ancestors were.'

'Your ancestors were *what*?'

'Jats. Isn't that your caste?'

I nodded. 'But how . . .'

'My great great great-grandfather was a Jat. From Punjab.'

'Then how come you're Muslim?'

'My ancestors became Muslims because of the bad treatment they received from the Brahmins.'

'I had no idea, Salim, that even the Jats were at the receiving end of the Brahminical stick. Farmers?'

'Oh yes. And a lot turned to Islam – and Sikhism – as a result. Why do you think pre-partition Punjab had a Muslim majority?'

I was in a daze. The news that Salim's ancestors were members of my community put me completely off balance.

Salim walked to the bar and returned with two small glasses. 'Let's drink to our common past, Hari.' He lifted his glass. 'To the reunion of Jats.'

'To, uh, brothers.'

'Brothers,' said Salim, 'Once and forever.'

I rode away, slightly tipsy, filled with a feeling of dread. I have to tell you, Col. Pai, that I had never been in the home of a Muslim before. My entire experience of Muslims had been based on a few families in my village from the Meo tribe – a small and fierce Muslim community that has traditionally earned its livelihood by stealing cattle and robbing people's houses. But the Meos have many admirable qualities, Col. Pai, and as a soldier it will interest you to know that they have a very high sense of loyalty, of which my family had first-hand experience.

It so happened that my father, in keeping with his ideal of service before self, used to give free tuition to a Meo boy in the village – one of the handful of Meos who ever made it to school. My father got into a land dispute with a powerful Muslim landlord who, one night, dispatched a couple of his men to beat him up. The toughs encircled our house and threatened to burn it if my father didn't come out. My father was about to comply when he heard shouts and the sound of stick fighting. It was the Meos. They sent the landlord's men packing within minutes. And not just that, Col. Pai: they insisted on guarding our house round the clock until the dispute with the landlord was resolved, which took a week. All because of my father's kindness to the Meo boy. Meanwhile, the rest of the villagers – all Hindus like my father – sided with the landlord.

Yet, Col. Pai, despite all the gratitude my father owed the Meos, he never visited them at their homes. He feared that they might return the call. And how, as Hindus, could we have entertained them?

My meeting with Salim belied all the malicious stories I'd ever heard about Muslims. I didn't notice a single object in his living room that was even remotely connected with religion. There was no Arabic calligraphy on the wall and none of those hard, longish cushions with shiny covers that one sees in movies about Muslims. On the contrary, Col. Pai, Salim's wife was wearing a saree, which really surprised me. And I was astonished to see that both Salim and his wife drank alcohol, so strictly forbidden in their religion.

But I felt something nagging in my mind. It was an unpleasant feeling I couldn't readily identify. I thought about it for a while. Then, like a flash of lightning, I had a sudden clarity of vision: If I were Salim, I would have become insane living with the knowledge that my ancestors had a different religious and cultural heritage.

It's not that I look down on Islam, or that I consider Hinduism superior to other religions. (In fact, I'm an agnostic: I don't pray to God and can count on my fingertips the number of times I've been to a temple.) What disturbed me about Salim was the idea that his religion was 'artificial' – something grafted on to his family tree by a quirk of history generations ago. Salim was like a guava growing on a mango tree – freaky and somehow frightening.

That night I had an upsetting dream. I dreamt that my father was dying. I was standing by his bed. 'Son,' he whispered weakly. 'Sit down. I have to tell you something.' I sat on the bed and gently took his fleshless hand. 'It's a secret your mother and I never planned to burden you with.' He looked at me. 'Now that I'm dying and your mother is no more, I feel it's better you learn the secret from me than from somebody else after I'm gone.' He looked away and spoke in a voice filled with emotion. 'Son, you are not our natural child.'

I wanted to scream but I couldn't find my voice.

'We found you on the river bank one night.'

I wanted to run away but my legs felt like lead.

'You were barely a few days old and were crying loudly. We took you home and brought you up like our own child.'

I felt, in the dream, that I wouldn't survive if I heard more. But my father went on.

'One day, when you were hardly five years old, Makhmool, the Meo from our village, stopped me on my way to school. He talked of the night that we took you from the river bank. I asked him how he knew about that night. He said he was the one who left you there, on the river bank, hoping that some good soul would pick you up. He said you were the son of his sister, who abandoned you because she was too poor to bring you up. For all these years, Makhmool said, he had watched with joy as you grew into a healthy, school-going child. But Makhmool said he had bad news. Your natural parents had died of some disease in a far-away village. He wanted you to attend their last rites. I refused. I told him how traumatic it would be for you to discover you were a Muslim. And he agreed. But he begged me to bring you to the funeral as a mourner. He touched my feet. I couldn't agree; but I said I'd bring you to your parents' grave after the funeral was over and there was no one in sight.'

My father shut his eyes as if trying to suppress some painful memory. 'Son, that night I brought you to your past. Makhmool and I accompanied you to your parents' graves. Fortunately, you were too young to understand anything.' My father folded his trembling hands. 'God.' He looked up at the ceiling. 'We did our best for our son. Forgive us if we made any mistakes.'

I awoke, bathed in sweat. My heart was beating so fast I thought I would suffer a heart attack. By the time the morning came I had a slight fever. Ordinarily I would have called in sick. But that was impossible on this critical day.

When I reached the bureau the Bengali was sitting in the newsroom, sipping tea and staring at his wall. Omi Chand was mopping the floor. Both had come in early. Ellen was also in; her office door was shut.

The Bengali was wearing an old and ill-fitting dark blue suit with thin red stripes and a red tie. The suit looked like it might have belonged to his father. As soon as he saw me he leaped from his chair and waved me into the kitchen.

'Hari,' he panted, 'we must talk before the others come.' His eyes were bleary and his breath smelled of liquor. He grabbed my arm and forced me to sit on the kitchen stool. 'Tell me, Hari: What happened?'

'With Salim?'

'Hari,' he said exasperatedly.

Let me tell you from the beginning . . .'

'Just tell me if the bloody mullah is going to vote with us

or not. Is he going to join the rest of the country or will he huddle up in his own bloody mosque, wailing away on his bloody prayer rug, asking advice from his bloody Allah the Arab . . .'

'I'm not sure, Dada, how Salim will vote.'

The Bengali's mouth tightened.

'I tried, Dada.'

'You're joking.'

'I tried my best.'

'What did he say?'

'I showed him the letters . . .' I hesitated and then went on: 'He said the first letter was all right.'

'The second one?'

'He said it might get us into trouble.'

'Mother-fucking son of a prostitute!'

'Don't get so hot, Dada.'

The Bengali's teeth were clenched tightly together. He poked a finger in my face. 'The bloody fate of the country is being threatened and you are telling me not to get hot!'

'He said he would think about it.'

'Think about it? Whether to vote for India? Ha!' He made a spitting sound. 'Those sister-fucking, circumcised mother-fucking pigs. I'll stamp out every last one of them from the face of this earth.'

'Sorry, Dada.'

The Bengali turned on me. 'I sent you to convince that back-stabbing mullah to vote for the country. And you let the Motherland down. You let her down when she needed you. A couple of hundred more people like you and India will be up for grabs.' He turned around and headed for the door. 'Take my advice, Hari. Drown yourself in a handful of water.'

He stormed out into the hallway. 'I'll be in the coffee shop downstairs. Call me as soon as the rest come in.' He slammed the door and left.

I was standing in the newsroom, lost in thought, when

Gopalacharya walked in. 'All ready for the vote?' He arched his eyebrows and took a long suck on his cigarette.

'It's not ten yet.'

'Where's the Bengali?'

'In the coffee shop.'

'How's his mood?

'Bad.'

Gopalacharya let out a sigh.

I changed the paper spools in the teleprinters. Gopalacharya sidled up next to me.

'Here we go. PTI says twelve killed in bus mishap in Simla.' Gopalacharya read the news rattling out of the machines. 'I don't know why our agencies call every accident a mishap.' He shook his head. 'Fifty people drown and PTI calls it a boat mishap. It's like saying fifty people drowned because they got unlucky.'

'It's a big country, Gopalacharya. It's their way of saying life goes on.'

'Wish we could say the same at UNI.' Gopalacharya ripped off a sheet of the news copy.

'Especially today.'

'That's right. We could have a voting mishap.'

'Seven injured.'

'Bengali absconding.'

Soon, Arun, P.K. and Matthew arrived. Arun's eye contact was at an all-time low. He headed for his desk and hid behind the pages of a newspaper. P.K. scurried into his cubicle like a rabbit into his burrow and turned on his pocket transistor radio. Matthew sat stolid and sphinx-like in front of the telex machine, punching out a message to New York.

I counted the number of people in the bureau. Except for Salim, everyone had arrived. The time was 9.50 – only ten minutes before voting was scheduled to start. I picked up the phone and called the Bengali.

'The mullah hasn't shown up?' His voice boomed over the

receiver. 'We can't wait. I'm coming up. Hari, instruct everyone to assemble in your room.'

When the Bengali came into the communications room we were sitting in a loose semi-circle facing the door. Arun was staring at the floor, nervously bouncing his knees. Omi Chand sat sideways in a chair, his back to everyone and his chin resting on the palm of his hand. The only sounds in the room came from P.K.'s transistor radio, which was glued to his ear, and Gopalacharya's suckings on his cigarette. The Bengali pulled himself up, his worn-out suit stretched tightly over his square frame. He put his hands in his pockets and started.

'Brothers, Indians and fellow countrymen. For the staff of a 24-hours-a-day, seven-days-a-week, 52-weeks-a-year news bureau to be present together at the same place and time is as significant an achievement as the meeting of Churchill, Roosevelt and Lenin during World War II.' He looked at us intently.

The door opened and Salim came tip-toeing in, cameras dangling from his shoulders. The Bengali jerked his head in his direction. Salim sat on a vacant chair next to Omi Chand.

'The seven samurai have just been joined by James Bond.' The Bengali sneered at Salim. 'Whether it is special agent 007 or double agent 666 only time will tell. Anyway.' He bowed his head briefly and paused to concentrate. 'We are here today to fight the agents of a hostile power . . .' He pointed towards Ellen's office. 'A power whose sole aim is to subjugate our beloved Motherland once again.' He pulled papers from his trouser pocket. 'These are our responses. Our first salvo' – he held up the letter to Ellen – 'will prepare the ground for battle. It will give the enemy ample warning and prove that we are not cowards to attack unawares.' Then he waved the letter to the Press Information Bureau. 'The second salvo. This will take the wind out of Ellen's sails.' He placed the two letters on a table in front of him.

'But friends,' A sly smile came on his face, 'In our haste we forgot about the main enemy battleship.' He eyed us one by

one like a school teacher expecting an answer to a problem.
'The mother ship in New York.'

'New York?' P.K. looked shell-shocked.

'You mean the UNI head office, Dada?' asked Gopalacharya.

'Exactly. The Seventh Fleet itself.' The Bengali whipped
out an envelope from his inner coat pocket and held it up. 'It
would be a big tactical mistake not to write to New York.' He
opened the envelope, pulled a sheet of paper and gave us a
wink. 'The third salvo – I worked on it last night.'

To Jonathan Wilkins, President, Union News International;
Mark Rosenthal, International Editor, Union News
International

Dear Mr Wilkins and Rosenthal:
As journalists dedicated to the ideals of a free press we are
accustomed to investigating and reporting issues of
inequality, injustice and exploitation of every kind.
Therefore, we think it is our professional duty to bring
to your attention certain compelling injustices needing
immediate redressal at the UNI New Delhi bureau.

We must state at the outset that urgent problems require
urgent and permanent solutions, not sweeping under the
carpet. Sugar coated pilliatives may be cheaper in the short
term but they kill the patient in the long run. Whereas
non-action is nothing but a stepping stone to anger,
despair and anomie, turning professional and loyal staff
members into the opposite, besides contributing to
nihilistic and destructive impulses which effect
everybody.

Let us come straight to the point rather than beating
around the bush. We were shocked and dismayed to
receive a message from Steve Brubeck on October 29,
questioning the term 'First War of Independence.' (See
enclosed photostat copy of our bureau chief's memo.) Mr

Brubeck's knowledge of history naturally stops where
ours begins – or vise versa. His implication was clear.
According to the slanted Western view of Indian history
there is no such thing as 'First War of Independence'. If
the White missayahs of history are to be believed, the correct
term is 'Indian Mutiny' or 'Sepoy Mutiny'.

But there is no mention of these terms in the UNI
stylebook, which implies that there is no UNI policy on the
issue. Under the circumstances, the matter must be left in
the hands of the local bureau staff. Why then did Ellen
Newcomb suggest in her memo that a correction should
be made?

A bureau chief is the bureau chief, but it is intolerable
when he or she barks up the wrong tree. Besides, if there
is any country in the world – after Great Britain – that
should correct its history it is USA. Americans are guilty
of more atrocities than all other countries put together.
From the massacre of Red Indians to the genocide in
Vietnam, Americans have left a long and bloody trail of
blood. So much so that blood has become a saleable
commodity today, as is evident from Hollywood films and
the Arms Race. But have these facts been entered by
obliging historians in your history books? No? Ha! Nothing
surprising. Money can buy anything. No wonder that
Henry Ford, one of the leading sons of your soil – or
should I say astro-turf – declared that 'history is bunk'.
A clear case of guilty conscious.

Or take another diplorable example of Western bias and
Racism in the coverage of India. During the past five
years, the White reporters at UNI have written more than
100 stories on tigers, Maharajas, cows, beggars, dacoits,
snake charmers and the like. Of course, nothing wrong in
that per se – Indian government's stand on freedom of
speech and expression is well known. What is shocking
nevertheless is that to date, the Whitemen have not
produced a single story highlighting India's positive side,

such as its role in promoting World Peace, the giant strides made in peaceful nuclear weapon technology, space research etc.

Like other American news organisations, UNI has a different way of speling and writing. In our capacity as the Indian staff, we are having to conform to this 'style' in letter, although thankfully not in spirit. For example, we are forced to write 'color' insted of 'colour'; 'reazon' insted of 'reason'; and 'fever' insted of 'feever'. This 'style' is contrary to our English, which is based on the British system. Moreover, it is mucking up our over-all spelings as well.

Indians are being paid a pittance in comparison to the salaries of White reporters despite the wide gap in their knowledge of the country. In fact a Whiteman's monthly salary is equivalent to the annual salary of an Indian reporter. Moreover, the Whiteman gets paid in foreign exchange whereas the Indians are paid in rupees which are falling regularly vis-a-vis the dollar. For many years we have been demanding payment in dollars but to no awail.

Two years ago Ellen Newcomb promised that Indians will be sent one-by-one to New York for training. Every time we bring up the subject she changes the topic or goes to the bathroom. The ball is in your court.

The British were nearly defeated in World War II because of these very same policies. (Luckily for them, more than 100,000 Indian troops bailed them out.) Mark these words: UNI will surely pay a heavy price if it rubs colonial salt in Indian wounds. And this time no Indian troops will come to the rescue.

The Bengali folded the letter carefully and put it in his coat pocket. Except for a crackling hiss from P.K.'s pocket radio there wasn't a sound in the room.

'*Arey Dada, pagla gaye ho kya?*' asked Gopalacharya. (This,

Col. Pai, is polite Hindi as it's spoken in the East. It means, roughly, 'Have you lost your mind?')

'What do you mean *pagla gaye ho*!' the Bengali thundered. 'It's an important letter and it must be sent.'

'But Dada.' P.K. scratched his balding head. 'This letter will definitely complicate everything. I mean *chutti ho jaye gi* – we will lose our jobs.'

'Look at P.K!' The Bengali pointed. 'Always thinking of his job first.' He made a rude sound. 'There's a saying in English: cowards are killed many times but the brave die only once. I don't know about you people, but I am ready to die for the Motherland over and over again.'

'But patriotism is not the issue here,' said Gopalacharya. 'P.K. is right: Your letter to New York is even more dangerous than . . .'

'What do you Tamils know about patriotism? What has Tamil Nadu done for India except teaching other states how to secede?'

A flash of anger overcame Gopalacharya. He tried to control it – an effort that lasted no more than a second – but failed. 'You are a disgusting man, Chatterjee, disgusting and diabolical. How *dare* you get personal!' He got up and walked towards the door.

'Truth hurts.' The Bengali watched Gopalacharya's back. 'I challenge you to say anything unpatriotic about the Bengalis.'

'I won't descend into your gutter. I'm taking the day off. Tell Ellen I'll be out of town.' He walked out of the room, leaving the door open.

'He who goes should never be stopped.' The Bengali faced his audience with folded arms. 'No war was ever halted because of one – what do they call it? – conscious objector.'

'You have just struck at your own foot.' Omi Chand was standing erect with head high, looking defiantly at the Bengali. 'You are drunk on your arrogance. No general ever won a battle by alienating his men.'

The Bengali gave his Genghis Khan stare. Omi Chand made a spitting sound and stormed out of the room.

It took the Bengali some time to recover from the shock of Omi Chand's insubordination. 'So we have two defectors now,' he said. 'I don't know if that's a setback or . . .'

'*Suno!*' The Bengali was interrupted by P.K.'s hysterical cry. 'Listen! Listen!' P.K. raised one hand in the air, index finger pointing to the ceiling. With the other, he pressed the radio set to his ear.

'What happened?' asked the Bengali.

'Indira Gandhi has been shot!'

'Who?'

'Mrs Gandhi!'

'*What?*' The Bengali's voice was both a squeal and a shout. 'Who says?'

'BBC.'

'Who did it?'

'Her bodyguards.'

'*What* bodyguards?'

'I don't know . . . BBC is saying it was her bodyguards. Maybe Delhi Police.' P.K.'s hands were shaking.

'Where?'

'Her residence.'

'We have to get moving.' The Bengali mopped his brow with a handkerchief. 'But before we do anything let's have the vote. It'll hardly take . . .'

'The vote can wait, Dada.' Salim picked up his bags. 'The other agencies must be on the story.' He vanished.

The Bengali ordered Arun to see if Ellen and Sam were in the bureau. Arun scampered away and returned to say Ellen's office and the newsroom were empty. 'We're fucked!' The Bengali looked very scared. 'Ellen isn't there and neither is *Daanav*. Son of a whore.' He turned to me. 'Get on the phone, Hari, and tell Ellen what's happened. I'll call Sam from the newsroom.'

I got through to Ellen's house on the first try. Her cook

told me she had gone to the vet's ten minutes ago with all her three dogs.

I went to the newsroom and told the Bengali.

'Indira Gandhi has been shot and our bureau chief is at the bloody vet's? I can't believe this!' He wiped his brow. 'Anyway, I got hold of Sam. He's going to the PM's house. Luckily the bastard was at home and not at the American club.'

The Bengali stared at the floor, thinking. He lifted his head. 'Does anyone know Ellen's vet?' Arun and I shook our heads. 'Arun, check Ellen's diary. Fast!' He turned to me. 'And Hari, check the wires to see what PTI is saying. He lifted a telephone receiver. 'And turn on the radio.'

I flicked the switch of the newsroom radio, which was perpetually tuned to the BBC. Then I went to the teleprinters to watch the news coming over. Arun came from Ellen's office to say he couldn't find the vet's number.

'Take a taxi and go to that vet in Kaka Nagar.' The Bengali caught Arun by the arm. 'You know where it is – opposite the golf club.' Arun nodded. 'That vet is the closest to her house. And tell the dog-fucking bitch to get her cunt back here fast. Go!'

The Bengali frantically dialled a number for the sixth time. 'Hello, police control room? I am calling from the press . . . yes . . . we just wanted to confirm whether the PM has been shot this morning. What? You have got no news of this sort? BBC is saying she has been shot. This is absolutely preposterous.' He slammed the phone down. 'Bloody pongos. The country's prime minister has been shot and they have no information.'

I told the Bengali there was nothing on the local wires.

'Of course – they must be waiting for clearance from the Information Ministry. Cock-sucking hacks.' He dialled another number. 'Hari, tell Matthew to send a message to New York. Take this down. "Beebs reporting Prime Minister Indira Gandhi shot in New Delhi by her bodyguards. No official confirmation yet. Two staffers in field. Will file as soon as we hear from them or have something official. FYI: I am alone in buro. Trying to reach Ellen and Sam whose whereabouts unknown. Regards, Chatterjee."'

I ran with the message and told Matthew to send it immediately. When I returned the Bengali was sitting on his desk, legs crossed tightly, shouting into the telephone.

'. . . Indira Gandhi, not Mahatma Gandhi. Yes, she has *also* been shot . . . today . . . the BBC is reporting it. What? There is no official word so far. Come on Mr Natrajan . . . you must have heard *something*. What is this, the Soviet Union?' He slammed the phone down.

A BBC news bulletin came on the radio. A clipped voice said: '. . . Indian Prime Minister Indira Gandhi was assassinated by two Sikh bodyguards today.' The Bengali rushed across the newsroom and increased the volume. 'Mrs Gandhi was killed in her official residence in New Delhi as she was walking across a garden to meet visitors, according to police officials who spoke on condition of anonymity. She was accompanied by two armed Sikh bodyguards who fired at her from close range, the officials said.'

The Bengali scribbled notes on a piece of paper.

'. . . Mrs Gandhi was hit by more than a dozen bullets, said the officials. She was immediately rushed to hospital in critical condition. A senior police official told the BBC that she died on the way to the All India Institute of Medical Sciences where hundreds of sympathisers and curious passersby have begun to gather. The assassination appeared to be in retaliation for the attack by the Indian army last June on the Golden Temple, the holiest Sikh shrine . . .'

'Fucking shit!' The Bengali's face was crimson. 'BBC is saying she's dead and we haven't even reported the shooting.' The Bengali rushed to his typewriter. He looked at his notes from the BBC broadcast and started typing furiously. I watched the local wires but, incredibly, there was no news about the shooting of the prime minister.

Soon, the Bengali handed me a piece of paper containing

five paragraphs. 'Tell Matthew to punch it and keep the tape ready for transmission. And don't forget to mark it "FLASH". He should run the tape as soon as the assassination is confirmed. All we need is the phone call from Sam.'

The Bengali leaned back in his chair. 'Can you believe this, Hari? Biggest story of the decade and the bureau chief is out getting screwed by her dogs and who knows, the bloody vet as well.' He laughed at his own joke. 'Our top reporter, rushing to Mrs Gandhi's death site, is a man who has trouble remembering his own birth date from one day to the next.'

The telephone on the Bengali's desk rang. The Bengali picked up the receiver.

'*What*?' He gave me a nervous look. 'Where *is* she then? Where are you? At her house?' I told you to go to the damned vet, not her fucking house. What? She uses a vet in *where*? That's across town. Okay, take the taxi and go there immediately. And then head for AIMS. Beebs says Mrs Gandhi copped it at AIMS. I want you to get confirmation. That's all. We have the story all written out and ready to send.' The Bengali turned to me. 'Has that fucking papist punched the tape?' I nodded. 'The story's ready to go, Arun. *Just get the confirmation*, understand?' The Bengali slammed the receiver down. He turned wearily to me.

'What Dada?'

'We could all lose our jobs, you know.'

'Where is Ellen?'

'She's changed vets. Of all days. Hari, are you sure that tape is punched? That story has got to go as soon as we get confirmation.'

A telephone rang across the room. I answered it. It was Sam, sounding breathless and rattled. 'Give me that!' The Bengali moved his bulk across the room in three giant strides. He yanked the receiver from my hand. 'Yes Sam . . . do you have . . . ? Is she . . . ?' He looked at me and lifted his arm in the air, finger extended like a referee. 'What?' The Bengali's mouth dropped and he shook his head in a gesture of shock and disbelief. His arm protruded in the air uselessly. 'Hurry Sam! AFP and Reuters must be sniffing Mrs Gandhi's blood by now.' He hung up. '*Daanav* has done it again.'

'What's the problem?'

'The idiot went to South Block instead of Safdarjang Road. I told him to go to the PM's *house*, not the *office*. He said he forgot. We're screwed. I'm going to the PM's house, Hari.'

'But Dada . . .'

'I know it's risky, but there's no other alternative.' He put a notebook in his coat pocket. 'Sam may never find the PM's house. He'll forget again.'

'The bureau will be empty. No newsmen. P.K. and me only . . .'

'You're useless, I know. I mean that in the nicest way, Hari. But sometimes these things have to be done. Just monitor BBC and the wires.' The Bengali seemed to be under some kind of spell. He was tightening his shoelaces. 'I should be calling you in about half an hour with confirmation of Mrs Gandhi's death. As soon as you hear about the assassination from me – or from Arun or Sam – press the button and send the story out.'

'But Dada.'

'There's nothing to worry about, Hari. If you screw up, you may lose your job, of course. But if we don't get this story out, we may all be unemployed by morning.'

I nodded.

'Good luck.' The Bengali strode out of the newsroom, flinging his tie over his shoulder.

I had never been entrusted such enormous responsibility before, Col. Pai. As I recovered from the shock of being left alone in the newsroom, I heard an ominous noise. It came from the hotel corridor. I ran into the hallway and opened the bureau door. What I saw stopped me in my tracks. The Bengali, ashen-faced, was standing in the corridor surrounded by a mob of rough-looking men. They were carrying sticks and iron rods and were shouting, 'Death to the killers of Indira

Gandhi' and 'Death to CIA agents'. It didn't take me long to understand: these were Congress Party activists hungry to avenge their leader's murder. I knew from past experiences that foreign organisations, especially American ones, were a natural target of marauding mobs.

As I stood in the doorway, paralysed with fright, the mob began raining blows on the Bengali. He screeched. I saw a placard smash into his skull. And then I noticed a figure in the far distance behind the mob. It was Omi Chand, running down the corridor with a broomstick in his hands. He swung the thick bamboo in a wide arc and uttered an appalling, war-like cry, plunging into the mob. I watched the broomstick land on the head of a burly man who instantly collapsed, a ribbon of blood oozing from his head. Then, in a smooth motion and without the slightest pause, Omi Chand swung the broomstick to his right. The bamboo struck an attacker on the knee. I heard the sound of bone cracking, followed by a shriek. Omi Chand grabbed the Bengali by the lapels of his coat, pushed him against the wall, and positioned himself between the Bengali and the attackers. He swung again, hitting a third man on the face. The mob moved back several paces, out of his reach.

Omi Chand took a step forward. 'Come,' he bellowed. 'If you have drunk your mother's milk, come and fight. We have nothing to fear here. At UNI!'

The mob immediately retreated, pulling their wounded behind them.

Omi Chand put an arm around the Bengali and escorted him to the bureau. He positioned himself outside the door with the broomstick in one hand. '*Sa'hb*, you continue with your work. I'll stay here and see who has the guts to attack again.'

'Omi Chand, I owe you my life.' The Bengali had tears in his eyes.

'It's my duty, *sa'hb* . . .'

The Bengali clasped Omi Chand's hands with his and shook them.

'. . . My duty to my country.'

I saw the Bengali pull away slightly. He coughed and started brushing off his lumpy suit.

I heard the ring of a telephone in the newsroom and ran inside. It was Salim on the line. He was calling from the prime minister's residence: a source in the home ministry had told him that Mrs Gandhi was indeed dead. I ran to the communications room and gave Matthew the command. He pressed a single button and the telex tape started curling through the machine. We had our news flash, thanks to a photographer. A Muslim at that.

Nonetheless, UNI was behind the other agencies. By the time Sam reached the prime minister's residence the place was swarming with Congress supporters looking for Sikhs and white men. Sam got roughed up and had to make a run for it. Arun managed to reach Ellen and she showed up breathless at the bureau with her three dogs. The next day, AP swept the news play throughout the United States on the Gandhi assassination story. In Europe and Asia we were beaten hollow by Reuters and AFP.

As for the vote on the letters, the Bengali never mentioned it again.

Yours truly,

Hari Rana

Mr Jeevan Shinde
President, Indian Letter Writers' Association (Regd.)
A 2/32 Greenfields
Mahakali Caves Road
Andheri East
Bombay 400 094

Dear Mr Shinde,
Drop by drop an ocean makes. I joined your good association
shortly after my letter on the Nellie incident was published.
Since then, with your fatherly support and encouragement,
my letter-writing 'career' has gone from strength-to-strength.
I now have to my credit 87 published letters in leading news-
papers. Recent topics include:
  – Why Amnesty is Unwelcome in India
  – Too Many Bird-Hits
  – Intellectuals' Lost Voice
  – Are All Illnesses Psychosomatic?
  – Plight of Night Soil Carriers
While it will be my endeavour to write on socially-relevant
and thought-provoking topics, this may not be possible at all
times. This is because I am also aiming at the Guinness record
for the maximum number of letters to the editor published by
anybody. As your life-long member, I hope I will have your
full co-operation. For your information: I plan to send my
candidature to the Guinness office in London, duly attested
by you, as soon as I cross the 300-letter mark. This should
not take too long. I am planning to boost my score by sending
out duplicate letters to regional newspapers.
    Let's make India proud!
    Yours truly,
    Hari Rana

Mr Jeevan Shinde, President
Indian Letter Writers' Association (Regd.)
A 2/32 Greenfields
Mahakali Caves Road
Andheri East
Bombay 400 094

Dear Mr Shinde,

I was outraged to receive your letter, which arrived just now, stating that one Mr Anthony Parakal of Bombay is already holding the Guinness record for the highest number of letters – over 2,000 – published in newspapers. Why did you not inform me of this before, especially since you now claim he is a founding member of ILWA? Is this any way for a senior citizen like you to behave towards the youngers? And what business have you got to tell me that 'in this business of letter writing there are no overnight successes'?

I have a strong suspicion that Parakal and you – both being senior Bombay-based citizens – are hand-in-glove. I have never heard or read about this Parakal and neither have my various friends in the media. You say that Parakal started writing letters after retiring as a railway clerk. That means he started writing after 60. How, may I ask, is it humanly possible for any human being, especially a decrepit-old pensioner, to publish over 2,000 letters within 12 years?! (An average of about one letter every other day!) In any case, he sounds like a publicity seeker rather than a true letter writer.

I am sure that like everything else in our corrupt society, the real facts of this case will never see the light of day. I am therefore tendering my resignation from your bogus organisation forthwith. I am also informing Guinness of this situation and suggesting to them that the category be amended to 'Most prolific LIVING letter writer,' so you and your organisation can't monopolise the honours from beyond the graveyard.

Hari Rana

The Times of India
Perverted Pleasures

Sir:

There are a host of reasons why the average reader writes letters to the editor. He may be angry, anxious, disputative or simply bored. Whatever the reason, most letters do a service to society (as when complaints are made about mosquitoes or potholes). But there is a nasty breed of letter-writers that writes solely for the sake of getting their names in the papers. These people get a perverted pleasure in seeing their names in the papers every day.

Most readers and editors are totally ignorant of these vultures of the letter page. This is because they keep hopping from one newspaper to the next just like a criminal changing his modus-operandi with every crime. In a free-wheeling city like Bombay, with 50 daily newspapers in six languages, this is easy to do. In Delhi, under the watchful eyes of the Press Council and with far lesser newspapers, this is an almost impossible task.

Little wonder that the Indian Letter Writers Association (ILWA) is based in Bombay. An investigation by this writer reveals that almost all the big names in this publicity-seeking racket are allied to the ILWA.

The ILWA is a fraud, a drain on imported newsprint and nothing but a menace to society.

Hari Rana
New Delhi

The Times of India
Ridiculous Feats

Sir:

Just as people get the politicians they deserve, a country gets the parasites it deserves. I refer to the millions of Indians who day in and day out do nothing but aspire to ridiculous human feats like balancing on one leg, eating 600 *idlis* and writing the longest letter.

It is such lay-abouts – and not the politicians – that are the real scourges of our society. Go to any district of India and you will find any number of dumb folk engaged in the most wasteful exercises – such as drinking 100 glasses of water – or insanely dangerous feats such as putting poisonous scorpions on one's face.

The reason for all this is a widely respected English institution called the Guinness Book of World Records. This book, which is more popular than the Holy Bible, is wreaking havoc in poor countries like India by encouraging people to waste their time and energy in setting records.

Just the other day I came across a thin village lad standing on his head in a public park. I asked him what he was doing and he told me he was preparing to break the Guinness – he pronounced it 'Ghinnsa' – world record for the longest headstand.

'Why?' I asked him.

The boy flicked his finger against his thumb in the international sign for money.

'But Guinness doesn't pay any money to record holders,' I explained.

When he heard that he almost fell down and broke his neck.

Some record holders waste other people's time as well. I am thinking of Mr Anthony Parakal, who clutters the letters page of all Indian newspapers in a swollen-headed attempt to corner the letter-writing record, which he claims to hold for time immemorial. Something should be done to reverse this sorry trend before it becomes a ruinous national habit.

Hari Rana
New Delhi

Mr S.L. Madhubhani
President, The Letter Writer (Regd.)
20/3 New Marine Lines
Bombay 400 020

Dear Mr Madhubhani,
Thank you for your letter congratulating me for exposing the
'crooks masquerading as men of letters'. (Your description is
most apt.) Thank you also for your kind offer to join The
Letter Writer. I like the straightforward name you have chosen
for your organisation. It sounds far more compelling than your
rival group, the Indian Letter Writers' Association.

The 'dope' that you supplied me on your rival organisation
made interesting reading. But I regret that I will not be able
to launch any campaign – open or subtle – against them in
the letter columns of newspapers. It is not that I am afraid
of the ILWA. To be frank, I am sick of this whole business. I
am writing my letters strictly for high-minded purposes from
now on: to world leaders and heads of educational institutions.
(As there can be no world peace without education and no
proper education without world peace.) Thus, I must keep
myself detached and will not be able to ally myself with any
letter writing group whatsoever.

Yours truly,
Hari Rana

Col. Narendra Pai
Lancer's Lodge
P.O. Urulikanchan
Dist. Pune 412 202

Dear Col. Pai,
I haven't written since Ellen, our bureau chief, was posted to Norway. Everyone was relieved to see her go, especially the Bengali, who claims his blood pressure has come down considerably.

Ellen was replaced, Col. Pai, by an American called Bernard Katz. They swapped jobs: Bernie hated winter and wanted a posting to a sunnier place. At first we pitied our colleagues in Norway, thinking they got the worse part of the bargain. Later we weren't sure.

Bernie, 35, is goofy, with spectacles, fuzzy hair, buck teeth and a nose so long that it tends to make people look in the direction it is pointing. Bernie liked India from the start. He decorated his office with Indian posters and sculptures. Soon he was coming to the office in Indian clothes: *kurtas* and *salwar-kameez*. Once he came in a *dhoti*, nervously twisting it all day long to make sure nothing vital was hanging out.

Then Bernie went overboard: within four months of arriving he got married to a Parsee woman named Lilette.

The wedding was a curious affair. Lilette wanted a Western ceremony – you know Parsees, Col. Pai – while Bernie insisted on Indian rites with incense, garlands and ruptured coconuts. Lilette wanted a five-star hotel to impress her family; Bernie wanted a temple on a river. Lilette dreamed of gold and a diamond; Bernie desired a sacred thread. Finally, when time started to run out, the couple compromised: the wedding would be held in the bureau itself, which is, after all, located in what was once one of the best hotels in New Delhi. To satisfy Bernie it was decided to bring in a bus-load of people from an Indian village, along with musicians and the requisite priest. We also decided to hire an elephant to greet the guests. Omi Chand was the only person from a village nearby and he was delighted. His villagemates would enjoy a free trip to Delhi, he said, and they weren't doing anything anyway, what with the drought.

On the day of the wedding, Omi Chand stood guard at the hotel entrance, next to the elephant, to await his villagers. The rest of us waited in the bureau. Two hours went by and there was no sign of the bus from Rajasthan. Bernie delayed the rites as long as possible but the foreign guests became impatient, as did the Parsee priest and the rabbi from the local synagogue. (It was supposed to be a ceremony performed by a holy trinity: Parsee, Jew and Hindu.) Finally the wedding proceeded without representation from rural India. Bernie was disappointed and so was Lilette in her own right: the hotel had promised shrimp canapés but served *samosas* and potato *tikkis*.

The bride and groom left a little after midnight and the bureau staff accompanied them downstairs. In the lobby the hotel manager was engaged in a heated argument with an elderly Punjabi gentleman. I made enquiries from a security guard. He told me that the old man had just concluded the wedding of his daughter in a function room and was trying to settle the bill. The number of dinner guests had far exceeded the number of invitees. The manager was shouting at the old man, threatening to call the police unless he paid for the extra guests.

'What do you mean you didn't invite the guests? What about those people who came in a bus?'

'What bus?' The old man looked totally bewildered. 'What people?'

'The bus!' The manager gestured angrily. 'With that band.'

'I thought *you* provided the band. As a gratuity.'

'Even mud,' said the manager, 'costs money these days.'

We all realised simultaneously that Omi Chand's villagemates had attended the wrong wedding. A security guard told me a bus-load of well-fed, singing villagers had left the hotel a few minutes earlier – from the rear entrance, which is why Omi Chand missed them.

To his credit, Bernie interceded and paid the difference. He looked unhappy, Col. Pai, when he got in the car to drive away to his wedding night. Although not as unhappy as Omi Chand the following day who said: '*Hamari naak kat gayi, sa'hb.*' (This North Indian expression – literally 'my nose has been cut' – means that the person concerned has been humiliated or shamed.) He said he was determined to make amends for his villagers' expensive 'mistake' and he immediately set off for his village.

He returned a week later. Bernie was also back and, judging from his expression, the honeymoon hadn't been the finest.

'Chief.' Omi Chand stood to attention and saluted smartly. 'Please come.' Bernie allowed himself to be led out of the bureau to the hotel corridor. He was greeted by half-a-dozen burly, moustachioed villagers in colourful turbans, who folded their hands, bowed their heads and mumbled something in unison.

'*Sa'hb,*' said Omi Chand in his broken English. 'They are sorry' – he pronounced sorry 'sorie' – 'bhery sorie.'

Bernie looked overwhelmed by this spectacle of apology. 'It was a mistake, Omi Chand. Tell them it doesn't matter.'

Omi Chand said something to the villagers and they swayed their heads up and down several times, bowing and touching their folded hands to their foreheads. Then they stood up straight and started to leave.

Omi Chand caught Bernie by the arm. '*Sa'hb,* you please come. Outsie now. Jus minit. Jus outsie.'

Beneath a tree outside the hotel we found a camel. The villagers untied the beast and brought it to Bernie. They bowed again with folded hands.

'*Sa'hb,* this camel phor you,' said Omi Chand.

'But Omi Chand . . .' said Bernie. 'How can I?'

'Prey-jent phor you *sa'hb,*' continued Omi Chand. 'Pleej.'

Bernie was hesitant to accept such a gift. But Omi Chand was undaunted: '*Sa'hb*, bhillagers not go behk iph you not take camel.'

'Okay,' said Bernie. 'How much?'

'No want munny *sa'hb*.'

'It's no use, Bernie,' I said. 'These people will not accept money. And they're not taking the camel back either.'

'All right,' said Bernie. 'I'll take it.' He held the rope around the camel's neck and patted its head. The beast slouched forward with an air of indifference. 'Does he have a name?'

'Sultan, *Sa'hb*,' said Omi Chand. 'King oph dejert.'

The villagers folded their hands and bowed at Bernie. Some puffed on *hukkas*.

'*Sa'hb*,' said Omi Chand, his face glowing. 'Whol the bhillage hay-ppi now.'

And Bernie was happy, too. For ever since he had come to India he had wanted his own pet, 'I wonder if I could ride him to work,' he said, stroking the camel's long snout. 'Wait 'til Lilette sees this.'

Lilette, it transpired, did not take to Sultan at all, which the Bengali found surprising. 'They look alike,' he said. 'And have virtually the same personality.' He was accurate on both counts. When we first met Lilette, she was the model of modesty and reserve. She only came to the office behind her fiancé and treated everyone in the bureau with shy respect. The Bengali found this a fault: he was reminded, he said, of Ellen's lame dog Nibble and soon he was calling Lilette 'Nibble' behind her back.

But then came the marriage, and the shy Lilette of courtship days was vanquished by a new creature known as Mrs Katz. The day after the honeymoon, Lilette stayed in the bureau for four hours, barging into rooms without knocking and shooting questions at the staff as if she owned the place. She commanded a cup of tea from Omi Chand and addressed him as 'bearer'. (Omi Chand said nothing, but he put salt in her tea instead of sugar.) Since then she has attended the bureau every day. Even her look changed. Prior to her marriage, Lilette wore sarees and *salwar-kameez*. Now, she comes to the bureau in shiny leather pants and boots. Earlier, she had waist-length hair. Now it's so short that if you saw her face, Col. Pai, with its prominent nose – we wonder how the two manage to kiss – you wouldn't be sure if she was a woman or a man.

No one, of course, detests her more than the Bengali, who has abandoned his former nickname for her. Instead of Nibble he now calls her Bite.

Women trouble. That's our problem at UNI. Recently, New York created a new position in the bureau. The assassination of Mrs Gandhi boosted Western interest in India – the Bengali says the Americans are drooling over the possibility of its disintegration – and we have been given a photo editor from New York. He is a Texan named Sean Carmichael. Sean arrived in India with his own female companion: a redhead by the name of Isadora, who is half Portuguese and half Greek. I have to say, Col. Pai, that Isadora has been rated by the Indian staff as the rattiest, least attractive and least cheerful white woman they have ever set eyes upon. Isadora favours a pair of Levis – she owns only one – work shirts and a commodious leather jacket. She smokes a nervous chain of pungent, European cigarettes. She has trouble meeting people's gaze and often steps away when addressed, as if she might be attacked. According to some people in the bureau, we are lucky for the latter habit: apparently Isadora's personal grooming leaves something to be desired. I wouldn't know: I've kept my distance.

But Isadora's personal offensiveness is not our main problem. It's her professional aspirations.

You see, Col. Pai, Isadora is also a photographer. And Sean, her boyfriend, has started awarding her assignments, which cuts into the income of Salim. Technically, Salim is a stringer, a kind of part-time employee in journalistic parlance, who gets paid by the number of assignments he does. In the past that didn't matter because he was the only photographer. It's possible he made more than he would have on a salary. Now Salim has been both demoted and sidelined. The good assignments are snapped up by Sean; secondary assignments go to Isadora. Salim gets the crumbs and his working hours have been cut by more than half.

Isadora's assignments have to be approved by Bernie, which always happens because the two couples are social friends. They hang out at the Foreign Correspondents Club together and, once, were seen by P.K. strolling in Lodi Gardens. The Bengali is most perturbed about this new alliance, which he calls the Gang of Four. 'This Turkish whore is particularly dangerous.'

'Portuguese,' corrected Arun.

The Bengali rolled his eyes as if to say: What's the difference? 'If we don't watch out, there will be a cultural revolution very soon in this bureau. And afterwards our Gang of Four will be having orgies in the bureau chief's office while we will sweep the newsroom floor and clean the toilets.'

Omi Chand gave the Bengali a look.

'Okay,' he said. 'There's nothing wrong with sweeping floors and cleaning toilets.' He nodded at Omi Chand. 'Work, as Pandit Nehru said, is sacred. They'll have us cremating dead bodies before long.'

'That's work too,' said P.K.

'Get out of here,' said the Bengali. '*Sala kabadi.*'

And then last week the Bengali's prediction about the Gang of Four came true.

We were at my desk in the communications room, where we normally gather at lunchtime. Present at the table were the Bengali, Gopalacharya, Arun, P.K., Matthew and me. Salim was in the darkroom, repairing photo equipment. As a Muslim, he eats with us only occasionally. The white people never eat with the Indian staff, excepting Sam who was working on a story that afternoon. The Bengali distributed on to six plates portions of food from everyone's tiffin box. (He always served a little extra for himself.) 'Gopalacharya, here, you have the nose of the fish.'

'I had it the last time, Dada.'

'That was the tail, stupid. You South Indians don't know your noses from your tails.'

We had just begun to eat when P.K. nudged the Bengali and whispered, 'Here she comes.'

'Bite,' said the Bengali. 'Everybody protect your plates.'

Lilette came into the room, swaying her hips and thrusting her chin out. She ignored us, threw a sheet of paper on the telex machine and left without saying a word.

(Before the wedding, Lilette never failed to compliment our food. When we invited her to eat with us she accepted most thankfully. But since then she hasn't even glanced at our food or at us when we are eating it.)

We heard a voice in the hallway and a distinct clicking sound on the tiles. It was Sean, who always wore cowboy boots.

'When did the son of a bitch come back?' growled the Bengali.

'Last night.' P.K. put a big piece of *roti* wrapped around dry potatoes in his mouth.

The Bengali did a count on his fingers. 'The fucker spent two full weeks in Kathmandu? While we were rotting in the heat here?'

'He takes all these trips and his photos don't even sell,' said Arun.

P.K., whose mouth was full, waved his hands as if wanting to interrupt.

'You don't have to stuff your mouth, P.K.,' said the Bengali.

P.K. continued to wave frantically.

'If you only put so much in your mouth . . . like this.' Demonstrating, the Bengali placed a large spoonful of chickpeas into the right side of his mouth and said, in a slightly muffled tone: 'See? You can eat and *still* talk.'

'Sorry.' P.K. swallowed contritely. 'I wanted to mention that darkroom expenses have gone up 150 per cent since Sean arrived.'

'There's nothing extraordinary about that,' said Gopalacharya. 'We have three photographers now.'

'But Salim's assignments have been drastically cut,' I countered. 'And Sean hasn't been taking that many pictures.'

'That's right.' P.K. blinked rapidly. 'Almost all the pictures are being taken by Isadora.'

'Isadora.' The Bengali spat mockingly on the floor. 'You have ruined my lunch by taking her name.'

P.K. looked nervous. 'I think there's something wrong.'

'What do you mean wrong?' The Bengali leaned forward in his chair.

'I mean the expenses are too high. I think this Sean and his girlfriend are up to something. Hanky-panky.'

Gopalacharya lifted an eyebrow. 'You mean to say they are misappropriating money?'

'I . . . don't know.'

'If anyone has guts in this bureau, he would investigate.' The Bengali licked curry from his fingers. 'To expose this White Devil and his Parsee witch wife in her leather pants. This fucking galloping Texan – I've read that corruption is rampant in Texas. And Turks! My God, the word probably comes from the Turkish. Korupt. With a K.'

'Why don't *you* launch an investigation, Dada?' challenged Gopalacharya.

'I would' – the Bengali emitted a burp – 'but I'm off to Dhaka this evening.'

There was silence at the table.

He stood and stretched. 'I may go home for a nap before my plane.'

The silence had an ashamed quality. Gopalacharya munched distractedly; Arun looked at the food on his plate with the concentration of a scientist. P.K. cleared the table. 'What does it matter?' he said, sweeping crumbs. 'We probably can't prove anything anyway.'

I don't know what came over me, Col. Pai, but suddenly I stood.

'I'll do it.'

'What, Hari?' asked P.K.

'I'll do the investigation.'

'The Bengali looked astonished. 'You, Hari?'

'Me, Dada.' I looked the Bengali in the eye.

'I think we're seeing a reawakening of the martial spirit in our Hari,' said Gopalacharya.

'There's something wrong in the bureau and it needs to be investigated.' I gave a small thump with my fist on the table. 'I'll do it.'

Arun looked at me like he was seeing a ghost.

'I mean, if everybody's busy with other things . . .'

'Bravo, my boy.' The Bengali stood and gave another burp. 'I always knew that if anyone could grow into my boots some day it would be Hari. He walked away chuckling. 'Maybe.' It wasn't long before he left the bureau for his nap and the plane to Dhaka.

Arun and Gopalacharya came to my office in the afternoon. 'Hari?' asked Arun. 'Are you really going to do it?'

Actually, Col. Pai, I wanted to investigate the alleged hanky-panky in the darkroom – I say alleged because nothing had been proven yet and this is UNI style – in order to help Salim. I felt a bond with him since visiting his flat. I felt that Indians should somehow all pull together – especially Hindus and Muslims. And if I could establish that film costs had gone up unnecessarily, it might prove that Salim had done as good a job at a lower cost before the arrival of Sean and Isadora. Perhaps it would help Salim get more assignments and income: I wondered whether he might have been forced to quit drinking for budgetary reasons.

'Yes, Arun. And I want to begin immediately. Get me the play reports.'

The play report is a daily record of how the bureau's photos compare to those of competing international news agencies. It didn't take me long to find out that since Sean and Isadora had taken charge of the photo department six months earlier, the play report had become only slightly better than in Salim's days. Next, I asked P.K. for the filing records – a list of all the photos sent to New York.

'Did we have a photo feature on the riot victims?'

'Isadora did it,' said P.K. 'I remember her taxi bills being too high.'

'What about the truckers' strike? You think she really went to the Delhi-Ghaziabad border?'

'The greater the distance,' said P.K., 'the more she can inflate her taxi bills.'

I found that the total number of photos filed by the bureau had gone up 30 per cent in the past six months. But this didn't account for a 150 per cent increase in costs.

'Fifty per cent may have been justified,' said P.K. 'But 150?'

Next I asked P.K. for the darkroom expenses. He opened a file and handed me about a dozen sheets of paper held by a clip. I went through them one by one, jotting down the expenses incurred during the past six months and comparing them with the preceding six months. I found that developing costs had gone up 20 per cent.

'Didn't Sean authorise the purchase of new equipment?'

'That's on a different ledger. Capital expenditures.'

'What other expenses are there?'

'Well, there's film.'

'Let me see.'

P.K. pulled out a thin folder from his drawer. 'Film accounts for the past eight months.'

The folder contained eight one-page entries of the number of boxes of film purchased and their prices.

'There's a 145 per cent increase in the purchase of film,' I said.

P.K.'s mouth fell open.

'Check.' I closed the folder and slid it across the desk. P.K. turned the pages with one hand and fingered a calculator with the other. 'You're absolutely correct, Hari. Who said Jats don't have a figure for heads?'

'It's the other way around, P.K.'

P.K. and I marched into the newsroom. Gopalacharya sat hunched over his typewriter with a cigarette protruding from his right fist. Arun was checking the news coming over the wires. I told them what I had discovered.

'Film.' Gopalacharya became pensive.

'Film,' repeated Arun.

'Isn't the film imported?' asked Gopalacharya.

'Of course,' said P.K. proudly.

'That means someone could make a packet selling it in the black market.'

The bureau door swung open: Bernie and Lilette were returning from lunch. The reporters dashed to their desks; P.K. slunk off to his cubicle. I made pretend I was checking the teleprinters. When the door to the bureau chief's office was shut, P.K. came scuttling back.

'We used to get two boxes a month.' P.K., whispering, made a V-like sign with his fingers. 'Even that was too much. We would have a surplus every few months. Now we get three.'

'How much was the surplus?' asked Arun in a whisper. 'Here – write on this. And over how many months did it accumulate?'

'Well, let's see.' P.K. poised a pen over the paper. 'We had an extra box every three months. Provided there were no big stories.' He wrote some numbers on the paper with Arun watching.

Lilette came out of Bernie's office. 'Where is Omi Chand, please? We would like some tea.'

'Certainly madam,' I said.

She gave me a dubious look and returned to the bureau chief's office, slamming the door.

'Okay,' announced Arun, reading from the paper. 'There's a box of film unaccounted for every month.' He waved his paper in the air. 'Missing.'

There was hushed silence.

'A whole box?' P.K.'s voice was incredulous.

'Precisely.'

'My God,' said P.K. 'Do you know how much that's worth? We could pay our rents with that money.'

'If anyone is stealing film,' said Gopalacharya, 'it is probably Isadora.'

'Why?' asked Arun.

'I just feel it.'

'She is the one who gets the film,' said P.K.

'She gets the film?'

'She moves it.'

A buzzer sounded on Gopalacharya's desk. 'My God,' he said. 'We forgot her bloody tea.' He ran to find Omi Chand.

'What do you mean she moves the film?' I asked. 'From where?'

'From the bureau chief's office,' replied P.K. 'I place it there – in that cabinet behind the desk – once a month. And Isadora moves it to the darkroom as and when she needs film.'

'How often?' Arun sounded excited.

'I told you,' said P.K. 'On a need basis.'

Gopalacharya returned and we filled him in. 'Well, how often do you put it in Bernie's office?'

'Once a month,' said P.K.

'And how often does she . . .'

'We're going bloody backwards,' cried P.K.

'Guys,' I said. Everyone looked at me. It must have been my tone. I have to admit that at that moment I found it difficult to swallow. 'I propose we catch her.'

'Catch her?' asked Gopalacharya. 'How?'

'Hold on a minute,' said Arun. 'For something like this we really need . . . we better wait until Dada comes back.'

'He'd hate to miss it,' said Gopalacharya.

'It'll be too late,' said P.K.

'He'll be back on Sunday,' said Gopalacharya.

'She has to be caught this week.'

'Why?'

'Because Bernie has proposed Isadora as a staffer,' announced P.K. solemnly. 'Her six-month probation period is about to end.' He paused, lowering his head mournfully. 'It ends in four days. *Friday.*'

'*What?*' A look of disbelief came over Gopalacharya's face. 'Are you sure?'

P.K. looked a little sick. 'I saw Bernie's letter to New York on the confirmation. It's post-dated Friday.'

'That means if we don't catch her by Friday she'll be confirmed as staff?' I asked.

'That's right.'

'*Four days.*' Gopalacharya was thinking hard.

'Ninety-six hours.' Arun looked at me.

I said: 'We have to do it! To help Salim. If Isadora becomes a staffer he'll be in a soup.'

'We'll all help, Hari,' said Gopalacharya.

'I agree,' said Arun.

The conversation ceased as Omi Chand came across the newsroom with Bernie and Lilette's tea. He went into Bernie's office and returned with an empty tray.

'Look at that.' Gopalacharya adopted a professorial tone. 'Did you all notice that?'

'What?' asked Arun.

'Omi Chand. Just now. Going in and out of Bernie's office.'

'Yes, we saw it.'

'That just proves the point. How could anyone, except a ghost, smuggle a whole box of film out of that room every month? How does Isadora do it – without being seen?'

'Um,' said Arun. 'Excuse me a second. I have an idea. Back in a few minutes.'

'Gosh, where's he going in such a rush?' Gopalacharya lit a fresh cigarette. 'Let's begin from the beginning. Where is the film kept?'

'In Bernie's office,' P.K. pointed to the closed door. 'In the cupboard on the right. Behind the desk.'

'Hmm . . .' Gopalacharya turned to P.K. 'Let's say Isadora carried a whole box of film through the newsroom. Let's assume that the newsroom is deserted for some reason. Wouldn't she be spotted on her way to the darkroom?'

'Certainly,' I replied. 'Omi Chand could see her through the kitchen, Matthew or me through the communications room, and P.K. from his cubicle.'

'Then how can the film be smuggled out?'

There was a moment of silence as the three of us pondered the question.

'By dividing the contents of the box into a number of packages,' I suggested.

'How would that help?'

'The packages could then be brought out one by one over several days. Nobody would notice.'

'That would be suspicious too,' said P.K. 'Photographers go into the bureau chief's office once a fortnight to collect film.'

'Not if they are friends with the bureau chief,' I said.

'Even if your theory is correct,' countered P.K., 'someone would have definitely seen her carrying the packages.'

'P.K.'s right.' Gopalacharya blew a blast of cigarette smoke.

A depressing silence followed. Just then we heard the sound of footsteps in the hallway. Arun marched into the room like an emperor. Behind him was a hotel bellboy, a diminutive Gurkha from Nepal.

'We better do this in my room,' I said.

When we were in the communications room – door bolted against intruders – Arun introduced the liveried bellboy. 'Bir Bahadur,' said Arun in a commanding tone. 'Tell them what you saw.'

'Sir . . .' The bellboy hesitated.

'Don't worry, Bir Bahadur. Nothing will happen to you. This is between us all.'

'I saw the madam, sir.'

'Which madam?' said P.K.

The bellboy made a low motion with his hand.

'That's her height,' said P.K.

The bellboy moved his hands frantically around his head.

'That's her hair,' said Gopalacharya.

He waved the air before his face, grimaced and pinched his nose.

'Okay, it's Isadora,' I said. 'Now what did you see?'

'Sir, I saw the madam carrying a box out of the lobby. A heavy box.'

'And . . .' prompted Arun.

'I tried to help her but she waved me away.' The bellboy made a dismissing gesture. 'Then she put the box in the trunk of her car.'

'Tell them what her face looked like, Bir Bahadur.'

'She looked scared.' The bellboy cupped his face with his hands.

'When did this happen?' I asked.

'About a month ago, sir.'

'And what time of the day was it?'

'Night time, sir.'

'Of course,' exclaimed P.K. 'She comes in when the bureau is closed.'

'No sir, it wasn't that late. It was around 8 o'clock in the night.'

We thanked the bellboy and Arun escorted him out. When he returned, I said: 'Isadora's our thief. She's doing it on her own.' Gopalacharya, Arun and P.K. embarked on an animated discussion on how she could have entered the bureau chief's office without being seen.

'She probably sneaks into Bernie's office when the night duty man goes to the bathroom,' said Arun.

'Kumar? You know Kumar,' said P.K. 'He never leaves his desk.'

'He must go to the bathroom.'

'I have never seen him go to the bathroom,' insisted P.K. 'Ever.'

'Then how on earth is it done?' Gopalacharya sounded frustrated.

He must wait until he gets home.'

'Not Kumar,' said Arun. 'Isadora.'

We heard the clicking of Lilette's high heels in the hallway. Bernie's face pushed through the doorway.

'I'll be back in a bit,' said Bernie. 'Just dropping Lilette home.' He turned to leave and then stopped. 'I think you guys ought to get some work done.'

As soon as the couple left, we moved to the newsroom.

'Look, as we have emphasised again and again, *someone would surely see her*,' said Gopalacharya. 'Even if she knew when the bureau chief would not be around, someone would see her hauling the box through the newsroom.'

P.K. rubbed his bald pate in a slow, circular motion, as if massaging his brain cells. Arun nervously drummed his fingers on the desk.

'Wait!' I shouted. 'Darts!'

'Darts?' P.K. screwed up his face.

'At the FCC. Every month. The darts tournament.'

'Ohhh!' Gopalacharya's face brightened.

'Everyone goes for it,' I continued, 'The bureau chief, his wife, the photo editor, Sam, Salim.'

'Except . . .' said Gopalacharya.

'Isadora!' said Arun. 'She takes darkroom duty on those evenings.'

'Exactly.' Gopalacharya's face lit up. 'She's alone in the bureau on darts nights, except for Kumar.' He took a long pull on his cigarette. 'And that explains the once-a-month theft. She has only one night a month' – his tone became urgent – 'Arun, go check the bulletin board.'

'For what?'

'Check the schedule. For the next darts night.'

Arun was already at the bulletin board. 'Tonight!'

'Tonight?' squealed P.K.

As if on cue, the door opened slowly and everyone fell

silent. A figure came tentatively into the newsroom. It was Isadora, dressed in her faded Levis with ragged holes at the knees. Fastened across her waist was a brown leather pouch containing money, rolling tobacco, cigarette paper, and according to the Bengali, enough Afghani hashish to get a whole regiment high. A crumpled white cotton men's shirt hung loosely over her scrawny frame. There were large, permanent sweat stains at the armpits. Over the shirt was an old, embroidered waistcoat. Its colour matched the rouge that Isadora thickly applied to hide the scores of pockmarks pitting her face.

She stood in the doorway sniffing nervously, her eyes darting like a trapped rat. Her fists were clenched like tiny balls. She walked unsteadily past us towards Bernie's office and stopped at the closed door.

'Are Bernie and Lilette . . . ?' Isadora's hand was on the doorknob.

'Gopalacharya looked up and said in a tired voice: 'They are out.'

'Not een?' Her hand started turning the doorknob.

'They're *out*.' Gopalacharya spoke as if Isadora was simple or partially deaf.

She blinked at him.

We all looked at her hand on the doorknob. Her gaze followed ours until everyone in the room, Isadora included, was looking at a small hand, with cracked fingernails, clenched tightly on a doorknob.

'They out,' she repeated in a dubious tone. The hand loosened. She took a long sniff of the air and wheeled around. 'Tell Bernie I here, in darkroom, when he come back?' She left the newsroom door ajar.

Arun jumped up to close it. 'We still don't know how she does it,' he whispered.

'Kumar's on casual leave.' P.K. turned to Arun. 'You're filling in, right?'

Arun nodded.

Gopalacharya beckoned us to follow him into the bureau chief's office. We crowded through the door and he opened the cabinet where the film was stored.

'The film is here. Isadora has to carry a very large box past Kumar. Now Kumar is getting old but he's not blind.'

'What are you doing, Hari?' asked Arun.

'Look.' I was standing beside a pair of dusty curtains in a corner of Bernie's office. I separated the curtains and pointed at a painted-over door.

'Oh my god,' gasped P.K. 'Check the bolt.'

'It's secured.' I gave the bolt a tug. 'But the paint is broken, cracked all along the door. It can be opened. And it leads . . .'

'To the hotel corridor,' said P.K. 'She comes in here on some pretax and . . .'

'Pretext,' prompted Gopalacharya.

'Okay,' said P.K. 'She takes the film and escapes into the corridor . . .'

'Or she – that's it!' Gopalacharya snapped his fingers. 'She comes in sometime during the day and draws the bolt. Then she can enter the bureau chief's office anytime *from* the corridor; she takes the film and leaves without anyone witnessing anything. Then she returns to the bureau through the regular door . . .'

'Sherlock!' I gave Gopalacharya a pat on his back. 'She says she's going out for dinner. Instead she comes in here, gets the film, puts it in her car and comes back without anyone being the wiser.'

'How much would a box of film sell for in the black market?' asked Arun.

'At least 12,000 rupees,' replied P.K.

'Imagine amassing that every month,' said Gopalacharya.

'*Luteri, sali,*' said P.K.

'Guys, I know how we can catch her,' I said.

Arun was trying the bolt on the painted door when we heard a horrifying sound. A familiar voice said: 'What's going on?' It was Bernie, back sooner than we expected.

Arun hid himself behind the curtains.

'Uh, we were looking at the office chairs,' lied Gopalacharya. 'There's a repairman coming in tomorrow to fix them.'

Just then, Isadora entered Bernie's office.

Gopalacharya, P.K. and I excused ourselves and went into the newsroom.

Ten minutes later Bernie and Isadora came out of the office.

'I'll be gone for a couple of hours,' said Bernie to Gopalacharya. 'Come on.' Isadora gave us a sick little smile and followed him out of the bureau.

When they were gone, Gopalacharya cried: 'Arun!' We charged into Bernie's office like a SWAT team. 'Arun,' whispered Gopalacharya. 'You can come out now.'

Slowly, the curtains parted and Arun stepped out. His face was ashen.

'They didn't see you, did they?'

He shook his head.

I said: 'Why didn't you slip out through the door?'

'I was too scared,' said Arun haltingly. 'The bolt is noisy. So I just stayed behind the curtains. I thought it was only Bernie. But then I heard Isadora. I was scared this may be her moment – to fiddle with the door. With the bolt. For tonight's theft.'

'Did she?' asked Gopalacharya.

'No. But Bernie did.'

'Bernie fiddled with the door?' said Gopalacharya.

'No,' said Arun. 'He fiddled with Isadora.'

There was silence in the room. Everyone had sour looks on their faces. I suggested we move to the newsroom.

'He fiddled with Isadora?' asked Gopalacharya, pulling up a chair. 'I don't want to know.'

'Everybody sit down,' I said. 'We have a long night ahead.'

'She was standing in front of Bernie's desk reading something. Bernie crept up from behind.' Arun did an imitation of Bernie with his arms in the air. 'He grabbed her from behind.' Arun's face flushed. 'I mean, he touched her breasts.'

(I'm telling you these details, Col. Pai, because surely as an army man you will have heard such things before.)

'Her *breasts*?' said Gopalacharya. 'She *has* no breasts.'

'She has nipples,' cackled P.K.

'What did Isadora do?' Gopalacharya had become interested.

'I couldn't see. Bernie was blocking her.'

'He must be screwing her,' said Gopalacharya.

'From behind,' said P.K.

'Carry on, Arun.'

'Well, Bernie rubbed her breasts and said: "Let's do it tonight honey. In the darkroom. After darts." '

'They do it in the darkroom?' P.K. let out a low whistle and said in a sing-song voice: *Jab andhera hota hai . . .*'

'We're running out of time.' I stood. 'Here's how it stands. We know that Isadora comes into Bernie's office on darts night and unbolts the old door. Then, instead of going for dinner, she enters the office from the hotel corridor, takes the box of film and leaves through the same door. She carries the film to her car and returns to the bureau. Sometime later, she makes some excuse to enter Bernie's office and rebolts the door.'

'How do you plan to trap her?' asked P.K.

'As long as we know where she is at any given point of time, trapping her shouldn't be difficult.' I paused. 'Here's what I propose. We know for a fact that she has not yet unbolted the old door, right?'

Everyone nodded.

'So that means she has to go through the newsroom to get to the office.' I pointed to the door of Bernie's office. 'This will be witnessed by Gopalacharya and Arun.'

Gopalacharya and Arun nodded.

'Next, she leaves the newsroom and heads for the darkroom. She walks past P.K.'s cubicle and my office.' I looked at P.K. 'P.K. and I will be sitting in our respective rooms at that time with our doors open.'

'No problem,' said P.K.

'That's phase one. Phase two is the critical part: monitoring Isadora's movements just before the theft.' I looked at my audience. 'There's no guarantee that she will announce she's going out for dinner. Which is why P.K. or I must see her leaving the darkroom and heading out of the bureau. Otherwise we're finished.'

'Don't worry, Hari,' said P.K. 'I have the eyes of an eagle and ears of a peacock.'

'One more important thing: we have to give her time to get into Bernie's office. How long would that be?'

'Twenty seconds,' said P.K.

'We don't want to be too fast,' I warned. 'She has to be through the old door and in Bernie's office before we rush into the corridor.'

'A minute,' said P.K.

'But we don't want to lose her.'

'Thirty seconds!' cried P.K.

'Okay, we wait thirty seconds and then you, me and Gopalacharya will go out into the hotel corridor without making a sound. We'll wait outside the old door. We should catch her coming out with the box of film.'

'A posse,' said Gopalacharya.

'A pussy,' said P.K.

We all looked at him.

'Sorry,' he said. 'All this bawdy talk.'

'Hey, what about me?' asked Arun.

'Someone has to be on guard in the newsroom,' I said. 'Just in case she uses the regular door to escape.'

We practised my plan five times with Arun acting as Isadora. That night the Indian staff stayed in the bureau. Arun was already scheduled to fill in for Kumar, the night-shift man; Gopalacharya declared he was working on an urgent feature story; P.K. said he was completing the bureau's monthly accounts; I said I was staying back to help P.K. tabulate the communications expenses.

At 7.15 p.m., Bernie, Lilette, Sam, Sean and Salim left for

the FCC. Our countdown had begun. Gopalacharya, Arun, P.K. and I synchronised our watches and went into our respective rooms. At 7.20 p.m., Isadora came into the bureau, cameras dangling from both shoulders, and headed straight for Bernie's office. She said to Gopalacharya: 'I use telephone. Private call.' A few minutes later she emerged, explaining: 'Number bizzy.' When I saw her pass my office towards the darkroom, I strolled to the newsroom and pushed my head inside the door. Gopalacharya was sitting at his desk, typing. Arun was standing by the teleprinters, reading the incoming wires. They both looked up at me and smiled. Arun gave a thumbs-up signal. On the way back to my office I stopped at P.K.'s cubicle and whispered: 'Phase one complete.' He twisted excitedly in his seat.

I went into the communications room, leaving the door open, and sat at my desk. Matthew was at his usual place in front of the telex machine.

'We're going to get her,' I said. Matthew nodded perfunctorily. It was hard to get Matthew excited about anything, Col. Pai. Sometimes I wondered if he was human.

Twenty minutes passed and there was no sign of Isadora leaving the darkroom. I went to the door and peeped into the hallway: the darkroom door was shut. Five minutes passed. I crept into the hallway and found P.K. looking anxiously out of his cubicle. To my surprise, even Matthew became infected with nervousness. He joined me in the hallway. 'Put your ear to the door,' I said. 'Silently.'

Matthew walked gingerly to the darkroom door and carefully applied his ear. P.K. was waving his hand: he thought the manoeuvre over-risky. But Matthew returned safely. 'She's working hard in there. I can hear sounds, like the moving of furniture or something.' P.K. stared at us anxiously from across the hallway.

It was 7.50 p.m. I started pacing the hallway. Sweat trickled down my armpits like water from a fountain. The time was 8 p.m. now – Isadora had 45 minutes before Bernie, Lilette,

Sam, Sean and Salim returned. P.K. joined me and the two of us walked up and down the hallway like soldiers on patrol.

'She's running out of time,' whispered P.K.

'Could she be taking some other route?'

He gave me a blank stare.

'The window ledge!'

We raced to my office. 'Matthew,' I said. 'Check the ledge! She might have snuck out from the window.'

Matthew went to the window and looked out. 'There's no one out there.'

'We're too late. Maybe she's already crossed over into Bernie's office.'

'Matthew.' I snapped my fingers. 'You're a mountaineer, aren't you?'

'Spelunker.'

'What?'

'It's like mountaineering.'

'Can you climb along that ledge?'

Matthew grinned. 'Piece of cake.'

It took all three of us to loosen the window, which hadn't been opened in decades. Then Matthew straddled the window-sill and lowered himself onto the ledge, which protruded no more than six inches from the wall. He shuffled sideways, the tip of his nose touching the wall. The darkroom was about fifteen feet to his left, and he inched along, grasping a water pipe. After what seemed like an eternity, Matthew reached the darkroom window and squinted inside. He turned in our direction and made a gesture as if saying he could see nothing. I called incredulously: 'No one's there?'

He shook his head.

'Is the window open?'

He shook his head again. 'It's locked from inside.'

I turned to P.K. 'Go knock on the darkroom door.'

'Are you sure?'

'Do it, P.K.!'

He was out of breath when he returned. 'There's no answer. And guess what?'

I looked at him.

'I tried the darkroom door. Very gently, of course. Hari: the door is locked!'

'Matthew,' I called in a desperate tone. 'Can you get to Bernie's window?'

He grabbed the pipe and inched back towards me.

'Hurry!'

He passed me, then the kitchen window and those of the newsroom. There was a lump in my throat when he reached the first window in Bernie's office. He peered into the room, ducked his head and moved his lips to form silent words.

I extended my top half out the window. I called quietly: 'What? What do you see?'

I could barely hear Matthew's words.

'*Whaaat?*'

The words came as a shock. 'She's inside!'

I pulled myself back in.

'She's fooled us.'

P.K. did a double take.

'Come on!'

With P.K. in my wake, I barged into the newsroom like a storm-trooper. There was a tension in the room and both Gopalacharya and Arun had alarmed expressions on their faces. Gopalacharya said, 'Um, Hari.' He pointed. I looked at the teleprinters. Sam was standing there. He had obviously come back early.

'What on earth's going on?' said Sam in a startled voice.

'Shut up!' I shouted.

I felt full of power, Col. Pai. Like a general sensing victory in battle, I marched towards the door of the bureau chief's office. Just as I reached for the doorknob I heard a shout.

'Look!' Arun was pointing at the doorknob.

The lock on the door was turning from within.

'She's locked herself in,' said Arun.

'How did she get in there?' spluttered Gopalacharya.

'How did she get out of the darkroom?' asked P.K. 'The door is locked.'

'What is going on?' asked Sam.

'Everyone – follow me!' I charged out of the newsroom and into the hotel corridor. Everybody followed, including Sam.

We stood huddled in a group, about ten feet from the old door leading to Bernie's office. There was pin-drop silence. 'I don't get this,' said Sam. 'What are we . . .'

'Shhh,' said P.K. Then he pointed.

The painted-over door opened, inch by excruciating inch, exposing a few strands of dirty red hair. Then Isadora stepped into the corridor. Her eyes were narrowed with painful exertion. The box of film was placed on her head, like a construction worker carrying a load of bricks. She quietly closed the door behind her and started walking slowly down the corridor. I stepped forward and entered her peripheral vision. Isadora stopped in her tracks. She jerked her head towards our group with such force that the box crashed to the floor, spilling dozens of rolls of film.

'Good evening Isadora,' I said.

She gulped.

'Going somewhere?'

'I . . . just . . .' Her face turned scarlet.

'Just stealing.'

'It's all over Isadora,' said Gopalacharya lighting a cigarette.

'Sheet,' she said. And then Isadora burst into tears.

We hauled her into the newsroom. She sat at Arun's desk, wailing loudly and cradling her head in her hands as if she were too ashamed to expose her face. I asked her for the key to the darkroom and told Matthew and Arun to guard her. Gopalacharya, P.K. and I walked to the darkroom.

P.K. said: 'If the door is locked, how on earth . . .'

I unlocked the door. In the centre of the room lay a large heap of boxes.

'What the hell is this?' asked Gopalacharya.

'Look!' P.K. pointed at an old door in a corner of the room.

'My God,' whispered Gopalacharya. 'A *second* secret door.'

The door was open. I went through it. It was pitch dark. A stale, musty smell hung in the vacuum. I say vacuum because Gopalacharya lit several matches but the flames died instantly because of lack of air. P.K. fetched a flashlight from his cubicle.

In front of us was a set of out-of-use service stairs. We followed it down to a store-room full of broken chairs. At the other end of the room was a door and a window with filthy, cobwebbed panes. The door was locked. The window was shut but not bolted. I opened it a few inches and found myself looking into the corridor one floor below that of the bureau.

We rushed back to the newsroom and confronted Isadora, who was wreathed in a cloud of smoke from her filterless cigarettes. We told her about the door in the darkroom and, coughing and snivelling, she quickly confessed.

It turned out, Col. Pai, that the secret door in the darkroom had been covered with boxes and equipment for decades. Nobody but Isadora knew of its existence. Each month on darts night, she shifted the equipment to get to the door. Then she descended the stairs to the room with the chairs.

'Then what did you do?' asked Gopalacharya.

'I climbed out window.'

There was silence as we all imagined Isadora crawling out from the window, once a month, and dropping to the corridor rug.

'And the rest is history,' said P.K.

'Hold on, P.K.' Gopalacharya gave him an admonishing look. 'How long did it take you to do all this?'

'Forty-eight minutes to shift boxes,' said Isadora. 'Seven minutes to make downstairs and to Bernie's place.'

'You've got to hand it to her,' said Gopalacharya with a sigh. 'She worked hard for her film.'

Soon, we heard the voices of Bernie, Lilette, Sean and Salim in the hotel corridor. Bernie was singing a Bruce Springsteen song: 'Ooh-oh-oh pooooint-blaaaank . . . right between the eyes . . .'

The moment they entered the newsroom, we presented our catch. Bernie scarcely breathed as I narrated the sequence of events that led to Isadora's capture: our suspicion about the missing film, the investigation, the trap and the final denouement. When I finished, Bernie asked Sean, Lilette and Isadora to accompany him into his office.

We waited in the newsroom, all eyes on the door of Bernie's office. Sam sat in a corner, a dazed expression on his face.

The door opened after fifteen minutes. Bernie stood in front of it as if guarding the occupants inside from attackers.

'Gentlemen,' he said in a low voice. 'I've heard both sides of the story and would like to make an appeal.' He gave everyone a quick glance. 'Let me begin by saying that Isadora was wrong in what she did and that she is feeling very pained and ashamed. She is also very depressed.' He paused to think, biting his lip. 'Gentlemen, in light of the circumstances, and for the sake of both humanity and bureau loyalty, I urge you all to accept her sincere apology.' Bernie studied our expressions. 'I hope you will find it in your large, Indian hearts to forgive her.'

Gopalacharya was staring at the floor. Arun was thin-lipped. P.K. looked at me out of the corner of his eye.

'I'm afraid that's out of the question, Bernie.'

'Hari, you of all of us!' said Bernie. 'Everyone makes mistakes. And after all, Isadora is popular in the bureau. Everyone *likes* Isadora.'

Arun said: 'None as much as you.' Gopalacharya started to laugh and cough at the same time.

'What's this all about?'

'Justice, Bernie,' I said. 'Justice. What would have happened if *you* had discovered the theft? Who would have been blamed? One of us Indians? And what would you have done to him?'

Bernie looked at the floor.

'What form the punishment takes is up to the bureau chief,' I continued. 'And if he can't decide, then the matter must be referred to New York.'

Bernie kept his head down for several minutes without uttering a word. Finally, he looked up. 'What do you guys think?'

'This is a news bureau, Bernie.' Gopalacharya was standing stiffly with his arms folded across his chest. 'There is no place here for thieves.'

'I agree with Gopalacharya,' answered Arun.

'And Hari,' interjected P.K. 'Me, too.'

There was pin-drop silence. Bernie stood with hands deep in the pockets of his trousers. Sam said, in a low mutter: 'Oh boy oh boy oh boy.' Then Bernie slowly turned around and, without saying a word, went into his office.

After a while, the door opened and the four friends emerged. Bernie and Sean flanked Isadora – whether for support or restraint we couldn't tell – and led her swiftly through the newsroom without looking right or left. Isadora was hiccuping violently. Sam left, taking up the rear.

Only Lilette was left behind and she carefully closed and locked Bernie's office door. Then, looking stately in her fashionable blouse, leather pants and towering heels, she glided through the newsroom, a curious smile on her face. When she reached me, she continued looking straight ahead. I viewed her jutting nose, her queer smile, a single eye. She said, quite simply: 'Congratulations, guys.' And then she was gone.

It was a strange remark, Col. Pai, neither bitter nor ironic. Lilette spoke not as a rival or opponent but as an ally, though one removed by certain unavoidable circumstances. It was as if she were acknowledging a long-term battle with the white men in which we were all engaged. And she was forced to pay homage to our unexpected victory.

The next day there was a notice on the bulletin board about a 'rotation' of staff. Sean was transferred to the Islamabad

bureau. Isadora didn't get her confirmation on the staff of the
New Delhi bureau. The following week, we learned, she flew
back to the United States.

Yours truly,
Hari Rana

Young Enchanting German Beauty
Box 3498, IHT
Friedrichstr
15, D-60323
Frankfurt/Main
Germany

Dear Madame,

I am responding to your advertisement for FRIENDSHIP in the International Herald Tribune newspaper. I am a young and handsome man from India interested in a long-term friendship with a 'good-looking, fun-loving and care-free' woman like you.

This is my first-ever missive to a woman. But that does not mean I am lacking in confidence – it is purely a matter of cultural upbringing. As you must be knowing, India is a conservative society, although times are changing and more and more Indian men are having girl-friends and vice versa. Needless to say, this is a positive trend. If Indians want to integrate with the modern world they must open their hearts as well as their minds to foreigners.

I am waiting for your frank reply at the top address.

Yours affectionately,

Hari Rana

The Editor
International Herald Tribune
5 Canterbury Rd
Singapore 0511

Dear Sir,

Recently I responded to one of the advertisements for FRIENDSHIP in your respected newspaper. The advertisement was inserted by a certain 'Young Enchanting German Beauty' in Box 3498, c/o IHT, Friedrichstr, 15, D-60323, Frankfurt/Main, Germany. The said advertiser said she was looking for a 'smart, broadminded companion'. I was therefore extremely thrilled the other day when I got an Air Mail letter from Germany. When I opened the letter it was completely in German, which being a foreign language, I was unable to understand.

It makes no sense for an advertiser in an English-language newspaper to reply to respondents in a foreign tongue. How would the advertisers feel if they got letters in Hindi? Or Tamil, which is even more *klisht*. For the protection of your readers, I think you should enquire into the English-language skills of your advertisers in advance. This would protect them from much disappointment.

Yours truly,
Hari Rana

Attractive Lady
Box 2347
International Herald Tribune
92521 Neuilly Cedex
France

Dear Madame,

Thank you for your reply, which I was heartwarmed to receive. I apologise for sending such a short initial letter, but I wasn't sure you would respond or, if you did, whether or not it would be in a language I could comprehend.

Thank you also for the surprise present of your beautiful photo, which I did indeed find very 'moving' (as you suggest). You are a very beautiful lady, as is obvious even from such a unique angle. The photo appears to be taken from a magazine (judging from the condom ad on the reverse). Are you a model?

Well begun is half done. So let me go on to the preliminaries right away.

I am a warm, young and caring bachelor of almost 30 years, having proportionate height and weight as per international standards. Currently, I am working as Chief of Communications in the South Asia bureau of Union News International, the world-famous American news agency. I am getting attractive salary plus health benefits and other perks. I have a degree in B.Sc. from Delhi University.

To put my personal self in a nut shell, I believe in no 'isms' – except for humanism and, of course, romanticism. What about you? I understand French people are highly romantic. I first came to know about French romance in 'Evening in Paris', a Hindi film in which tall handsome French men were kissing their girl friends openly in public while the Indian hero and heroine were running around the Ifell Tower like school kids. Alas, in India, even kissing on cheeks is considered taboo.

What a contrast from France where even 'Last Tango in Paris' is peanuts. The French Kiss is world famous. (Somebody told me it is two kisses on the lip followed by a thrusting tongue. Is this true?)

My sun sign is Taurus, which is famous for its loyalty. What is your sign? As a general rule, Taurus gets along beautifully with Virgo and Pisces. In the Chinese horoscope I am a Pig.

This letter is slightly delayed because I had trouble furnishing the photo you requested. I had to make special arrangements with our own photographer in the bureau because a photo of the sort requested by you could not be just brought down to any local photo shop. But I enclose the snap and hope you look at it long and hard, so to speak. If you examine it closely, you'll see I am holding your photo in left hand and looking to same.

I am eagerly looking forward to your reaction and your reply post-haste.

Affectionately yours,
Hari Rana

Attractive Lady
Box 2347, IHT
92521 Neuilly Cedex
France

Dear Madame,

Exactly two months month ago I wrote to you a letter extending my friendship and enclosing a photo specially requested by you. One month ago I sent another letter, enclosing a second photo (not quite as good as first but from the same batch). Despite daily perusal of office mail I have not received any letter from you. Normally an Air Mail letter reaches India in a week to ten days. Presuming that my letters reached you in minimum two weeks and assuming that you responded, I should have received your letter by now. But I have been waiting in vain.

I hope some tragedy in your life has caused this break in communication – a death in the family, say – and not what I suspect to be the case: that you did not like my photographs and are even right now laughing at them and showing to friends. It wouldn't surprise me if I stumbled across my own photo in one of the disgusting magazines you 'model' for. I must therefore demand return of said photos forthwith and post-haste as they are my personal property and there is nothing wrong with them. The messages I wrote on the reverse side of the photos were not sincere and should be ignored entirely. You should also know that my address is false: I do not work for the company heretofore stated and no one at that office has ever heard of Hari Rana. Further, I have told the post office not to deliver any letters from France to the above-said address and to take them to the police instead. (Incidentally, India is having a tie-up with Interpol.)

It would be to your advantage to return my possessions

immediately and before I am forced to move the High Court in this matter, with all the expense thereto involved.

Your former penfriend,

Hari Rana

The Times of India
Enchanting Frauds

Sir:

I would like to warn all readers seeking to make foreign pen-friends about a fraud being practised by some advertisers in international newspapers. Under the guise of 'friendship', certain women invite correspondence from innocent men in countries around the world. But what happens when one innocently accepts this proffered hand of friendship?

– One German lady, self-described as 'enchanting', wrote back to me in German!

– A letter from a French woman, called 'Attractive Lady', was delivered to me with pornographic materials enclosed, certainly breaking international laws.

– And recently, I answered an advertisement by a Dutch lady interested in making friends with readers of the International Herald Tribune newspaper. I wrote two letters to the said lady and when I got a reply I was shocked to find the so-called 'Dutch' lady was actually a Moluccan. When she sent me her snap I noted to my horror that she was ugly, having dark curly hair and pimples on her face, even though she was technically a Dutch national. (The photo showed her holding up a Dutch passport.)

One can understand such things happening in India, where the evil dowry system forces advertisers to call themselves tall, fair, handsome and charming even if they happen to be midgets, jet black, hideous and cunning. International newspapers are being affected by this same dishonesty disease. This is nothing but cashing in on the reader's loneliness and gullibleness. Those looking for international friendships should beware.

Hari Rana
New Delhi

Col. Narendra Pai
Lancer's Lodge
P.O. Urulikanchan
Dist. Pune 412 202

Dear Col. Pai,

Strange are the relations among men and among races. Strange, too, are human perceptions and how they alter. As I told you in my previous letters, the UNI staff used to believe that Ellen was the worst bureau chief we ever had. Then we got Bernie Katz for five years and our attitudes about Ellen softened. Now we have a new bureau chief, Col. Pai. His name is Damon Hatcher. And once more, we find ourselves revising our views. Just today, at lunch, the Bengali was saying:

'This bloody *kutta*.' He stuffed food in his mouth and scratched his armpit. 'I would do anything to have Bernie back for a single day.'

'Now, Dada.'

'Bernie was an ordinary Joe. Human. Married, at least, and therefore not destined to hell like *this* fellow.'

'You despised his wife,' I said.

'She was a bitch, no doubt. But her capacity for harm was limited. And Bernie . . . well, Bernie showed an interest in the country.'

'You couldn't stand his love for the country. You called him – I remember your exact words – "a rootless American upstart wallowing in the timeless grandeur of India . . ." '

'That's true for every American.'

'And his clothes. Remember the day he wore a *dhoti*?'

'*Dhoti* be damned *sala*!' The Bengali thumped the table, knocking over a glass of water. 'I say Ellen was the best bureau chief we've had in my time here.'

Everybody at the table was dumbfounded. Arun left to get a glass of water. P.K. sucked on a large bone. Gopalacharya tilted his head towards the ceiling and started to whistle. Even the Bengali seemed a little shy after our awed reaction.

'She had a heart, old Ellen,' he said. 'Loved animals.'

There were defeated sighs from all quarters. The Bengali despised animals and animal lovers. One of his favourite pastimes was calling shelters in the city and yelling animal-related obscenities to volunteers over the phone.

Gopalacharya said, 'Dada, why do you hate Damon Hatcher?'

'It's not that I hate Damon Hatcher so much,' said the Bengali, picking his teeth. 'I *fear* him.'

The Bengali's fear, Col. Pai, was rooted in the fact that Damon Hatcher was the complete opposite of his predecessors. First and foremost, he was a man of severe character. A chronic bachelor – I say chronic because he is edging fifty, although he looks younger – Damon Hatcher always dresses in a coat and tie, no matter how hot the weather. (The Bengali, who has been reading up on American sociology to understand him, has nicknamed Damon Hatcher 'The Mormon'.) Unlike Ellen, who was always closeted in her office, Damon Hatcher spends nearly all his time in the newsroom, scanning the wires with one eye and observing the reporters with the other. He has a total lack of interest in India. As you probably know, Col. Pai, most foreign journalists are either star-struck or excessively critical of India. Damon Hatcher doesn't give a damn: If a thousand people were to die of starvation at his doorstep tomorrow, Damon Hatcher wouldn't be moved. He has been posted to Cairo, Managua, Manila and, most recently, Johannesburg. He has shown no interest in any of these countries. What does interest him, however, is a country's military history. The book shelf in his office is crammed with books on India's colonial period. His special love is the first Anglo-Afghan War and the British retreat of 1841.

'I too couldn't care about Nicaragua,' said the Bengali. 'Or the blooming Philippines. But India? *Ram, Ram, Ram* – only a man without a heart could be neutral towards a country like India.'

'Damon Hatcher detests India,' said Gopalacharya. 'I heard him say something very nasty to that American diplomat at the welcoming party.'

'What?' said the Bengali.

'I don't remember how it came up. But Damon Hatcher said to the man: "The Indians believe in karma, right? They believe that in their current life a person gains or suffers from the actions of his past life?"'

'And the diplomat said yes,' sneered the Bengali, 'as diplomats in India normally do.'

'He did. And then Damon Hatcher said: "In that case, you have to believe that the Indians were very, very bad in their past lives – all 800 million." The diplomat almost spilled his drink. He said: "What makes you think so?" And Damon replied: "That's why they were born in India. They came in last in the karmic sweepstakes."'

There was silence at the table.

'"Otherwise," he went on, "they would have been born in the States. Or England. Germany even. Anyone with a halfway decent past life would have been born with a visa."'

'He said that?' The Bengali was the first to speak. '*Aisa bola*!'

'The motherfucker!' said P.K. 'Excuse my language.'

'He does hate India,' said Arun.

'He's neutral in his stories though.' Gopalacharya flicked cigarette ash on the floor.

'Do you know what he says about our having lunch together?' asked P.K.

The Bengali straightened in his chair.

'"These Indians never fail to have lunch."' P.K. did a bad imitation of an American accent. '"You could set your watch by it."'

'He hates the smell when we heat our food in the kitchen,' said Arun.

'Just yesterday,' P.K. said, 'he told me: "Smells like cabbage."'

'Nobody brought cabbage yesterday,' said Gopalacharya.

'He might have said *garbage*,' said Arun.

Everyone looked shocked.

'I will show this Damon Hatcher.' The Bengali was seething. 'If I don't stick a hot iron rod in his heart my name is not Ashit Chatterjee.'

'He has no heart,' said P.K.

'I tell you this day.' The Bengali stood with a curious expression on his face. His chest bulged with every breath. I wondered if he might be having a stroke. 'I will get the better of this man. Take that as my personal vow.' He slammed his hand on the table, making the serving spoons jump in their dishes.

Heart or no, what Damon Hatcher did have was a phenomenal memory. The man remembered every duty schedule, every story filed, every press conference, even the number of times a staff member reported sick or came late for work. On his very first day in the bureau he knew the entire staff by name. This was a record: bureau chiefs normally take a month on average to get everybody's name right. Sam, our news editor, still hasn't conquered the names after eight years.

Damon Hatcher had been bureau chief for barely three months when Kumar, the night-shift man, announced his retirement. Kumar had another two years before he turned sixty, the company retirement age, but he was throwing in the towel because, he said, he was too old to get used to another foreign bureau chief. That's how he put it. We tried our best to dissuade Kumar but he was adamant.

'It's only two years, Kumar,' said the Bengali.

'Years, months, days, seconds are all man-made measurements of time,' said Kumar, who liked his philosophy. 'Time itself cannot be measured. It is eternal.'

Said the Bengali: 'Especially with another foreign hyena.'

At Kumar's farewell party, Damon Hatcher announced that

a new night-shift schedule would be enforced. From the end of the month, he said, night duties would be distributed among the Bengali, Gopalacharya and Arun. What this meant was that the Indian staff, and the Indian staff alone, would be responsible for night duties. The bureau chief and news editor would never have to work during the night. 'Except,' said Damon Hatcher, adjusting the knot of his peacock-blue silk tie, 'on stories of overweening importance.'

We could not have been more shocked than if a bomb had exploded under our desks. The night-shift, or the graveyard shift as the old-timers called it, is hated at all wire services, Col. Pai. At UNI we had been lucky: Kumar had actually enjoyed working at night. Earlier in his career he had done double shifts to support a large family, infirm parents and several deadbeat aunts. Over the years, the family had grown and prospered; the aunts had not only died but left agricultural property. Kumar, meanwhile, had become an incurable insomniac and begged for the night duty. He got a veteran's salary; and, to tell the truth, didn't do all that much from seven-to-four – many have questioned the veracity of his insomnia – and wasn't famous for his accuracy either.

The point is that once he departed, no one wanted his duties. And the Indian staff didn't expect to shoulder them alone. In no other foreign news agency in Delhi were the night duties delegated exclusively to the local staff.

We staggered out of the bureau that night like prisoners set to meet a firing squad. When we reached the parking lot the Bengali roused.

'Bloody hell! We can't accept this! Can you imagine us doing nights while the Whiteman has dinner with his wives? I say this is absolute bloody nonsense and something should be done. *Nahin* – something *must* be done!'

We turned back and went to the bar of the hotel. Over pegs of whisky, the Bengali enunciated his strategy. To cut a long story short, Col. Pai, a letter was posted on the newsroom bulletin board the following morning, well before the bureau chief arrived. It read:

Dear Damon Hatcher:

As a new man to India, we think you may be making big mistakes in your dealings with very local conditions.

Your plan for an all-Indian staff at the night-shift is extremely distressing. While we are not opposed to hard work or working against deadline well into the night, the fact is that regular night duty takes a toll and reduces mental ability, immunity, sexual desire and expectancy of life.

Your decision is utterly unacceptable to us also in principle, since it singles out only the Indian staff for what is decidedly an ill and cruel fate. It must be pointed out that Mr Prasana Pratap Kumar, night editor, preferred night duty because he also worked in the day in order to support his large family, including two expensive aunts, and, later, his sleeping preferences. As you may know, none of the other members of the current news bureau have relatives of that variety in their homes or queer bed habits and, as goes without saying, camaraderie is an important component of running an international news bureau and it is hardly possible to expect cordial relations among Indians and the Whites if the former are consigned to the dreaded 'graveyard shift' while the latter go out to dinner with their wives.

Your new rule is the latest addition in a long list of inequities and insults heaped on the loyal Indian staff of the UNI New Delhi bureau. For many years now we have been repeatedly promised salaries in dollars, but we continue to be paid in the inflation-burdened rupee. We were assured trips to New York for training but nothing whatsoever has become of that. Our daily allowance on news trips is less than one-third of the Whites, which forces us to eat cheap, unhygienic food while our White colleagues eat six-coarse meals in the air-conditioned comfort of five-star hotels, usually with missuses.

The new policy on the night shift not only strikes at the heart of UNI's democratic functioning, it is also grossly unhumanitarian. We therefore urge you to reconsider your decision, failing which the responsibility for the consequences will be entirely yours.

– Signed

The UNI staff

It was with great difficulty, Col. Pai, that we persuaded the Bengali to desist from a longer, more emotional outpouring. We tried to edit out the final remark about Damon Hatcher being responsible for the consequences of his decision, but the Bengali held firm.

Damon Hatcher saw the note on the bulletin board upon entering the newsroom. The Bengali, Gopalacharya and Arun were at their respective desks. I was servicing the teleprinters. Damon Hatcher stood in front of the bulletin board, read the note, stiffened, turned, retired to his office and, quite uncharacteristically, closed a door that hadn't been shut since Bernie Katz's departure four months before.

Sam, our news editor, came in, smoothing his hair with his fingers. He stopped dead in his tracks when he saw Damon Hatcher's shut door. He went to his desk, sat, and waited for something to happen. Four minutes later, the intercom on Sam's desk beeped. He picked it up, nodded and said in a choked voice: 'Um, yes.' Then he stood, looking worried, and went into Damon Hatcher's office.

'The Mormon is holding a conference,' whispered Gopalacharya, a mischievous grin on his face.

'Not an international conference,' said Arun. 'Strictly American.'

' "Danger Hatcher," ' boomed the Bengali. 'That's his nick-

name from now. Let "Danger" Hatcher hold his conference –
on terrorism in India if he's smart.'

Ten minutes later, the door opened and Sam came back to
the newsroom. The look of worry had been replaced by one
of guilt. He walked to his desk holding his head down.

Gopalacharya gave the Bengali a perplexed look. The
Bengali responded with a low cackle. We could hear the sound
of typing from Damon Hatcher's office.

At 11 a.m., Damon Hatcher emerged from his office and
pinned a piece of paper on the bulletin board. As soon as he
went back into his office, the Bengali leaped from his seat. We
joined him.

> The present management of the UNI New Delhi bureau
> cannot be held responsible for the alleged 'unfulfilled
> promises' of past managements. In the context of UNI's
> financial woes, it seems highly unlikely that any changes
> in policy on salary or training trips will take place in the
> foreseeable future.
>
> As regards night duties, several other foreign bureaus
> have similar systems, including Cairo, Managua, Manila
> and, soon to be instituted, Johannesburg.

The Bengali, Gopalacharya and Arun went back to their desks
looking sullen. I went to the communications room and told
P.K. and Matthew about the letter.

The Indian staff gathered at lunch-time. At 2 p.m., the
following letter was pinned over Damon Hatcher's letter:

> We fully appreciate the current management's difficulty in
> fulfilling the promises of the previous management and
> nowhere has it been our intention to blame it for the same.
> However, we do think that the management has been
> callous, uncaring and harsh, not to mention generally
> insensitive and neglectful, if not denying of basic human
> rights in the first place and at every point along the line.

It is clear from your response that you not only favour the idea of night duty by Indians but are unrelenting in your enthusiasm to enforce it, evincing an unfortunate bias in the matter.

Unless the night shift is shared equally by the White and Indian reporters, the entire Indian staff of the bureau will be forced to take the extreme step of going on an indefinite strike on the day the new schedule comes into effect, which is July 1.

The Bengali wanted to go for broke, Col. Pai, and demand foreign exchange payments, training trips to the U.S., daily allowances on par with the whites, as well as a 30 per cent hike in salary. But we argued him down. Everyone was willing to resign if the letter made a single demand on a very firm principle: bureau duties should be shared equally regardless of race. Even Matthew, sitting in his usual spot – at the telex machine with tightly crossed legs – agreed to sign such a petition. He said, and rather good-humouredly I thought: 'Indians are no more or less nocturnal than Americans.'

The Indian staff was too excited to do any real work but pretended to be busy. Damon Hatcher and Sam returned from lunch. They walked across the room to the teleprinters. Sam pointed to a news piece popping up from one of the machines. He laughed. Damon Hatcher pretended to notice but couldn't keep from swivelling to the bulletin board. He took three rapid steps forward. He read the notice, arms folded tightly across his suit jacket. Sam, sensing that something was amiss, stepped away from the teleprinters and looked about.

Damon Hatcher slowly removed the letter from the bulletin board, gave us all a fish-eyed look and said: 'Sam.'

Sam's eyes dropped to the ground. He said: 'I'm sorry, Damon. I have to . . . I was just going to the bank.'

Damon Hatcher paused for a second, a look of irritation on his face. He turned and walked to his office, shutting the door behind him. Sam, his head drooping, left the bureau with dangling hands.

'Point one,' said the Bengali. 'We split them!'

'I feel sorry for Sam,' said Arun.

From Damon Hatcher's office we heard the sound of typing. Then came a dead silence. Finally, we heard a strange, whirring noise from behind the closed door.

'What the hell . . . ?' The Bengali got up and approached Gopalacharya's desk, which was near Damon Hatcher's door.

'It sounds like a fax machine,' said Gopalacharya.

'*Fax* machine?' The Bengali made a face. 'We don't *have* a fax machine.'

'I guess we do now,' said Gopalacharya. 'Damon Hatcher got approval last month. It must have come by DHL.'

'What the hell is he faxing?'

'I think he's faxing our letter.'

'To New York,' added Arun.

'*New York*?' The Bengali said New York in the usual incredulous tone he reserved for that city. 'If we have a fax – I mean if *he* has a fax – we can't rely on the wires anymore.'

Arun gave me a doleful look.

'We can't see all the messages,' said Gopalacharya. 'No more running to the communications room. No more "Did you see this?" or "Pull out the overnight traffic, Hari."'

'That's true,' I said.

The Bengali flopped into an empty chair. 'Now *that* is dangerousness.'

Sam returned, walking through the newsroom as if he were treading barefoot on broken glass. He came to the knot of assembled reporters. 'I sure hope you guys ain't leaving.' His tone was one of genuine concern. 'And I just want to tell you that I understand how you all feel.'

I caught a flicker of emotion on the Bengali's face – the first I had ever seen him show for a white man.

Sam continued: 'I would've reacted in the same way. Janet too – I don't think I've ever seen her so outraged.' Then he looked at Damon Hatcher's door. 'But . . .' He lifted his palms to the ceiling, shrugged, rolled his eyes and gave a long, languorous sigh. He brought his hands down to his thighs, slapped them, inhaled sharply, walked back to his seat and started riffling through the papers on his desk, talking to himself in the usual low undertone. (Janet, Col. Pai, is Sam's wife. She is a miniature American woman with arms so short they look like stubs.)

An hour passed and nothing happened. Then the phone rang in the newsroom. Sam answered. It was a long-distance call for Damon Hatcher. Sam put the call on hold and buzzed him.

Again we heard the sound of typing through the closed door. A couple of minutes later Damon Hatcher emerged, pinned our letter on the bulletin board and a sheet of paper next to it. Then he returned to his office, shutting the door behind him.

We looked at each other. The question was obvious: Who would stand to read the letter? There was a pained awkwardness as everyone looked around the newsroom. Finally, the Bengali started to rise. And I said: 'Sam?'

Sam looked up with surprise.

'Wouldn't you . . .'

He looked as if he'd won the lottery.

'As the news editor, after all.'

He stood.

'An important moment . . .'

He shambled to the bulletin board.

'Because I think, when it's all said and done, you've behaved . . .'

'Oh shut up, Hari!' boomed the Bengali.

'Holy shit!' cried Sam.

Damon Hatcher's letter read as follows:

I have consulted with my superiors in New York on the

matter of your threatened resignations. They do not think such an example of insubordination should be tolerated.

The night duty schedule, as drawn up, will not and cannot be amended. That is the most important point. Anyone wishing to resign as of the end of this month is welcome to do so. In that case, however, since proper notice will not have been served, there will be no severance/separation pay. Additionally, those employees who have taken loans from UNI will not receive their pay checks until after the end of this month. This is a precautionary measure.

I am authorized by New York to announce that any employee in the New Delhi bureau who goes on strike will be terminated immediately.

'We are Indians first.' The Bengali's voice boomed in the interior of the aged monument. 'And Brahmins, Jats, Goojars and Kabir-panthis last.'

The Bengali was making an impassioned speech. It was the lunch break and the staff had gathered at the Lodi Gardens, New Delhi's most beautiful park, a ten-minute walk from the bureau. Flowers bloomed on the lawns surrounding the stately tombs of the Sayyid and Lodi kings who ruled Delhi during the 15th and early 16th centuries. We were in a tomb in the middle of the park, listening to the Bengali speak. The tall stone dome gave his voice an impressive resonance. He recognised this and became all the more loquacious.

'We know at least what we are.' He pointed a finger upward. 'We are the world's greatest civilisation.' His hand curled into a fist. 'Bar none!'

The Bengali stood while the rest of us sat with our lunch boxes.

'Historians say Egypt was the greatest civilisation. What nonsense!' He made a dismissing gesture similar to a backhand table tennis shot. 'The Taj Mahal is any day superior to a pyramid. Bloody ugly, if you ask me. Others say the Chinese were great. But the entire Chinese civilisation was at one time addicted to opium, according to historians. They allowed the British into their country thinking they would never fight – couldn't fight! – because their trousers were too tight. Bloody nincompoops! We wear loose trousers in Bengal and we never thought that it would make us better fighters. Quite the contrary.'

Outside the monument, young lovers wandered in search of a private bench or glade. Voyeuristic men, in turn, prowled in search of couples in transport. Through an arch I espied a balding, pot-bellied man tip-toeing around some foliage. The man stiffened at the edge of a bush, bent forward, and began rapturously eavesdropping on a young couple on the other side.

The Bengali mopped his face with a dirty old handkerchief, followed by his neck. Then he continued.

'Now, take the case of one Mr "Danger" Hatcher. The fellow has been a bureau chief for fifteen years, which is a peanuts position. We are forced to put up with him. Why? Because economically we are a poor country. But we are survivors; we have been surviving for millions of years. Our race survives, like, I don't know, cockroaches. We certainly cannot be humiliated in *this* manner.' The Bengali shook his head as if he were having a fit. 'Not because we are human beings, or people, or citizens of the world's largest democracy or any such First World bullshit. We cannot and will not be humiliated because' – the Bengali gave a thump to his chest – 'we are Indians.'

He pointed a finger at Omi Chand. 'You – you are an Indian!'

Omi Chand squirmed.

'And you!' He pointed at Matthew. 'Even though you are a Christian from the south, you are an Indian. Cent per cent Indian.'

This was the first time, Col. Pai, that the Bengali had not

disparaged Omi Chand or the lower castes in general. He was also being uncharacteristically kind towards Matthew.

'This monument' – his voice turned low and sombre – 'is the grave of Ibrahim Lodi, the third and last king of the Lodi dynasty. The Lodis ruled India just before the Mughal invasion . . .'

'They didn't rule the whole of India, Dada,' interrupted Gopalacharya in a lecturing tone. 'Only the Sultanate of Delhi, which included parts of Punjab and U.P.'

'Thank you, Gopalacharya.' The Bengali bowed mockingly. 'Please to correct me at any point.' He walked to the raised cement casket and touched it reverently. 'The Lodis were Afghans and the Afghans are very . . . what is the word?'

'Fierce,' prompted Gopalacharya.

'No, not fierce.'

'Blue-eyed?' suggested Arun.

'I don't care about their eyes!'

'Faction-ridden,' said Gopalacharya.

'That's it!' The Bengali snapped his fingers. 'Faction riddled. Like we Indians.' He sniffed. 'We too don't get along with people who are not from our religion, caste, *gotra*, village, state, etcetera, etcetera.' He paused for a moment, as if recollecting his thoughts. 'Anyway, it so happened that the Afghan chieftains in the Lodi empire were not unconditionally loyal to their king. There was always the threat of revolt. Isn't that right, Gopalacharya?'

'Yes, in Afghan custom loyalty seldom extends beyond the tribe.'

'The first two Lodi kings realised that the only way they could win the loyalty of their chieftains was by giving them some power, some independent control over a part of the kingdom. Give and take, gentlemen. Give and take. But the third Lodi king' – the Bengali pointed to the tomb – 'old Ibrahim, wanted it all. He asserted his full susu . . .'

'Suzerainty,' said Gopalacharya.

' . . . over his chieftains. He ignored their tribal sentiments.

The chieftains got pissed off. They invited Babur to invade Delhi. Babur killed Lodi in the first battle of Panipat. 1526. I still remember that date from school. It was the beginning of the Mughal empire.' For a moment, there was a faraway look in the Bengali's eyes.

And India was in the soup for 400 years,' said Gopalacharya.

'Exactly!' The Bengali jumped in the air and landed atop the casket of the Lodi king. 'The moral of the story, gentlemen, is that without unity we too will be in the same soup. And Damon Fucking Hatcher is the modern equivalent of Babur.' He started waving his arms like an electoral candidate at the hustings. 'There is no other way to win this battle with "Danger" Hatcher and New York but to stick together, even if it means losing our jobs.' He looked down at the Indian staff. 'Your job, Gopalacharya. Your job, Arun. Your job, P.K., Matthew, Omi Chand. And your job, Hari.'

There was silence in the tomb.

'And . . .' He straightened suddenly. 'My job. I will be the first to take the fall. This I am promising. In this, no one will ever find me wanting.'

'It's a question of principles,' I said.

'Listen to Hari,' said the Bengali. 'We can't backtrack now. If one of us defects, the strike will be over and our weakness exposed to the ridicule of all those *goras* in New York. And in Delhi too. I don't know about you people, but I would not be able to go within two miles of the Press Club.'

Everybody nodded their heads in unison.

'Let us take a pledge, in this historic tomb, to be thoroughly loyal to each other. To fight for a single right: to abolish a night shift staffed by Indians only!'

The Bengali jumped down from the tomb and extended his right hand with the palm upturned. One by one, starting with Gopalacharya, the Indian staff placed their hands on his palm, one on top of the other. The Bengali shut his eyes, his body very still, and everybody did the same. There was silence.

'And whenever you are plagued by doubts,' he said,

'remember the fate of Ibrahim Lodi.' The Bengali opened his eyes. 'May he dwell in hell with the British, the Mughals, all the fucking Pathans and Benazir bloody Bhutto as well.'

We went back to the bureau and assembled in the communications room. As soon as the door was shut, I asked the others: 'Who has taken loans?' There was some initial hesitation and then the hands went up. It turned out that except for Matthew, Omi Chand and me, everybody had taken loans from the company. The Bengali owed the most – a whopping 25,000 rupees. P.K. came next with 20,000.

'How are we going to live?' P.K. whimpered.

'Use your gratuity and provident fund,' said Gopalacharya.

'But what will I do when my daughters grow,' pleaded P.K. 'With dowry so high these days? None of you have daughters!'

'What would happen if someone in the family needed an operation?' asked Matthew.

'Find a job,' said Arun. 'I'm sure we're not going to be idle for long.'

'Dada owes more than any of us and you don't see him worrying,' said Gopalacharya. 'Isn't that right, Dada?'

The Bengali hunched his shoulders and let them drop.

As I drove home on my scooter, I felt proud of the staff. Even those of us unaffected by the night shift, such as P.K., Matthew and myself, were standing behind reporters condemned to an ignoble fate. We were sacrificing salaries, the future of our families – indeed our very survival – for the sake of a principle. As you know, Col. Pai, white-collar jobs in Delhi are few and far between. The least affected was probably Omi Chand: If things got tough for him, he could always find another job or go back to his village.

The next morning, I went to P.K.'s cubicle. 'How do you feel today, P.K.?'

'I feel just great, Hari. Have a seat.' P.K. took a big sip from a cup of tea.

'Just great? P.K. – I'm on tenterhooks.'

'Hari, you should be a professor of English. Tenterhooks!

It's the first time I've heard the word in my whole life. I tell you you're wasting your time at UNI.'

'P.K., why are you smiling?'

'There is another phrase in English, Hari.' P.K. leaned over his desk. ' "Every cloud has a silver line." '

'Lining.' I didn't like his look.

'I have a fall back, Hari. A great fall back. I don't need to worry if I lose my job at UNI. In fact I might be quite happy.'

'Have you been drinking?'

'Have you been drinking? You can't hear properly? Bloody jackass.'

'Don't do this, P.K. We've been friends for years.'

'My brother-in-law, Hari, is the works manager in Jindal Cables. They need an accountant.'

'They need an accountant?'

'I wouldn't have thought of it except for the strike. I was perfectly happy. But I have these blasted daughters, you know.'

I said I knew.

'The work is dull, I admit. But I'd have my own office, Hari. Two hundred square feet.' P.K. looked disapprovingly at his little cabin. 'I've always wanted a real office. I think at a certain age everyone deserves an office. And Hari, I will be fifty next month. I'm tired of working in this dump.'

'But what about the strike?'

'If we win, well and good. If we lose' – he folded his hands and sniffed – '*Jai Ram ji ki*. Bye-bye.'

I couldn't bear to sit with P.K. any longer. I went straight to the newsroom. Arun was at his desk reading a newspaper. I asked: 'Have you talked to P.K.?'

Arun looked up, startled.

'He's abandoning us. He's got another company.'

'I don't get you, Hari.'

'P.K.'s going to work in his brother-in-law's firm if the strike fails.' I gripped the top of Arun's desk. 'He says he'll get a proper office.'

Arun stared at his desk, thinking.

'Arun, did you hear what I said?'

'You know, Hari, I always thought P.K. was smart.'

'Smart?'

'Good for him *yaar.*' Arun gave me a strange look. 'If we were half as clever we'd be looking for jobs ourselves.'

I was stunned by Arun's words. P.K.'s plans were a shock; now Arun was thinking on the same lines. If even one of them resigned the strike would be over.

'Do *you* have similar plans, Arun?'

'I was just thinking, Hari. It would be a good idea to go back to my home town.'

'Nagpur?'

'It's nothing like Delhi, but Delhi costs money. I have an MA in political science. Maybe I should try to get a teaching job in a university. It shouldn't be too difficult. Besides, it would please my in-laws-to-be. They've always wanted me to settle in Nagpur. My father-in-law is a mathematics professor.'

My brain whirred. Something had to be done quickly. P.K. and Arun were poised to ruin the strike at any moment by resigning.

'Father-in-law-to-be,' he corrected.

'You're getting married?'

'Yes,' said Arun.

'Congratulations.'

Arun reached for the telephone and started dialling a number. As I left the newsroom, I heard him asking for the registrar of Nagpur University.

I waited anxiously in the hallway. Gopalacharya showed up first, wheezing from the climb up the stairs. I whisked him into the kitchen.

'I have something very important to tell you,' I whispered. 'It's about the strike.'

As soon as he heard the word strike, Gopalacharya became alert. He lit a cigarette and sucked in a lungful of smoke.

'There's a serious threat to the strike, Gopalacharya.'

'What?'

'P.K. wants to leave UNI.'

'He has another job?'

'Some cable company in which his brother-in-law works.'

'Hmm.' Gopalacharya pursed his lips. 'Interesting.' He rocked forward and backward on his feet, one hand thrust in a trouser pocket. 'What else did he say?'

'Well, he said he would be getting an office . . . two hundred square feet.'

'An awfice!' Gopalacharya pronounced the word in a mocking tone of voice. 'Trust P.K. to be attracted to something like that.'

'The strike, Gopalacharya: what will happen?'

He gave me a guilty look. 'Hari, I contacted Penn last night.'

'Penn?'

'Don't you know Penn? Andrew Penn? The Reuters bureau chief? Beckwith's replacement.'

I shook my head.

'Reuters has a vacancy.'

My stomach fell.

'They're expanding the bureau. Penn – he sounded like a nice chap – offered me a job.'

'But . . .'

'And d'you know? I'd get a much higher salary at Reuters – thirty per cent more. Plus . . .' – Gopalacharya raised his forefinger like a conductor's baton – 'I'll be paid in dollars.'

'What about our strike?'

'Oh, the strike. That's not a problem. Reuters has given me six weeks to decide. The strike will be over by then. One way or the other.' He gave a short laugh. 'Now get this, Hari, at Reuters . . .'

By the time Gopalacharya finished his discourse on the glories of working at Reuters I felt as if I was going to be ill. We parted and Gopalacharya went into P.K.'s cubicle. I heard them talking animatedly.

I went back to my chair. Not one, or two, but *three* treacherous allies. I wanted to talk to the Bengali. But he was out covering an anti-World Bank rally – probably leading it – and wasn't expected until noon.

When he arrived in the bureau, he immediately sat down to write his story. Then the collegial daily lunch was served.

The group was strangely silent. I tapped my water glass with a fork. 'I have an announcement to make,' I said. 'As you all know, this new rule about the night shift has created a great deal of insecurity in our lives. Nobody knows if that new rule will become a reality or not – it depends on the outcome of the strike.' I paused, studying the bewildered faces around me.

'Some of us have started thinking about their futures even before the strike is begun. People at this table are already in the job market.' I looked at Gopalacharya. 'One has been offered a job by Reuters.' I swung my fork at P.K. 'The other is joining his brother-in-law's company. And yet another' – I turned to Arun and gave him a nod – 'is casting his hook about in the colleges of Nagpur. Isn't that right, Arun?'

Arun sniffed, giving a nervous nod.

'I didn't say I am joining,' said P.K. 'I said I *want* to join . . . I mean I *might* join . . .'

'All right,' I said, 'P.K. *might* join his brother-in-law.'

'Wait a minute, Hari,' cut in Gopalacharya. 'Are you imputing mala-fide motives to our job-seeking endeavours?'

'You don't think you are doing something very wrong? Our threat to strike is not even twenty-four hours old and you guys are lining up new jobs!' I was shouting now. 'How do you expect the strike to succeed? You people are a disgrace.'

There was a heavy silence at the table. I looked to the Bengali, expecting him to say something. But he sat stolid, chewing away like a cow. Gopalacharya ended the silence. 'We're just looking,' he said. 'What's wrong with . . . ?'

The Bengali cut him short. 'Hari has made a point. Sometimes battles are lost for want of single-mindedness. We should be thankful to Hari, not angry at him, for making us aware of that.'

The Bengali smoothed his curry-stained moustache with

his fingers. 'I am personally not in favour of Gopalacharya or P.K. or Arun or anybody for that matter looking for jobs while the strike is coming on. It is not good for the strike. It is not good for us all. However, I trust the Indian staff completely and am confident that none of you will resign before the end of the month, until July first, when the strike will officially begin.'

'But Dada . . .'

The Bengali held up a silencing hand. 'You and I are in the same boat, Hari. We are too involved in the strike to think of anything else. To think of our lives, our families, our futures. Some are this way. But not every brother in a family is of the same temperament.' He placed the palm of his hand on the table. 'The five fingers of one hand are not equal.'

'What will *you* do, Dada,' asked Gopalacharya. 'If the strike fails?'

'Whatever I do, this much I promise: I will never, *ever* work in a bureau where the night shift is a racist tool.'

I lay awake that night, realising how wrong I had been to place such pride in the Indian staff. I had considered every member of the staff a hero for supporting the strike. In fact they had turned out to be spineless cowards, with the exception of Matthew, Omi Chand and, most surprisingly, the Bengali. The struggle in the bureau wasn't a moral challenge for P.K., Arun or Gopalacharya. P.K.'s situation was perhaps understandable – he had three daughters whose marriages hinged on his financial support. Arun's volte-face didn't shock me too much – he always had lacked grit. But I was greatly disappointed in Gopalacharya. Suddenly, all his intellectualism and idealism looked hollow.

I was particularly disillusioned by the prospect of our lost unity. *Ekta*. Mahatma Gandhi had cried himself hoarse over the unity of Hindus and Muslims, but in the end the country split into two. We were in a similar position: The Bengali had left no stone unturned in emphasising the importance of unity. Only time would tell whether or not his efforts came to naught.

The next day, over lunch, Gopalacharya asked Omi Chand about his future plans.

'*Sa'hb*, I only know about my karma. As long as it is good, I have nothing to fear.'

I nodded vigorously in an attempt to inculcate some moral values in the rest of the staff.

'But aren't you worried,' asked Gopalacharya, 'about your family if you resign?'

'It is my duty to resign, *sa'hb*.' Omi Chand stiffened to attention, flexing his chest. 'I believe that where there is injustice a man should not stay.'

I said: '*Shabash*, Omi Chand. '*Himmat ho to aisi.*'

'*Satyamev jayate*,' said the Bengali. 'Or as they say in English, truth shall prevail. This is the tragedy of modern India: only uneducated people like Omi Chand believe in truth.'

There was an awkward silence at the table. Gopalacharya fingered his nose. P.K. stared into his empty cup as if seeking his future in it.

My respect for Omi Chand, Col. Pai, knew no bounds at that moment. Surely this poor man from a desert village was the bravest of us all. He may have been sacrificing less in material terms, but for him it was everything. And he had been at UNI longer than anyone: it must have broken his heart to threaten to quit.

Omi Chand gathered our plates. I volunteered to help. In the kitchen, he started humming a song.

'Listen, Omi Chand.' I touched him on the shoulder. 'I could lend you money if you need it.'

'It's very kind of you, *sa'hb*.' Omi Chand wiped his hands with a towel and folded them in a greeting of respect. 'I'll manage.'

'Do you have any savings?'

He shook his head.

'What if you lose your job?'

'I'll go back to my village.'

'But there's no work in the desert.'

Omi Chand shrugged. 'All I need is two pieces of bread, *sa'hb*.'

I marvelled at such stoicism.

'It's also possible, *sa'hb*, that the office upstairs might need a new sweeper.' There was a gleam in Omi Chand's eyes. 'They promoted the last sweeper to driver.'

'Bearer?'

'No, *sa'hb*. *Driver*. I've always wanted to be a driver. Ever since I left the army . . .'

But I had stopped listening. Omi Chand was also hoping for a promotion as a result of the strike. All that talk about duty and the martial spirit was hogwash. I had considered him a man of fortitude. But like the others, he had failed the test.

At the lunch table a lively discussion was underway. Gopalacharya was exulting in the prospect of receiving dollar salary at Reuters: 'The exchange rate is going crazy . . . the bloody dollar is getting stronger every day . . .'

Arun was saying how easy teaching would be: 'Nobody does any work in the colleges these days. The students all want to skip classes and the lecturers couldn't care less. You get free housing . . .'

P.K. was thrilled at the prospect of a full-fledged office. 'Human rights activists should look into this cubicle business, I say . . . I will be asking for coffee at least thrice a day . . .'

Everybody was going to be better off except the Bengali and me. I became curious to know what he would do if the strike failed. Where would the Bengali go? Where *could* he go with his appalling personality and miserable references? The Bengali had always said UNI would be his last job in journalism. (He had worked in every other Western news agency in India.) Wasn't he terrified by the strike he had brought about?

As if he were reading my thoughts, Gopalacharya said:

'Dada, I know you don't like this question, but what will you do if you leave UNI?'

The Bengali, shutting his lunch box, gave Gopalacharya one of his cobra-lidded looks.

'*Bolo na* Dada,' persisted Gopalacharya. 'Or have you taken a vow of silence.'

The Bengali stared out the window, his face as impassive as a sage's. He opened his mouth to speak: 'You are asking me what I will do . . .'

Everybody held their breath.

'The answer is: I will do whatever is right.'

'And what is that, Dada?' implored Gopalacharya.

But the Bengali didn't say a word.

Next morning I came to work earlier than usual. Before I entered the newsroom, I saw something through the glass pane in the newsroom door that made me freeze: Arun was coming out of Damon Hatcher's office. I slunk out of the bureau and returned after a couple of minutes, pretending I hadn't noticed anything. When I asked Arun the usual bureau question – 'Anything going on?' – he answered in the negative. This meant nothing was happening news-wise. I asked him the latest on the strike. He said things were still the same. But I detected a guilty look on his face.

After lunch I saw Damon Hatcher, in his neat suit and tie, talking to P.K. in the bureau hallway. Late that evening, Damon Hatcher called Matthew into his office, ostensibly, according to Matthew, to give him a message to transmit to New York. But they were together for more than ten minutes. I felt something was fishy. Surely Damon Hatcher was trying to break the strike by offering separate deals to the Indian staff.

My suspicions were confirmed that night. I was in the parking lot unlocking my scooter when I saw Damon Hatcher's car pulling away. There were two people in the car, but, because it was raining, I failed to identify them. The car turned towards Khan Market; I ran after it to get a better look. Sitting at the wheel was Damon Hatcher. He was smiling and talking to the person on his left, who was smoking a cigarette in a familiar stove-pipe fashion. It was Gopalacharya.

I walked to my scooter in a daze, a single sentence reverberating in my mind: *One defection and it will all be over.* Was the strike already sunk?

In the next two days I noticed more hushed contacts between Damon Hatcher and the Indian staff. Eating lunch together turned into an embarrassing and hypocritical exercise. Gopalacharya, Arun and P.K. never brought up their meetings with Damon Hatcher. They had trouble making eye contact. I hoped the Bengali would ask them to come clean; if I had seen the contacts with Damon Hatcher, so had he. He had been painstakingly vigilant in avoiding Damon Hatcher, to the point of never remaining alone in the newsroom. But he was totally silent on the issue.

On the fourth day before the strike I was going out on an errand when I ran into Damon Hatcher on the hotel stairwell.

'Hari,' he said. 'Do you have a minute?'

I stopped.

'I've been watching you, Hari. And I have to say I'm impressed by your, shall I say, industriousness.' Damon Hatcher was extraordinarily tall – at least six-foot four – and dressed in a dark suit with a sumptuous red tie. His shoes were so well polished you could have combed your hair in them. He stood with one arm resting elegantly on the banister, the other hanging loosely by his side. His voice was a mix of haughtiness and concern.

'I've travelled the world, Hari, and been to every UNI bureau.' Damon Hatcher smiled. 'I've met every kind of character there is in the news business – good, bad and ugly.' He gave a short laugh. 'I thought I'd seen them all. Until I met you.' Damon Hatcher pointed. 'You, Hari, are the only communications man I've ever met at UNI who wanted to become a writer.'

How did Damon Hatcher know I wanted to become a writer? I had never discussed it with him.

'All that writing, day in and day out.' Damon Hatcher gave a smug shake of his head. 'This is a new one – only in India.'

'Well, I am Indian.'

'Indians want to be heard, don't they? They must be heard. What else do they have?'

We have our families, our ambitions, our loves, our conscience, our culture – that's what I wanted to say. But I merely nodded.

'You want to be a writer. You want your name on the news, Hari Rana, don't you? But you don't know politics. You don't know economics. You look like the type that would be too scared to talk to a policeman or a soldier.'

'I'm not demanding anything, sir.'

'Today is June 28. If you are working for UNI on July 1, Hari Rana, you will be named a reporter.' Damon Hatcher straightened. 'That's my offer.'

My heart was beating fast and my breathing was shallow. I couldn't have spoken if my life depended on it. I just stood there, four steps below the towering figure of Damon Hatcher. He turned and started walking up the stairs.

I said: 'But . . .'

He said, without bothering to turn back: 'Don't be stupid now, Hari.'

I was scared and outraged by Damon Hatcher's offer. The man was trying to buy me: no one had tried to do that before. I cursed myself for not putting him in his place – to show him that not every Indian is up for sale. At the same time I felt thrilled. I was a man whom someone needed. I was the bait – reclining on a white couch with long, soft cushions, as in the movies. And then I had a clear image, like a dream bubble in a cartoon, of my name atop a story:

By HARI RANA
Union News International Writer

My consciousness opened: If Damon Hatcher had promised me a writer's job, what gems had he thrown the way of the others? P.K. craved an office instead of a cubicle; Arun always wanted the feature beat, which would allow him to travel outside Delhi; Gopalacharya longed to go to Sri Lanka for a couple of months to do what he called that 'definitive piece' on the Tamil civil war.

When I got down to the parking lot, I saw Omi Chand backing the bureau car. I understood: come July 1 he would undoubtedly be sharing driving duties with Bhoop Singh – one more of Damon Hatcher's evil deals.

The suspense continued until we were only a day from the July 1 deadline. It was Tuesday, over lunch, when Matthew said he had an announcement. He was withdrawing his support for the strike. He couldn't afford to lose his job, he said, because his widowed mother was ill with cancer and he had to pay her medical bills. He said he had already communicated his withdrawal to Damon Hatcher.

'What did he offer you, Matthew?' I asked flatly.

He shook his head.

'Why didn't you tell us first?'

Matthew turned to me. There were tears in his eyes. 'Forgive me, Mr Rana, but I had no choice.' He got up and ran out of the room. His shoulders shook with sobbing.

Everybody looked to the Bengali. He was rotating his ring-studded fingers in a mound of rice and fish curry. When the rice had been reduced to a sticky mess, he scooped up a handful and sucked it hungrily into his mouth. He chewed slowly and soundlessly, which was most unusual: we were used to seeing him talk whenever his mouth was full. He gulped a whole glass of water. He burped. Finally, he spoke: 'So Jesus-fearing Matthew has withdrawn from the strike.' He wiped his lips with the back of his hand. 'I accept his decision.'

A stunned silence followed, broken only by the Bengali's renewed sloshing of rice.

'But Dada,' I said, 'you insisted that the strike be all or nothing from the start.'

The Bengali nodded like a guru about to unravel a great paradox. 'Matthew is the least of the staff. He's dispensable.' He licked rice from his fingers. 'Don't worry. The staff will hold together.'

'It's embarrassing,' I said with my eyes on the table, 'that the only defection came from my department.'

Gopalacharya gave a kind of hiccoughing laugh. 'That's the point, isn't it Hari?'

'What's the point?'

'Well, Matthew's expecting your job. Once the strike begins. And we're all fired.'

Col. Pai, I couldn't think. An opaque cloud the colour of blood spread across my vision. I felt close to fainting. Arun noticed there was something wrong and helped me out of the bureau to the hotel lawn. I don't recall the passage. All I remember is lying on the grass with Arun massaging my forehead.

'Should we go inside, Hari?'

'How long have we been here?'

'Forty-five minutes.'

'Is Matthew still inside?'

'Yes.'

'I'll wait.'

Arun excused himself and went back to the bureau. When he returned he said: 'I've told Matthew to take the rest of the day off.'

I stared blankly.

'Matthew's gone home, Hari. He left from the back gate.'

I walked back through the lobby and up the stairs to the bureau. Arun made me a cup of tea with extra sugar. The communications room was deserted. I don't know why, Col. Pai, but the idea of Matthew taking my job changed my view of everything. I had been willing to make big sacrifices for the sake of a lofty principle. The policies of Damon Hatcher were unfair and racist. We were fighting for the exact kind of independence and dignity that our fathers and grandfathers had fought for – and died for – in the struggle against the British.

But as soon as I heard that Matthew would benefit, would be sitting in my chair, I no longer wanted to go along with the strike. It sounds petty: I don't like to admit it. But that's how I felt.

As I sat there, I thought of my father. I've told you in previous letters, Col. Pai, he was a man of principle – a true karma yogi and a humanist to the core. I recall an incident from when I was a small boy. My mother sent our servant, a poor teenager from Bihar, to retrieve some expensive sarees from a laundress in the neighbourhood. When the servant returned, my mother found two sarees missing. She suspected the servant and asked my father to question him. The servant pleaded innocence. In a fit of anger, my father slapped him. The servant broke down and confessed to the theft: he had stolen the sarees. Just then my elder brother entered the house. In his hands were the two missing sarees. He had found them lying in a nearby park. The sarees, it turned out, had slipped from the servant's hands on his way home from the laundress's. He had confessed out of fear of my father, or worse, the police. My father was beside himself with remorse. He never laid a hand on anyone after that as long as he lived. But he made it a point to bring up the incident from time to time as a lesson in restraint to my brother and me.

Remembering my father, I decided to stand by the principle for which we had threatened to go on strike. I rose from my desk and walked robot-like to the newsroom. The bureau was deserted except for Kumar – on his last night at work – who was eating a plate of *vadas*. He nodded at me perfunctorily. I knocked on Damon Hatcher's door.

'Come in.'

I entered the office, shut the door behind me and stood two metres from Damon Hatcher's teak desk.

'Do you know what you are doing?'

'What is it you want, Hari?' Damon Hatcher shut a folder.

'I just wanted to ask you . . .' I looked at my feet and then into Damon Hatcher's eyes. 'Do you know how serious this situation is?'

'What situation?'

'Do you know what it means to recruit an entirely new staff?'

'I don't, to tell you the truth.' Damon Hatcher smiled thinly. 'But then I've never had cause to fire an entire staff.'

'Even if you get people from other agencies, it will take months before they can work together.' I was surprised at how easily the words came. 'Ellen used to say it often: getting along is very important in a wire service. Ellen Newcomb.'

'I know.'

'It will be years before the bureau is back to normal.'

'Yup.'

'Production will plummet. The news play will be terrible. It will reflect badly on you in New York.'

'I know all this, Hari.'

'It could be a disaster.'

'There's a tide in the affairs of men, Hari.'

'*Julius Caesar*,' I said. 'Brutus.'

'Wonderful, Hari. I hadn't expected you to know that.'

'I am educated.'

'Then do you remember the full quote?' I shook my head. '"There's a tide in the affairs of men – which taken at the flood *leads on to fortune*."'

'How do you know the tide is in your favour?'

He smiled again. 'You'll make a good writer for UNI, Hari Rana.'

'*If* I abandon the strike.'

'You don't have much time to decide.' He looked at the clock. 'Less than twenty-four hours.'

I said: 'Who's going to train me? Who's going to help me learn the ropes? I don't know if this is the right way to become a reporter – in a demolished agency.'

'You'll learn fast.'

'You're taking an enormous risk.'

'You think I like risks?' Damon Hatcher's amused demeanour disappeared with suddenness. 'I *hate* risks. I've avoided them all my life.'

'If you compromised . . .'

'What kind of compromise?'

'Night duties.'

'The night schedule is *absolutely* out of the bounds of nego- tiation.' Damon Hatcher sat forward in his seat. 'Anything else is negotiable. You go and tell that to your people.'

'My people?'

'You know what I mean.'

'The night shift schedule is our only demand.'

'I am *not* the kind of man who accepts demands. I can discuss. I can compromise. But I cannot imagine anything more dangerous than accepting demands from people who are my charges. One step along that road and we'll end up where the British ended up in 1841 in the Khyber Pass. Just one man returned to tell the story. One single soldier out of fifteen thousand – crawling on bloodied knees.' Damon Hatcher looked at the bookshelf stacked with his old books on India. 'Catastrophe.'

'Catastrophe for whom? The Americans or the Indians?'

'I think you understand me better now. The night shift is the one non-negotiable point. Other than that, I am willing to do anything and everything that needs to be done to resolve the situation.'

'Like?'

'You don't have a suggestion?'

'No.'

'Then why did you come in here?'

I shrugged.

Damon Hatcher sighed wearily. 'I hope I can turn things around.' He looked at the clock. 'Decisions have to be made. *I* have to make some decisions.' He looked down at his desk for a second, jerked his head up and gave me an intent look. 'We'll know soon enough, won't we?'

The next morning, Gopalacharya walked into the communications room and stood in front of my desk. I hadn't slept a wink the previous night and was half-dozing.

'Hari,' he said. 'Sam is leaving.'

I almost fell out of my chair.

'Janet and the kids are packing. The word is that Sam's leaving today.'

'Today?' It was D-day, June 30. In just a few short hours, at 7.00 p.m., the new night schedule went into effect. Kumar had worked his final night at UNI. If the staff held together, the bureau would be abandoned en masse at seven and the strike would begin. Then, presumably, we would all be unemployed by the morning. 'But how? Why?'

Gopalacharya shrugged.

I dashed out of the room to look for the Bengali. He was in the kitchen, squeezing the last drops out of a tea-bag with his fingers.

'Dada.' My voice cracked. 'I just heard that Sam is leaving.'

'Hmm.'

I waited for more.

The Bengali tossed the tea-bag into the sink. 'Going, going, gone.'

'When did you know about this, Dada?'

'I heard this morning.' The Bengali took a noisy sip from his mug. 'I believe it happened this morning. I can't say I was surprised.'

'You weren't?'

'Keep your hat on, Hari. There are bound to be lots of surprises today.'

I walked back to my office, feeling rivulets of sweat running down the inside of my arms. To my astonishment, Sam was sitting in my chair, an overstuffed sports bag on his lap.

'Sam!' I stretched my hand out. 'You're leaving?'

'Yup.' Sam gave my hand a weak shake.

'Why so suddenly?'

'Haven't a clue, Hari.' Sam's face drooped. 'Not a clue in the world.'

'Are you going to another country?'

'To the desk in New York.' Sam shrugged. 'It's better than dealing with asshole bureau chiefs abroad.'

'Who's replacing you?'

'Dunno.' Sam threw up his hands. 'I talked to the guy who was supposed to be coming here. Aw! what's his name now?' – Sam clawed at his head – 'In Cairo? Anyway, he said he ain't comin'.'

'That's strange.'

'I know.' Sam rubbed his face. 'The guy had been pitching for news editor in the Delhi bureau for ages. And suddenly – boom! – India's over for him.' He pushed the chair behind him and stood. 'Tell you what, Hari, between the two of us. Damon's behind it all. He hasn't talked to me since this whole mess began – you know, when I kinda sympathised with you guys.'

I felt bad for Sam and wished I could say something to make him feel better.

'It was nice knowing you, Hari.' Sam put his free hand on my shoulder and gave it a friendly squeeze. 'I always liked you best, though I can't say why. Keep up the letters: you'll be a writer someday.' We shook hands and Sam walked down the hallway. He looked back: 'Be in touch with you guys over the wires.'

What had Damon Hatcher done in the previous twelve hours? I couldn't make any sense out of it: getting rid of Sam hardly seemed a solution to any problem. I thought a little brainstorming with the reporters would help.

In the hallway, I stopped before the row of pigeonhole mailboxes. It was pay-day and there was a manila envelope in my cubby-hole. An identical pay envelope was jutting out of the Bengali's, which was directly above mine. That struck me as odd. The Bengali wasn't supposed to be getting his salary because he had taken a loan. I looked at Gopalacharya's, Arun's and P.K.'s cubby-holes. There were no envelopes. All had taken loans, like the Bengali.

There was another curious envelope in the Bengali's mailbox. It was made of expensive-looking white paper and the letters 'DH' were embossed in gold at the back – a letter to the Bengali from Damon Hatcher. I stepped into P.K.'s cubicle: for P.K. distributed the pay each month.

'He wasn't supposed to be getting a pay check as per Damon Hatcher's instructions.' P.K. scratched his jaw. 'In fact Damon Hatcher specifically reminded me yesterday evening' – P.K. wagged a finger in the air – ' "No pay envelopes for any loan takers, P.K. Got it?" But this morning he changed his mind.' P.K. lifted his hands in a gesture of despair. 'He told me to put an envelope in Ashit's mailbox. When I said what about the others who have taken loans, he got angry and told me "Don't you understand English? Do as I told you." *Harami sala*. I wish on him four marriageable daughters!'

'There's another envelope,' I said.

'What?'

'A letter from Damon Hatcher. On his stationery. Sealed.'

Just then the Bengali came into P.K.'s cubicle with the two envelopes in his hands.

'*Arey*, P.K. There must be some mistake.' The Bengali waved the pay envelope. 'This shouldn't have come to me. I'm one of the loan takers, remember? Here.' The Bengali dropped the envelope on an empty chair. 'And this.' He held up the white envelope. 'This letter is also a mistake. Please return it to the bureau chief.' The Bengali tossed the envelope on P.K.'s desk. 'I do not accept communications from him in this fashion.'

P.K. nodded rapidly and collected the two envelopes. The Bengali walked out.

'Admirative thing to do *yaar*,' said P.K. 'I've never seen him return money before.'

The morning wore on quietly. The Indian staff gathered in the communications room at one o'clock sharp, our usual time for lunch. The Bengali had ordered a huge amount of *chola-bhaturas* from a famous hawker at Parliament Street.

As he spooned the *cholas* into everybody's plates, the Bengali said in a sombre voice: 'This may be our last supper.' He looked at Matthew who was sitting with his eyes lowered to the floor. 'Let us hope there are no more Judases among us.'

The lunch lasted about an hour and a half, which besides being a record, was a sure sign of anxiety. After lunch everybody went back to work looking very depressed. We were all waiting for the 7 p.m. deadline.

At five minutes to seven I went into the newsroom. My body was so pumped with adrenaline that I thought I could taste it in my mouth. The Bengali, Gopalacharya and Arun were working at their desks. I went to Arun's desk and started flipping through a newspaper. I was just about to begin a conversation when Damon Hatcher's door swung open. He stepped to Gopalacharya's desk without looking at the rest of us. He said: 'Ask Ashit to come to my office.' Then Damon Hatcher turned, went into his office and shut the door.

The Bengali stopped his typing but remained frozen.

'Uh, Dada,' said Gopalacharya.

The Bengali nodded slightly.

'Our bureau chief would like to talk to you.'

The Bengali didn't move.

'In his office.'

'Dada,' said Arun. 'Damon Hatcher's calling you.'

'Calling *me*?' There was a quizzical expression on the Bengali's face.

'You.'

The Bengali heaved his heavy body out of the chair like a

wrestler getting up for an upcoming bout. He smoothed his bushy, white moustache with his fingers, swivelled his hips to tuck his shirt inside his pants and did a short tap dance. Then he stopped. 'In what capacity?'

'What?' asked Gopalacharya.

'In what capacity am I being called?'

Gopalacharya shook his head. 'I imagine in your usual capacity. As a UNI correspondent.'

The Bengali returned to his desk and took his seat. He looked up with an officious expression. 'If Mr Hatcher would like to consult me as the leader of the Indian staff, I would be happy to join him in a summit meeting. In any other capacity . . .' He froze for a second. Then he made a rude noise with his lips and tongue.

Arun burst out laughing. Gopalacharya, shaking his head disgustedly, went to Damon Hatcher's office, knocked, entered and shut the door behind him. He returned immediately.

'Yes, Dada. You are cordially invited as the leader of the Indian staff. To this holy summit meeting.' Gopalacharya gave a facetious bow and wave of his arm.

The Bengali scurried across the newsroom in record time and, without looking at anyone, dashed into Damon Hatcher's office, kicking the door shut with his foot.

Fifteen minutes later, the door opened and the Bengali stepped out. A pink-coloured file was tucked under one of his arms. He swaggered to the centre of the newsroom, holding his head high in the air. 'May I have your attention, gentlemen, please.'

Gopalacharya and Arun immediately stopped working. I put my newspaper down on Arun's desk.

'I am your news editor with immediate effect,' the Bengali declared.

A silence deep as death greeted the announcement.

'The strike is off as of this hour and all issues between the staff and the bureau chief have been resolved.'

'Oh God,' said Gopalacharya. Arun raised his palm to his mouth.

The Bengali pivoted on one heel and a toe, shifting his gaze from Gopalacharya to Arun and me. 'Is that clear?'

'Dada,' said Gopalacharya. 'I don't think anything is clear.'

'It was my decision to end the strike,' the Bengali said. 'Up until now I was your leader *ipso facto*. Now I am the real leader.' He craned his neck forward like a cobra about to strike. 'Our fond friend Sam is soon to leave these shores and, if he was here, I would pay him my highest respects, not just as my predecessor but as a fine UNI news-person.'

'Oh Dada, come on,' I said.

'Well, it is the proper thing to say. Especially since *Daanav* is gone. We all know the man had major problems.' He made circles with his right index finger around his temple. 'In any case, you will be happy to know that on account of my efforts, Damon *Sahib* has agreed to look into the foreign exchange issue. He will try to convince New York to pay the staff in dollars. It will be a tough fight, but what is more worthy an issue than being paid in greenbacks?' The Bengali eyed us shrewdly. 'Now, regarding the issue of foreign training trips.' He paused. 'Starting with me, everyone will be sent to New York for two months training. My trip will be scheduled for the next calendar year. Other trips will be scheduled for other calendar years.' His face glowed. 'I am planning to go in October because Damon *Sahib* will be taking his annual leave during the summer and the Number Two' – his fingers drummed on his chest – 'has to manage the bureau in his absence.' He cleared his throat. 'In any case, I have heard that New York is beautiful in the autumn. The scenery looks like it has been sprayed with Agent Orange!' The Bengali roared with laughter and looked at everyone, waiting for us to laugh. He got sour-looking when no one did. 'Humour was always your weak point, all of you. I suggest you work on it at home. Otherwise you won't survive a day in New York.'

The Bengali exhaled, sounding like a teacher in a class full of dull students. 'Daily allowance of staffers during news trips has been increased from 150 rupees per day to 200. I will try to make it 250 but can't promise anything. The budget is tight.' Gopalacharya and Arun sat with slack-jawed expressions. 'There are other concessions in the pipeline. Damon *Sahib* and I are meeting the chartered accountant tomorrow. I will propose that the company pick up at least twenty per cent of our house rents. That will be a great help to all of you who don't have their own houses, and I'm sure you will reciprocate by working twenty per cent harder, am I right? Give and take, gentlemen. Remember when I told you that? It's the key to life and the master key to success. Give and take.'

I interrupted: 'What about the night shift?'

'Here it is.' The Bengali opened the pink file and held out a piece of paper. 'The night schedule.'

I walked up to him and took the sheet of paper.

He said: 'Tonight's duty is Arun's.'

'It's the same schedule. The one Damon Hatcher put up before we threatened to strike.'

'It may *look* the same.' The Bengali gave a charming smile. 'But it's not.'

'How?' asked Arun.

'My slots are taken by him: Hari Rana, reporter.'

I handed the paper back. 'It's unchanged.'

'I think congratulations are in order . . .'

'I said it's unchanged, Mr Chatterjee.'

He looked at me dolefully. 'Hari. You speak like this on the biggest day of your life? You're a reporter now!'

'That's not the point.' Tears blurred my vision. My voice was thick with resentment. 'We fought a noble battle and we have lost. Because you gave in. The night schedule is the same. The Indians have been assigned the nigger work.'

'That's where you're wrong, Hari.' The Bengali smiled. 'Where you're *all* wrong. The Indians are not doing the nigger work – because it's no longer a racist schedule. All the Indians *don't* have to do night duty.' He brought the fingertips of both his hands to his chest. '*I* am an Indian.' He shook his head slowly. '*I* don't have to do the night duty. *I* am the news editor.'

The whole jigsaw puzzle fell into place. Damon Hatcher could not back down on the schedule: the Bengali perceived that early on. He gambled that if Damon Hatcher was brought to the point where the continuity of the bureau was threatened, he'd find only one way out: to come to the Bengali and offer terms. I imagine he was angling for a small promotion: a co-news editorship with Sam, perhaps. Fortune favoured him and Damon Hatcher took the excuse to axe Sam. It was a brilliant and audacious scheme, which required nothing more than wile and guile, which the Bengali had in spades, and, on our part, unwavering, principled, heroic – and thoroughly idiotic – support.

'I always said I would never work in a bureau where the night shift is a racist tool.' The Bengali waved the schedule like a flag. 'My friend Hari is not convinced that this schedule is just. He says it is still the same. But it is *not* the same.' The Bengali had begun to shout. 'Can't he see that I have made sacrifices, personally and professionally, to be made news editor? Who took all those trips to Dhaka? All those years?' He paused. 'And does any one dare to suggest that it was easy for me to go through there this evening?' He pointed at Damon Hatcher's door.

We all looked at the door with wonder. It was amazing it was still shut – with a human being inside – considering the racket going on in the newsroom. I imagined Damon Hatcher eavesdropping at the keyhole – or sitting at his desk, in suit and shiny tie, with his hands over his ears.

'*I* am proud that Hari Rana, chief of communications at UNI, has been become Hari Rana, UNI writer.' The Bengali swung his massive, shaggy head in my direction. 'Hari deserves this break. He is a born writer: you can't get him away from the typewriter. But instead of being overjoyed, Hari Rana is furious. Why? I ask you: *why*?'

The Bengali looked for a reaction. Gopalacharya was shaking his head.

'Why? I'll tell you why: because an Indian has been made news editor! This is the tragedy of our nation! Everybody is trying to pull the next man down! I get a little greatness in the sunset of my career and everybody's heart starts burning. There was a time when everything in this bureau was divided on racial lines. But that was when the bureau chief and the news editor were both Whitemen. From tonight there is going to be a different situation here. All that was needed, really, was give and take. Our forefathers had a term for it – *len-den*. We Indians have been giving too long. The tide has reversed: we are starting to *take*.'

I looked at Gopalacharya, whose cigarette tip had three inches of ash, and Arun, whose eyes were on the floor. I walked past the Bengali towards the front door.

'Hari: where do you think you are going?'

I turned around. 'I'm *taking* – taking my leave.'

'For tonight?'

'For ever.'

'Are you leaving UNI?'

'Yes.'

'You?' The Bengali gave an exasperated shout. 'What will you gain?'

I opened the door and left the bureau.

Yours truly,

Hari Rana

The Times of India
The 'Country of the Foolish'

Sir:

Once again, Mother India is on a collision course with Uncle Sam. Last time the bone of contention was textile quotas. This time it is Bhopal. Big or small, a certain word continually creeps into these acrimonious discussions: hypocrisy.

One does not have to be a professor to know what hypocrisy is. If a penny-pincher tells his friend to be generous, he is a hypocrite. If your Jain neighbour eats meat, sprays Flit all over the place and then lectures you on ahimsa, likewise. If a politician from a certain northern state (beginning with a K) denounces corruption but allows his wife to accept bribes from university applicants, he is a hypocrite of the highest order. And if a colleague exhorts you to join an office strike, and in the end the strike has been nothing but your colleague's ruse to get a promotion, he is not only a hypocrite but a traitor as well.

Globally, America zapped a million Japs at Hiroshima and Nagasaki. And yet America is trying to keep nuclear weapons from proliferating in other countries. The United Nations stands for the upliftment of the poor but its officials, many of them Marxists, get six-figure salaries and wave their UN passports under the noses of customs officers when bringing cases of Scotch whisky into the country. And what about India? Mahatma Gandhi is the father of a nation with a burgeoning arms industry – including nuclear weapons! We harangue South Africa on the evils of apartheid even though no people are more hung up about skin colour than us.

Which brings us to Bhopal. Thousands of people died inhaling iso-cynate gas from the Union Carbide factory. The world's sympathy is with them.

But who was truly right and who was wrong? India

charges America with exporting death in the pursuit of profits. If Bhopal is what capitalism brings, we couldn't be wiser than to continue in our anti-material, regulated, socialistic Nehruvian path, even if we remain the joke economy of the world.

But the Bhopal victims were, largely, illegal squatters. A callous multinational might have created the cloud of poison gas – but who put the Indians in its path? The poverty of our country, our political system, along with the corrupt officials who took bribes to allow the slum to exist and the politician who cultivated those squatter colony votes. The Indian government claims Union Carbide should pay the same compensation as they would to a victim in Switzerland or Monaco; the company would be bankrupt, they say, if Bhopal had occurred in Boston. But with income tax rates at 42%, it's no wonder why they are so demanding. And what compensation does the government itself pay when one of the workers at the leaky Narora nuclear power plant grows an extra head or when a houseboy dies of torture during a police investigation of a petty theft? Hardly enough to buy a bowl of Boston beans!

Hypocrisy is basically a moral charge. But do we Indians have the moral advantage we are always claiming? Does the mere fact of being born in India confer some transcendent holiness? Some superior karma?

I know a certain foreigner who claims the reverse. With better karma, wouldn't we have been born Australian or Belgian? Have we truly come in last in the karmic sweepstakes? (Or, to be precise, second to last, ahead of Bangladesh?) Much behaviour witnessed in the name of Indian unity would lead one to make that conclusion. And if so, aren't our protestations about morality and rightness not only hypocritical but ludicrous? Why should the rest of the world pay any heed to sanctimonious hypocrites like us? Wouldn't they be smarter to take the advice of our own Chanakya-Neeti-Darpana:

'Keep a distance of five feet from the cart, ten feet from the horse, a thousand feet from the elephant. The country of the foolish should be left altogether.'

These are words worth pondering over in a subject requiring more serious study.

Hari Rana
New Delhi

Part Two

Part Two

The John Dewey Foundation

'Knowledge is Action'
John Dewey

6 Panchsheel Marg
Chanakyapun
New Delhi 110 021

Telephone (91–11) 469–8682
Fax (91–11) 469–2072

September 12, 1992

Hari Rana
Union News International
Claridges Hotel
New Delhi 110 003

Dear Mr Rana,

This is to inform you that you have been awarded a John Dewey Foundation Fellowship. Every year, we receive thousands of applications from candidates in 146 countries from which less than 450 are selected. You are one – and we believe you have reason to be proud.

The aim of the John Dewey Foundation is to propagate the teachings of John Dewey, one of America's foremost educational reformers and philosophers. The scholarships are funded by the United States Department of State, with support from the Fulbright Foundation, the Ford Foundation and a number of private corporations.

Your fellowship consists of a three-month stay at any participating university, located in the American state of your choice. (Please see the attached form for details.) At the time of joining the university, you will receive the title of 'scholar-in-residence' in the field of your speciality. You will be expected to interact with students and faculty with a view to imparting unto them your practical knowledge. (The John Dewey Foundation is dedicated to practical solutions as opposed to theoretical ones.) Further details are in the enclosed literature.

All travel and living expenses are paid for by the John Dewey Foundation.

You may be surprised to hear of your selection for this scholarship, Mr Rana, especially since you didn't apply for it. In the 12 years that I've been Program Co-ordinator in the John Dewey Foundation I have never come across a case such as yours.

You were recommended for a scholarship by my superior, Mr Claude Zimblast, who is attached to the Council of Foreign Affairs at the American Embassy and is a former Regional Director of the John Dewey Foundation. Mr Zimblast learned about you from Mr Nicholas Schafer, the embassy's Cultural Counselor who screens all applications by Indian citizens for the USIS Scholarships, which, as you know, are similar in nature to the Dewey fellowships but less selective. When your file arrived on my desk I noticed that you had been referred to Mr Schafer by Mr David Brock, an official of the United States Information Service (USIS), which comes under the American Embassy but whose offices are at the American Center on Kasturba Gandhi Marg. It so happened that Mr Brock came to know of you through his boss. Mr Ernest F.X. Grimcase, Minister-Counselor for Public Affairs at the USIS mission in India. And Mr Grimcase heard about you at a cocktail party.

As Mr Grimcase put it, the American Ambassador, Dr Hamilton Edward Gunther III, stated at a recent cocktail party that he had discovered the most original modern philosopher in modern India since Gandhi. The Ambassador cited a letter you wrote to a local newspaper.

For that reason, Mr Grimcase recommended you to Mr Brock, Mr Brock recommended you to Mr Schafer, Mr Schafer recommended you to Mr Zimblast and, lastly, I recommended you for the last remaining, unfulfilled John

Dewey Foundation Fellowship – which happened to be in philosophy. You will be philosopher-in-residence in the university of your choice. (Please see the attached for details.)

Incidentally, I have not been able to track down the newspaper in which your letter was published. Could you please send me a copy?

For bureaucratic reasons, the fellowship must start before the end of the third fiscal quarter. If it is agreeable to you, we would like to send you to the United States in the next week to 10 days. Kindly fill in the attached form and send it to us at your earliest.

Yours sincerely,
Christopher Morrison

Col. Narendra Pai
Lancer's Lodge
P.O. Urulikanchan
Dist. Pune 412 202

Dear Col. Pai,
You probably opened this letter expecting bad news from your
recently unemployed pen-friend. Get ready for a surprise: I
have been awarded a three-month fellowship to live in the
United States of America!

I feel like I won a lottery – without even purchasing a ticket!
It all began with my letter on hypocrisy. (Many thanks for
your congratulatory sentiments regarding the same. I think it's
an excellent idea to have a public debate on 'Hypocrisy in
India' at the Pune Rotary Club. I hope to be able to attend
after my foreign journey. Please keep me informed as to dates,
etc.) As fate would have it, my letter was noticed by the
American Ambassador, Dr Hamilton Edward Gunther III,
who apparently is considered a man of great wit and hilarity.
(His sympathy to Indians, however, is questionable.)
Ambassador Gunther said I was 'the most original modern
philosopher in modern India since Gandhi'. Those words
echoed down the diplomatic corridors and soon I was offered
a fellowship as 'philosopher-in-residence' at the American university of my choice.

I was happy not just for myself but for the country as well.
India is too much the outcast and hermit of the international
community. It lives too much in itself. What it really needs,
far more than foreign technology and aid, is to reach out to
the outside world. This was the reason UNI was so important
to me: it was my link – India's link – with the outside world.
And it is my firm belief, Col. Pai, that we will be doomed
unless we realise that our future is with the world, not against
it. The Greek and Roman civilisations perished because of

their complacency and conceitedness. We will go their way, too, our 'superior' philosophy notwithstanding. As the poet said: No man is an island. We are living under an illusion if we think that the world will come to us to learn our great philosophy or help lift 80 per cent of our population from the pit of poverty. We will have to go to the world. (But first the government will have to dismantle foreign exchange regulations.) I am proud of my contribution in this regard and am sure that, as Swami Vivekananda did in the late 19th century, I will win over American hearts and minds and make them see the greatness of India.

The obvious place to carry out this massive task is Washington, the capital of America, the bastion of its politics, the home of George Bush (recently victorious in the Gulf War). How often I have stared at pictures of Washington: its monuments, the White House, vast numbers of people on lawns protesting the Vietnam War alongside a body of water that looked oddly like our very own Boat Club. That's why I decided to go to Washington.

But then I started to wonder. Washington seemed an unsophisticated choice. I wondered whether every foreigner chose Washington. The John Dewey Foundation viewed me as a renowned Indian philosopher, and philosophers are supposed to marvel at the smaller, unusual things ordinary people overlook.

So I said in my letter to the Foundation: 'With reference to your request for my idea of an ideal educational setting, my main consideration is the peace and quiet necessary to a philosopher in his philosophising, plus the requisite inspiration, which, for most of my philosopher friends, consists of trees and mountains and rivers . . .' Then I realised I knew nothing about Washington's natural surroundings. I slipped on my chappals, ran down to the market and pumped a rupee coin into a public phone. P.K., the office accountant, answered.

'Hello, P.K.'

'Hari! *Kya haal-chaal hai?*'

'Listen, P.K. Are any of the reporters around?'

'Busy. Since the Bengali became news editor there's no time to even fart.'

'*Accha*? *Yaar*, can you do me a favour?'

'*Bolo.*'

'Can you get the encyclopaedia? The volume including W?'

'Anything for an old friend like Hari.'

When he returned to the phone, sounding breathless, I said: 'Turn to Washington.'

I heard the sound of P.K. wheezing and muttering: it was the way he concentrated. 'Got it.'

'Read it out to me.'

'The whole thing?'

'The whole thing.'

I took notes as P.K. spoke, returned to my apartment and continued my letter.

' . . . My ideal educational setting is Washington, a place where I can ramble in green meadows awash with the delightful fragrance of wild flowers and to fondle beautiful cows while biting into juicy, ripe apples plucked straight from trees. I would like to go mountaineering in the well-known Mount Rainier National Park and to swim in the cool, blue waters of River Columbia. I would like to be able to walk in woods "lonely dark and deep" and forget about all the "promises to keep".' (The latter quote was in the Thesaurus under 'Woods', which P.K. also dug out for me.)

The next morning I delivered the application form personally to the John Dewey Foundation. Two days later I got the following reply:

We are pleased that you have chosen Washington, America's "Green State," as your temporary home during your fellowship. The natural beauty of Washington is among America's finest. We have made arrangements for you to join the University of Washington as philosopher-in-residence. Like most

American universities, the University of Washington has a good faculty, friendly students and also a splendid campus. Our reference materials state that its department of philosophy is unique in that it employs Aristotle's peripatetic method of teaching. The cost of living in Seattle is moderate.

The Foundation also made the arrangements for my trip. I trust that by the time you get this letter, Col. Pai, I will be on my way to Washington or perhaps even walking in the green meadows on Capitol Hill. Wish me luck!

Yours truly,

Hari Rana

American Letter
by Hari Rana

A strange evil has entered my body – the evil of prolonged slumber. I feel like the demon Kumbhkaran who was divinely cursed because of an error. The gods granted him a boon and he decided to remain awake for eleven months every year and spend the remaining month sleeping. But by mistake he reversed the order of his request. The gods said, 'So be it,' and that was that.

My mistake has been to cross the waters. The ancient Hindus were correct: I should never have left India. It was so exciting: the happy news from the Americans, the preparations in Delhi, the initial stages of the trip. And now, here I am, in a steel monster with a sprinting dog along each side, hurtling at a dizzying speed across a far-away continent – and somehow I can do nothing but sleep! Is it the drone of the engine? The foreign air: has it polluted me, as the ancients believed it would? Or some odd traveller's curse? The sensation is so overpowering that if the bus were to fall into a river I would drown without batting an eyelid. I don't feel a thing when the bus stops for meals or refreshments – not even the pangs of hunger or thirst. I have not had a bowel movement since leaving Delhi.

Whenever I awake it is night and the human population of the bus has altered. Faces I have come to recognise are gone. New shapes are in different positions, usually sleeping. I feel like the caretaker of a rolling graveyard. When one of the corpses coughs or talks in his or her sleep, I shiver. Once a passenger sitting next to me slammed his head into my chest. I shrieked so loudly the driver stopped the bus and the passengers, those who awoke, glared at me. I spend hours staring at the headlights illuminating the tunnel of road ahead. There is darkness all around, gloom, loneliness.

Perhaps I should never have come to America.

American Letter

by Hari Rana

'EAT OR BE EATEN.' I read these words on a T-shirt worn by an obese woman munching on a foot-long hamburger and sucking at a bottle of Mountain Doo. This is her midnight snack. The slogan on the shirt swells at its extremities, shrinks slightly in the centre (around the word 'be') and all the letters tend to shudder when the woman takes a laboured breath. Occupying two full seats, she is the most gigantic passenger in the bus: a veritable Mammoth among humans, round like the surface of the earth. Except for the hands that feed her and the ever-moving mouth, her other body parts are inert. She might be 30 years old but her figure suggests that she has already consumed enough food to feed 30 million people and enough aerated drinks to irrigate as many acres. When her meal is finished, she fishes out a chocolate called a Chunky and, with eyes fixed on the road, puts the entire, pyramid-shaped glob in her mouth.

A couple behind me has started to talk. The sound of human voices in the darkness, in normal social intercourse, startles and pleases me. I have to restrain myself from turning around and joining in. I think of my travels on Indian buses and trains, with their fascinating array of characters: the Westernised oriental gentleman, or WOG, who sits by the window reading his newspaper with an air of superiority. The Brahmin, recognised by his detached, meditative countenance. The *bania*, or the shopkeeper, whose unruly family can get nothing done without tearing their clothes and hair while simultaneously eyeing every snack hawker that passes by. The officious middle-aged man who peddles advice to everyone but has trouble deciding where and how to position his suitcase. And of course, the *dhoti* – or *pyjama*-clad villager – who sits cross-legged and puffs endlessly on his *bidis* while watching, as it were, the world going by.

On Indian trains, everyone shares food (with the possible exception of the WOG). A dozen people manage to squeeze into seats designed for three without a murmur of complaint. And no sooner does the journey begin than passengers start exchanging autobiographical information, replete with the number of brothers and sisters, uncles and aunts, the political situation back in their home towns, the price of vegetables in the market, etc. etc.

I tune into the couple's conversation.

The man's voice: 'The laws are far too liberal.'

The woman's: 'You reckon?'

'I'm a firm believer in castration for second-time rape offenders.'

'Don't you think castration is a bit harsh?'

'Everyone has the right to one mistake – I can buy that.'

It seems a difficult conversation to enter, but I take the plunge. I turn in my seat. 'Castration is for animals.'

He fixes me with piercing blue eyes and says: 'Are you a Democrat or something?'

Not quite understanding his question, I take out some peanut jaggery from my jacket that I brought from India. 'Here, please have some.'

'What in hell is that?' says the man.

'Jaggery. *Gujjak.*'

'Aaah!' The man recoils.

'Is it sugar-free?' asks the woman.

'Take it away, for God's sake.'

*

'You from India?'

I am roused from sleep by a young woman sitting on my right across the aisle. The night-light strikes her hair, giving her a blond halo.

'Very much so.' I smooth my ruffled hair.

'I was in India last year.' She gives me a smile and blinks large, blue eyes.

'How did you like it?'

'I haven't come up with a one-line statement but it was *interesting*.' She stretches the word 'interesting'.

'What did you like best?'

'The Taj Mahal. It was beautiful. In fact, I didn't know it was a hotel until I got to Bombay.'

'Oh, yes,' I said.

'I also liked the Maurya Sheraton in New Delhi – where I had the best tandoori food? The Fort Aguada in Goa was nice. It had its own beach? And all the rooms had a view of the sea? Even the bathrooms?'

'What about the rest of India? Did you like it?'

'That was the problem really. Like I was stuck in these five-star hotels all the time? I had these good friends, Indian friends, who insisted and, well, one of them owns this palace-hotel in Udaipur. So naturally, I didn't get to see the real thing. And I wouldn't want to say something about India without having seen the real India. If you know what I mean?'

I started feeling sleepy.

'I would have really liked to go into a slum and cuddle a baby, maybe even adopt one. But . . .' She sighs. 'My friends . . . I have all these friends . . .'

American Letter

by Hari Rana

I wake from a deadened sleep. The bus is hurtling down the highway. I look through the side window. Swollen clouds are floating across the dimly lit American sky. I have been asleep so long that I can't tell whether it's dawn or dusk. I enjoy a long, deep yawn. Out of the corner of my eye I catch a glimpse of a figure huddled in the seat next to me on the aisle.

I can't tell whether it's a man or a woman. All I can see is a weather-beaten face, eyes obscured by shaggy hair and a lumpy-potato nose with an intricate network of veins. The rest of the body is tightly wrapped in a blanket, like an Egyptian mummy. I lean forward to get a better view of this bizarre specimen of humanity.

'First time on Greyhound?'

I get such a jolt that I smack the sealed bus window with the back of my head.

'You all right?' The voice is hoarse but unmistakably that of a woman. I think the question must be directed at me even though her eyes seem to be looking forty-five degrees on either side. (She is cock-eyed.) She gives a twisted smile. 'I said first time on the dog?'

'Yes, but . . .' I touch my neck and grimace.

She cackles, exposing yellow teeth. 'Been long on the road?'

'It seems so.'

Another cackle. 'How long?'

'About twelve hours. I guess.' I look out at the horizon. 'Or maybe twenty-four.'

'Where you headed?'

'Seattle.'

'Been there.'

'You are well travelled?'

She nods. 'And I always take the dog. Cheapest bus fare in the world.' She lifts a silver flask. 'Drink?'

I shake my head. 'I'm afraid the cheapest bus fare would be in India.'

She brings the flask to her lips. I'm glad I refused when I see her greenish teeth scrape its rim.

'You could get off-loaded for drinking, you know. The driver made an announcement.'

She laughs. 'The drivers all know me – every one of them.' She winks and takes a long sip from the flask. 'The first Greyhound bus I took was in 1953. And since then, well . . .' She takes another sip. 'Maine to Mexico; Florida to – well, I already told you, Washington. I'd say I've been everywhere. I *live* on these buses. They're like home. You're from India?' Her eyes do an erratic dance.

I nod.

'Have you heard about the plague?'

'The plague?'

'Read about it at the last rest-stop. There's an outbreak of plague.'

'In India?'

'Your India.'

American Letter

by Hari Rana

Bubonic Plague Erupts in India

NEW DELHI, India (UNI) – Bubonic plague, the rat-borne disease that ravaged nearly half of medieval Europe, has erupted in a town in Western India, news reports said Thursday.

The *Times of India* newspaper said Indian health authorities had detected at least 23 cases of bubonic plague in the town of Bhor in Maharashtra state. The disease is curable but potentially fatal and is spread through rats infected with the plague bacillus.

A massive plague epidemic at the turn of the century killed 6 million people in India. During the 1940s and early 1950s the disease routinely claimed thousands of lives because of bad public health care in the country, according to the World Health Organization.

I am in a toilet stall in the back of the bus. It's like being stuck in a cupboard. The canary-yellow colour of my urine suggests I am dehydrated. The newspaper is called the *St Louis Post-Dispatch*, which I found abandoned next to the sink. I stare in disbelief at the story and return to my seat. I wonder how true it is, and who put it together at the UNI bureau. I wonder whether to take it seriously: Indian newspapers often indulge in rampant misreporting of facts. The plague: could it really make a comeback in the late 20th century, even in India?

I pick up my bags and move to a row far from the other passengers. I could be a carrier – the individual who brings the plague to America for the first time in centuries. On my way down the aisle, I sneak a glance at my fellow passengers: would they throw me off the bus if they discovered where I had come from?

American Letter

by Hari Rana

I have come from darkness into light. I am at the American version of a *dhaba*, bearing the wonderful label of a 'rest stop', in the very middle of America. We're in a town called Salina in Kansas state. I have made it through Washington, Pittsburgh, Columbus, Indianapolis and the historic city of St Louis, which is known, according to the bus driver, as the gateway to the West. I have indeed passed through the gateway to the West – and survived! I lift my tea in a snow-white, American Styrofoam cup. Cheers!

I feel alive for the first time in days. The sun is in my eyes, the wind in my nose and I've just eaten my first-ever cheeseburger, which is a bun with a fried cheese cutlet in it. It left me poorer by five dollars, nearly 150 rupees, which seemed a lot for cheese, but I was famished. Also, tiny pieces of cheese seem stuck between my molars, which never happens with Indian cheese. With prying, they come out black or grey. But no matter: I am standing under the open sky, happily sipping my free tea. (I brought along a packet from India and brewed it up with hot water from the rest stop bathroom.) To make it all heavenly, I feel a welcome stirring in my bowels!

Welcome, my friends, to America, the Land of Plenty. In my case, I thought it was a land of darkness, doubt and difficulty. But as anywhere, day follows night, good times follow bad. Many writers have tried to capture the spirit of this youthful, visionary land: British, French, Spanish, German, even Australian. They have left accounts of their travels that enriched the lives of whole generations. Now a new name is being added to this list of travellers: Hari Rana. Let me state in all humility that I am probably the first Indian to travel across this continent at breakneck speed, observing the manners, customs and predilections of the American people with only 100 dollars in my pocket. (About this, later.) The first Indian without a hatchet and wigwam, that is.

You will be wondering, dear reader, what is this all about and who is this Hari Rana anyway? Well, I am a journalist-cum-writer on a John Dewey Fellowship to America and I am writing a sequence of letters based on my trip to this most exciting and stimulating country. It's a project that was born of necessity or, shall I say, adversity. I hadn't planned such a project. I hit an unexpected snag, which put me, with no preparation, on this lengthy bus ride. I have felt as depressed as ever in my life. I've been hungry, sleepy, *kabzi* (constipated) and needy of a kind word or an interested glance. (No one looks at anyone in America!) But opportunity – doesn't it knock only once? What better exercise for an aspiring writer than to be thrust into a new land – and to let his thoughts come freely out on paper without undue hindrance. That's the idea: my 'American Letters' will be published in instalments, upon my return, in a major national daily, hopefully the Sunday supplement of *The Times of India*. The letters will be from my diary – a verbatim account of things as I see them. Each instalment will be fresh like morning dew since it will be published exactly as it was written at the time. Rest assured that 'American Letter' will include everything that happens to Hari Rana: good, bad, humiliating, and, of course, triumphant.

I am travelling in a Greyhound bus, which many readers will remember from James Hadley Chase novels. The landscape has been uninspiring: green fields and hills on both sides but absolutely no people on them – not even farmers or cowboys. (In India it's impossible to go a mile without seeing men, women and children jostling with cows, goats and pigs amidst a multitude of two-, three- and four-wheeled vehicles. But that is not to say everything is dull. For one, travelling in a comfortable, air-conditioned Greyhound bus is a dream compared to the hot, bumpy rides in ill-maintained govern-ment buses back in India. (Although the air-conditioning sometimes doesn't work and a peculiar smell of sweat and vomit hangs heavy inside these bus.) And there is the joy of not knowing what awaits you over the hill or around the corner.

One of the things I will be able to tell you is how the momentous events happening in our country are perceived from abroad. As I write this, the American media has been reporting an epidemic of the plague back home. Hardly half an hour ago I saw a CBS television report in a restaurant that showed a municipal rat catcher in Bombay holding a dead rat by its tail. The report then focused on a South Indian tribal village where rats are the staple diet. Needles to say, Americans in the restaurant recoiled in horror. Some of them left their food half eaten. The restaurant rang with cries of 'Disgusting!' and 'Yuk!'

American Letter
by Hari Rana

But first – how did I get here, from India to the middle of
the American continent, from New Delhi's Indira Gandhi
International Airport to Colonel Sander's Kentucky Fried
Chicken?

I was seen off – when was it? Just fifty-six hours ago? – by
three former colleagues of mine from Union News International, the prestigious international news agency, who
insisted on driving me in the office car. It was night time and
the exterior of the car was decked with marigolds, making it
look like the car of a bridegroom. I thought this was absurd
and told my friends so, only to have a thick garland of flowers
flung around my neck and a shining golden turban thrust on
my head by Omi Chand, the office driver. 'This occasion is
even more significant than a marriage,' said Omi Chand. I
smelled whisky on his breath.

Gopalacharya, a rising reporting star at UNI, was in agree-
ment. 'Hari,' he said putting his arm around my shoulder,
'you deserve a royal send-off because you are the first Indian
from the office to go West!'

Arun, a less stellar journalist but extremely reliable nonetheless and probably irreplaceable, agreed even more whole-
heartedly: 'It's a day of happiness not only for ex-colleagues
but for the whole country!'

I had never experienced such a send-off. I felt a little
choked. 'You know, guys, at times I just want to turn around
and go back. How could I be leaving UNI after all these years?'

'Hari,' lectured Gopalacharya, 'take another. Everyone gets
bombed when they travel abroad.'

'Go on, Hari,' said Arun.

'I don't want to use up your whole bottle.'

Gopalacharya waved unconcernedly. 'I'm putting it on expenses, Hari. Drink away!'

Omi Chand drove at top speed with constant, unnecessary blasts of the horn. We left New Delhi proper and drove down a floodlit highway through blackened, abandoned fields. The airport, seen from a distance, resembled a sprawling fortress with brilliant lights. The car accelerated up a steep, winding ramp and suddenly we were in a sea of chaos. The entire stretch of road in front of the terminal was blocked by scores of cars, taxis and buses from which passengers with enormous amounts of luggage were alighting. Thousands of people milled around. Policemen shouted and blew their whistles at errant drivers who either ignored them or simply shouted back. I was shocked. Could we not at least project a nice image to foreign tourists?

As my friends and I were making our way through the crowds of people, I felt a thump on my shoulder. Turning, I found a portly man wearing a *dhoti* and a half-sleeved under-vest. His forehead was smeared with a white *teeka* and tied around his right wrist were several red-coloured holy strings. The man gave me a toothless smile. At first I couldn't recognise him, until he spoke in a distinctive sing-song voice. It was my village priest, Lalji Ram, whom I hadn't seen in years! I touched his feet and he blessed me. I asked him what he was doing here but he just smiled and beckoned.

Lalji Ram led me to the edge of the road and pointed a finger. A group squatted on the sidewalk on the other side. The men were smoking *hukkas* and the faces of the women were covered with their sarees.

'*Pandit ji,*' I asked, 'who are these people?'

'*Beta,* your uncles could not come so they have sent your aunts. To wish you a happy journey!'

'But who are the others, *pandit ji*?'

'They are all from the village. They heard that you were going abroad and wanted to come. We hired a bus.'

As we approached, the women threw off their veils. The men jumped up to greet me. I touched the feet of my three aunts and they smothered my head with kisses, each one saying over and over again: 'May you have a long life, son.'

Somebody cleared his throat on my left. I turned. It was a short, severe man dressed in a spotless white *dhoti* and *kurta*. His thick, black hair was plastered to his scalp with oil.

'*Namaste*, Master *ji*,' I said with folded hands. His name was Devendra Sharma but everybody called him Master *ji*. He was the village teacher, specialising in Hindi, history, civics and Sanskrit. He was one of the most self-important men I had ever known.

'*Namaste, namaste, namaste.*' Master *ji* said with a little cough.

'Say, what are you doing these days?'

Master *ji* hadn't changed one bit. He had travelled a hundred kilometres to see me off and was pretending as if he didn't know what I did.

'I have just been selected by the John Dewey Foundation to . . .'

'All my three sons are well settled,' he interrupted. 'All three are engineers.'

'That's wonderful.'

'Of course,' coughed Master *ji*, 'I have no worries now.'

The villagers were looking impatient, hoping the interlude with Master *ji* would be auspicious, beneficial – and brief.

Master *ji* gave the villagers a haughty look and, with a bored expression on his face, said: 'You can meet these people also. They are waiting.'

Immediately, two well-built men caught hold of my legs and lifted me on their shoulders. The women broke out into a shrill song with a wavering tune. I couldn't follow the words, but it was something about a village boy going abroad while his family worried about his welfare.

The song ended amidst loud cheers. Lalji Ram pushed ahead of Master *ji* and held up his hand. The crowd quietened.

'I want to say something on behalf of our village to Hari, who is the star of our eyes.' The women listened with rapt attention. 'According to our scriptures, Hindus are not supposed to cross the seas to other countries. But times have changed and these days going abroad has not only become an acceptable practice but a welcome one. India must keep abreast with the world if it wants to progress.'

Lalji Ram paused, looking at his feet. 'However, there are dangers in going to foreign countries. Hari is probably an intelligent boy and is undoubtedly aware of these dangers. But there is no harm in repeating them once more.' He looked directly at me. 'The first danger is foreign women.' He uttered some mantra as if the very mention had defiled him. 'I have heard they spin a fine web to entice innocent men from the East, whom they covet. Be very careful of these women and befriend them only if you must. Keep a safe distance at all times.' Lalji Ram mumbled another mantra. 'Fifty metres should be sufficient.

'The second danger is the food and drink.' He looked up at the sky and shook his head. 'Hari, you have to be most cautious about what you eat. Stay away from restaurants because they must be serving cow meat in everything. I have heard that there is milk in America. As far as possible, drink milk and eat fresh fruits and vegetables. And keep away from alcohol, which does nothing but corrupt the soul.'

Gopalacharya, who had been watching the spectacle from a distance, staggered towards us, waving his bottle of whisky. I shooed him away.

Lalji Ram took a deep breath and continued. 'Now I come to the last point. The West is full of temptations. But perhaps the biggest temptation of them all is money and comfort. Many Indians who go abroad stay there. This you must avoid at all costs. You were born in this glorious country and you must work and die here. Otherwise your soul will never be at rest.' Lalji Ram took my hands in his. 'Promise me, Hari, that you will return.'

I said I would.

'Are you sure?'

'It's only a three-month fellowship, *Pandit ji.*'

Lalji Ram shook his head as if he'd heard this before. 'You know who you are, don't you, Hari Rana? You know who your father was.'

I nodded.

Lalji Ram blessed me. I touched his feet and turned to my aunts and the women from the village. Another round of embraces followed. I walked away with my colleagues. Minutes later, I was in the terminal. There were numerous formalities: Bags had to be X-rayed, taxes had to be paid. A corrupt-looking fatty in a khaki uniform asked why I had never been abroad – which I thought to be a very stupid question because there is always a first time for everything. Then a policeman asked me to raise my arms while he ran his hands all over my body. I joined hundreds of other passengers sitting in a lounge. Everyone suddenly got up and went through a door. After walking for about one hundred metres, I entered a narrower lounge crammed with colourful, comfortable seats. I was told by a pretty lady to take one of the seats, which I did. Then I looked out of the window on my left and got a shock. There was a huge wing below me: I was sitting in the airplane itself!

I kept to myself through the two flights and the stopover at London. Finally, we landed in Washington. The cotton-wool feeling in my ears ended. My heart felt light and there was a new-found energy in my legs. My spirits soared: the very air in the plane suddenly seemed different: the oxygen of a different country!

I walked through a chute, which led to a steel-coloured corridor. I noticed that the passengers ahead of me started, with some jostling, to form a single file. I assumed there was a narrow staircase ahead leading to a lower floor of the airport. As I moved forward, I heard a woman's shriek, followed by the sound of something tumbling. For a second, the line of passengers stopped, and except for the grinding growl of some machine, there was silence. A voice from ahead said, 'It's the lady in the saree.' I assumed that an Indian lady must have fallen on the stairs. The queue started moving again. After a while I heard a dull thud. Someone from behind asked if another passenger had fallen. 'You bet,' said a voice ahead. 'A man in a turban.'

With a few steps more I came into sight of the monster: a pulsating, descending staircase with black, rubbery, moving handrails. Without a moment to think, it was my turn to board the perpetual motion machine. I felt the pressure of impatient passengers behind me. I had no choice. I looked down at the first step. It was grooved, like a giant comb, and moving at what appeared to be an incredibly impatient rate. I tried to act casual and put my right foot forward. Instantly I felt my foot sinking and my body froze with fright. Somebody collided into me from behind and I slipped. But I managed to catch the rail and recover my balance. Except for a slight tear at the back of my pants there was no other damage. At least I hadn't fallen: one point for India!

I managed to leap off at the bottom with an involuntary cry and followed the flow of passengers through a wide corridor with a polished floor and clean, spotless walls. A uniformed man with a gun on his hip was saying over and over: 'American citizens this way, non-Americans this way.' I went in the non-American direction. Passengers were lining up in front of counters with passports in hand.

Soon, my turn came. I handed my passport to the officer. He flipped the pages and said: 'First visit to the United States?' I replied in the affirmative. He stared at me provocatively. 'What is the purpose of your visit?' I said I was on a John Dewey fellowship. He took several moments to study me. They were the most terrifying few seconds of my life. Finally, the officer nodded, stamped my passport and said with a smile: 'Have a nice stay, sir.'

I couldn't believe my ears. Not only was I allowed to enter the world's top country but I was called sir! And that too by an officer. I realised it was the first time anyone had called me sir. I walked away with my head held high, a tune on my lips, a jerk in my knees and, of course, the tear in my pants (covered by my jacket).

I followed the crowd out of the hall, wondering what sights and smells would await me in the city outside. A uniformed man blocked my path with a meaty arm. 'Do you have anything to declare?'

The only thing I wanted to declare, I said, was that everybody should not be forced to use the escalator.

'Wha-at?'

I said: 'I want to declare that I slipped on the escalator and was nearly injured.'

The officer snapped his fingers and another uniformed man came over. 'This gentleman's touchy about something,' he said. 'Says he fell off the escalator.'

The second officer asked me what nationality I was. I told him. He started laughing. 'Indians are always falling off the escalator.' He patted me on the back and, pointing ahead, said: 'Have a nice day.'

I walked into another lounge full of people – mostly big people with bizarre clothes and haircuts. It didn't take me long to find a public telephone. I dialled the contact number for the University of Washington. After a few seconds, a sweet female voice told me to put in four dollars and fifty cents. I only had twenty dollar notes. I told the operator but she just kept repeating, 'Four dollars and fifty cents, four dollars and fifty cents.'

I got change from a change machine, which turned out to be yet another First World technological marvel. Then I hurried back to the telephone booth and dialled the university number. I put in the required four dollars and fifty cents, and within seconds heard a ring.

'University of Washington.'

'Madam, I have just come from India. I am currently at the airport. You might be knowing about me, my name is Hari

Rana. I have been sent by the John Dewey Foundation on a fellowship as philosopher-in-residence at your esteemed university.'

'Sir, what can I do for you?'

'Actually I just wanted to know how to get to the university, madam.'

'The best way would be to take a cab.'

'Cab?'

'Uh, a cab. A taxi.'

'Thank you madam, I am looking forward to meeting you soon then.'

I headed out of the terminal. I stood on the kerbside and tried to flag half-a-dozen taxis. Finally, one pulled over. I hopped into the back seat with my suitcase and told the driver, a big black man, to take me to the University of Washington.

He looked at me with a scowl on his face.

I repeated: 'University of Washington, please.'

'What's the address?'

'It's the University of Washington.'

'Never heard of any such university.'

I said I had the name of the university and a telephone number.

'Well, I suggest you call that number and get an address.'

I ran back to the telephone booth. The same voice answered the phone.

'Sorry to disturb you, madam. It is Hari Rana from India. Can you give me your good address please? The taxi driver is wanting it.'

'They should know it,' said the voice, 'but I'll give it to you anyway.'

I wrote down the address and went out into the street. As luck would have it, a vacant taxi came along in an instant. The driver was a jolly looking man with a cigarette sticking out of his mouth.

'Excuse me, sir.' I put on my most polite voice. 'I would

like to go to the University of Washington.' I handed him the note on which I had scribbled the address.

'Never heard of it.'

'You are sure?'

'Lemme tell ya somethin' pal.' He took a drag from his cigarette. 'I've bin a cab driver twennytoo years an I ain't never herda no University of Washington on Olympia Boulevard. Georgetown University. American University. Catholic University. No University of Washington, pal.' He smiled, showing nicotine-stained teeth, and drove off.

I hailed another taxi. The driver popped his head out the window.

'I want to go to the u-née-ver-city of Washington,' I enunciated. 'Do you know where it is?'

The driver had pale blue eyes. He pursed his lips and slowly shook his head.

I pulled out the paper and read the address aloud.

'Zere is no sus place.'

'You mean there's no such university?'

'I said zere is no sus place.'

'The University of Washington . . .'

'Sori, no place like zees.'

'I don't understand . . .'

'Vere you from? Pakistan?'

'India.'

'Oh, Eendia!' The driver's face broke into a warm smile. 'Me from Raasia, braather of Eendia. You sink I tell lies? Nooooo. I help you. Frend to frend. I tell you, zere is no sus university. Now I go. *Namaaste*.'

My Russian friend zoomed off.

I was getting worried. I called the woman at the university once more.

'What's the problem now, Mr Rana?'

'All the taxis are refusing to go to the university.'

'I don't see why . . . this is most unusual.'

'The taxi drivers are saying there is no such university.'

'There's no such university?'

Just then we were interrupted by a voice on the telephone. 'If you want to extend this call,' it said, 'please deposit two dollars and fifty cents.'

I heard the woman at the university take a sharp breath. 'Isn't this a local call? Where are you calling from, Mr Rana?'

'From the airport.'

'But the airport is a local call. How much did you pay for the first three minutes?'

'Four dollars and fifty cents. I got change at a machine near the . . .'

'This is impossible.'

The operator interrupted again to demand her money.

'Operator,' said the woman. 'What city is this call originating from?'

'Bethesda, Maryland,' she replied. 'Two dollars and fifty cents for the next three minutes, please.'

'Where are you, Mr Rana?'

'I'm in Washington, of course.'

'Washington D.C.?'

'Yes.'

'Just one minute, Mr Rana. Operator, please hold the call.'

I heard music. The operator said: 'I'm not allowed to hold this call for much longer.' I started to apologise and then a new voice came on the line.

'Mr Rana? Hari Rana?'

'Yes?'

'I need two dollars, gentlemen,' said the operator, 'and fifty cents.'

'Mr Rana, this is Brandon Griggs, director of the John Dewey Fellowship programme. I understand you are in Washington D.C.'

'Looking for the University of Washington,' I said.

'Mr Rana, you are three thousand miles from the University of Washington. We are in Seattle.'

'How . . .'

'If you look at your ticket . . .'

The operator interrupted. 'I'm sorry gentlemen but I'm going to have to cut this line.' And she did so.

I stood, receiver in hand, in a state of shock, pondering the reasons for my error. My ticket was a round-the-world fare with numerous leaves and destinations: New Delhi – London. London – Washington. Washington – Seattle. There it was: the all-important ticket to Seattle. After that came Seattle – Tokyo, Tokyo – Singapore and Singapore – New Delhi. I had thought my trip broke in Washington and the final four legs were my return journey three months hence. A scrutiny of the ticket details revealed that I was correct about the final flights. But the ticket for Washington – Seattle was, indeed, for today. The flight left at 8.15 a.m. It was now 9.00. I had missed it! I was stranded on the wrong side of a continent.

In India, getting off at the wrong stop is not so serious. In America, you have to travel across three time zones. I assumed my Washington – Seattle ticket was now worth less than half its value. That was the case in India when a passenger missed a train or flight and didn't ensure that his ticket was cancelled several hours beforehand.

I approached three men who were talking animatedly near the exit door and told them about my problem. Could you tell me how I can get to Seattle?

'There are a million ways to go to Seattle,' answered a short, pale-looking man in shorts. He looked like Bugs Bunny with a Hitler moustache.

'A million ways?'

'You can fly.' Shorty sliced the air above his head with outstretched fingers. 'You can take a train.' He brought his fingers to chest level and pushed them straight ahead. 'Or drive.' He held his fists at arm's length and wheeled them.

'They all sound expensive.'

'In that case,' continued Shorty in his squeaky voice, 'you could bike' – he made a paddling motion with his hands –

'run' he moved his arms forward like pistons – 'or even walk' – he marched briefly on the spot.

'Is there a middle way?'

'The dog,' said a tall man wearing metal spectacles.

'The *dog*?'

'Greyhound,' said the man.

It is said that if a traveller's first experience in a foreign land is a bad one, it sours the whole trip. By that theory, my disastrous disembarkation in Washington was bound to ruin all that was to follow. But when I was settled on the bus, several hours outside of Washington, I didn't feel my trip had been soured. I was beginning to like being a stranger in a strange country. I was determined to learn new things about a new world. And it was a very new world indeed.

And when the bus made its first stop on the highway, at a sprawling restaurant complex, I thought it was time to rectify my false start. America had thrown me a loop: it was a new world, it needed adjustments, but that's what I came for. To see, to learn, to conquer. So I decided to start anew. My first wish: to ride an escalator successfully. And there it was – leading from the pavement to the restaurants with their neon lights and combined smells of cheese, oil and disinfectant. I strode through the doors of the complex and faced my enemy. I could hear its constant grinding. I positioned myself a foot away from its jaws. My heart was pounding and my palms were drenched with sweat. I saw the steps, looking like moving toast holders, popping up from the floor one after the other. With my right foot, I tested the air over the first step. I did the same with the left. I took a deep breath, steadied myself and lunged forward. My right foot landed squarely on the escalator. Immediately, I pulled up my other foot and before I knew it I was moving upwards just like everyone else.

American Letter

by Hari Rana

Another stretch of endless American road. Another fitful nap. Another rest stop and restaurant, this one a tribute to American sports. The walls are adorned with pictures of people wielding rackets and oversized gloves. A dozen TV screens show wide-shouldered men in helmets running with a *lauki*-shaped ball. Buoyant music fills the air, along with the smell of frying food.

I look for a place to sit. A middle-aged man with a striking white mane is eating alone in a corner of the restaurant. I recognise him as a busmate. He is dressed more fancily than any other Greyhound passenger I've seen. He wears a white bush-shirt. His trousers are of a matching white material. His moustache is bushy and white. He sits with a kind of ethereal alertness, chest bowed, with an expression that suggests he's listening to some inner music.

'May I sit here?' I ask.

He looks up, nods deliberately.

'What is the national sport of America?'

He finishes chewing, swallows and fixes me with alert, interested eyes. His face is at an angle, as if he's turning his good ear towards me. He clears his throat. 'You are alone. You feel out of place.' He wipes his mouth with the corner of a serviette. 'This is your very first time abroad!'

His words are surprising enough but so too is his accent: a classic Italian accent like you hear in the movies. 'Excuse me?'

'You feel like everything is' – he waves a hand – 'foreign. Every*body* is foreign.'

I look at him.

'You are a little depressed. No?'

'Are you a mind-reader?'

He points an index finger to his temple. 'There is no such thing as a mind-reader.' His voice is deep and melodious, like a mandolin.

'A psychologist?'

He expels contemptuous air from his nose.

'Do you do this for all the passengers?'

'These people?' His gesture becomes disparaging. 'They do not interest me. *You* interest me.'

'Why?'

He lifts his face sideways, although his eyes fix me directly. It's not a hearing problem, I realise. This is the way he concentrates. I notice he's deeply tanned. His hair, slicked back on top, erupts in soft white curls at the collar-line.

He looks at his watch. 'It's time.'

On the way to the bus I ask: 'How was the food?'

He looks at the clouds as if for an answer. He nods to signal the close of his deliberation. He proclaims: 'Acceptable.'

'You should have had the pizza.'

He looks at me like I'm crazy. 'You are from India? Or Pakistan?'

'India.'

He nods thoughtfully.

'You must have read about the plague,' he says.

'I've never been to the affected areas,' I stammer. 'They're not really on the main routes. I feel sorry for the tourists, actually. Imagine going to a foreign country and finding a plague. I'm sure no one would want to visit my country these days.'

'The *Pest*.' He stops me a few paces short of the bus door. 'I want to tell you, my friend, something. You are absolutely wrong.' Some other passengers approach and he pulls me out of their way, waving them into the bus with a gallant flourish. Then he whispers from the side of his mouth: 'Given a choice, your country is exactly the place I'd like to be right now. Right now!' And then he turns and climbs majestically into the bus.

American Letter

by Hari Rana

George is one of the most interesting individuals I have ever met. Despite his Italian accent (he pronounces *a* as *aa* and *i* as *ee*) he calls himself an American. 'A true blue Aa-mer-ee-caan,' he avows, sounding like someone on a spaghetti commercial. He refuses to tell me his profession. 'Not important,' he says dismissively. He refuses to disclose where he lives, where he comes from, where he is going on the bus, or why he is travelling.

'All I will say to you, Hari Rana, is that you will look around one minute' – he makes a sweeping gesture with his hands like a conductor telling the violins to come up – 'and I will be gone!' He would tell me, however, his philosophy of life – and at some length.

'The world is confusing. That is acceptable. It cannot be changed, no? I was confused, too, when I was young.' George gazes out of the window, a soft look in his eyes. 'But Hari Rana, I also had a grrreat curiosity about the world.' He claps his hands together, making a sound that turns a few heads in front of us. 'A *terrific* curiosity. I tell you: one day I put a blanket and some clothes, a bundle of clothes, in a bag and I left. Fffft – goodbye! I travelled everywhere. I went to India.' He gives me a curious look. 'Stayed a long time. And what did I learn? I will tell you, Hari Rana. I discovered the secret of happiness! Yes – you don't believe? The secret of life, enlightenment, call it what you like.' The dismissing gesture again. 'I will share my secret with you. It will save you much trouble in life. But not now. Laterwards. For now I take a nap.' And he does, with extraordinary swiftness. He begins again later, after having a glass of water and doing a number of spine stretches and neck exercises.

'I divide mankind into two groups.' He chops the air with his hand. 'Those who are content simply to *be*.' He waves his right hand towards the window. 'And those who strive to *become*.' His left hand moves towards me. 'These are very different, Hari. You see, to *be* is to accept your lot in life; to *become* is to create, to achieve, to discover. For example, a man who renounces the world, as they do in India. Is this man trying to *be* or *become*?'

'Be?'

'Excellent!' He slaps his thigh. 'Now. A man who paints? Is he being or becoming?'

'Becoming.'

'You and I – we are understanding each other. Excellent! The artist: he makes something from the paint, the bronze, the marble. He does the . . .' – George slices the air in front of him; he pinches the material of the seat before him – 'and when he makes changes, he changes himself. You see?'

'I don't know.'

'Hari.' His tone is one of disappointment. He touches my arm consolingly.

'What about you? Your life?'

George falls silent. We sit, each looking ahead, listening to the bus engine. Then he starts speaking softly. 'In my life, I've only found one way to continually *become*.'

'How?'

'Motion.'

'You mean . . .' I arch my eyebrows towards the landscape outside.

'Not just physical motion.' He makes a raspberry sound. 'Anyone can . . .' His hands scurry along his knees like mice. 'I . . . you could say I am in search of *experience*.' He shifts impatiently. 'You are familiar with the Buddha?'

'Of course.'

'He is from India. No?'

'Yes.'

'The Buddha taught man to work for his own salvation. To work every day, every minute. That's the kind of thing I have been doing for thirty years. Thirty years!'

'Wasn't the Buddha always sitting?'

'For an Indian you are very funny. You know that? Very good sense of humour. Very funny.'

'Thank you.'

'Hari,' he says sombrely. 'I am en route to an interesting experience. Don't ask what it is.' He wags a finger. 'And if I wasn't here, on this bus, I'd probably be on a plane to your country.'

'You mean for the plague?'

'Hari – think of it! Every soul in the middle of that *Pest* is going through an experience. A grrreat experience: to live through the biggest outbreak of the *Pest* in the 20th century!'

'But it's terrible.'

'Completely curable. A few pills.' He snaps his fingers. 'Everyone in the world takes pills. But how many will be able to say they were *there*?' George's eyes have a distant look. 'That they lived through that time? That they wore masks? And . . . oh . . . saw *bodies* burning in the streets?'

I excuse myself to go to the toilet. On the way I run into the Greyhound lady, alone at the back of the bus with her flask.

'Have a sip.'

I decline. I motion to the driver in front. 'Be careful.'

'To hell with him.' She takes a long pull and sighs. 'I'm glad you've found a friend, dear.'

'He's Italian. But he calls himself American.'

'Doesn't everyone?'

When I get back to George, I mention the Greyhound lady.

He swivels his head grandly. 'There?' He scrutinises her for several moments then returns his gaze to the front. 'She looks horrible.' He starts his neck exercises again.

'By the way,' I interject, 'is George your real name? I've

never heard of an Italian George. There was an Italian correspondent called Giorgio in Delhi.'

'I am Aa-mer-ee-caan,' answers George, thumping a fist to his chest. The next sentence came out with slow, metronomic solemnity. 'So . . . I . . . am . . . *George*.

'Twelve years ago I received my US citizenship. There is no need to go into anything before that.' George flicks a hand in front of his face as if swatting a fly. 'Why did I leave my country? Why did I come to this country? Meaningless. It's meaningless because of what I discovered when I came to this country. Change, Hari, Change. C-H-A-N-G-E. And freedom. F-R-E . . .' He waves a hand. 'You know how to spell. Back to my story. More than anything else, Hari, this is a country of change and freedom. It should have been called United States of Change and Freedom. How do I mean? You see that girl across the aisle? Where does she come from? What did her father do? Does it matter? In my country it matters. In your country it matters. But here? Pfffft. Why? Because of this.' He pounds the bus seat with his palm. 'She goes – *vroooom*.' He gyrates two clenched fists as if steering a stock car. 'That girl moves. She leaves her father and her place and goes . . . where? Anywhere. No questions.' George lowers his shoulders, cranes his neck and purses his lips seriously. 'She changes. That's her freedom. You understand? Take that man. What is he? A farmer from New Hampshire? Where is he going? To open an antique store in New Mexico? Who cares where he's from? What he did? What he's going to do. Pffft.' He faces me. 'I met a woman at a bus station the other day. Do you know what she does? She's a designer, an interior designer. A decorator. But now she's changing: she's becoming a yoga teacher. You know yoga.' He arches his back and looks like he's meditating for a moment. 'What is this, you ask? A decorator becomes a teacher of yoga? Imagine! The point, Hari: you can be what you want in America. You're selecting the wallpaper for people's toilets one day and the next day you're sitting cross-legged going, you know, *Ommmm*. Isn't that wonderful?' He smiles and moves his fingers in the air like a pianist. 'In America, everyone is a chameleon, changing their colours as they go along. That's why I'm interested in you. Before, you were the frog in the well: you thought the outside world was nothing but a patch of sky. Look Hari.' He points through the window. 'That's the outside world.'

American Letter
by Hari Rana

The bus comes to a halt at a desolate looking station on the highway. The landscape is sandy and dotted with thorny shrubs. The driver has made no announcement where we are or how long we will be stopping. A hissing sound from the front indicates that the door is opening. I hear a small commotion at the back and turn around. The Greyhound lady is trotting up the aisle.

'We are in Lansing!' Her tone is hushed, ominous, and I wonder if she is drunk. 'Where the penitentiary is!'

George gives her a scornful look.

'When they release the cons, they bring them here. To the bus station. With their twenty-five dollars and new suits.'

A wiry young man with cropped, blond hair gets on the bus, dressed in a new suit. The Greyhound lady comes back down the aisle. As she passes us, she whispers: 'There's one now.' The man looks around the bus furtively and quickly slips into an empty seat.

'Look, George, how does this affect me? I'm only a visitor here.'

'This country was founded by visitors. *I* was a visitor; I became American. You are a visitor; you can become American.'

'I'm here for three months!'

George's hand sweeps up in exasperation.

'George, I'm from India. I'm not from a rich family. How can I get along with, say, that man there? He may be a tycoon.'

'On Greyhound?'

'The professors at the university: how can I get along with them? They've been to Harvard or Yale or God knows where. The students: think of the differences in our lives. I'm just hoping they'll be kind.'

'And?'

'George, I'm a nobody. A nobody from plague-stricken India.'

'You throw away your passport once you get here. That is what I am trying to tell you. The only passport that works here is personality with a capital P.' George faces me. 'This is the point: You may not be an American citizen but you will be treated like one. That's the American way. So why not take them up on the offer?'

'George,' I say, 'why should I even try?'

'So you can *become*.' He switches to a whisper: 'I'm from America. You are from America, Hari. Because America is . . .' He pounds his heart. 'I have a grrreat idea. See that girl over there? The one with the auburn hair? I want you to go over to her and introduce yourself.'

I suck in my breath. 'Introduce myself?'

'And not as Hari. As *Harry*. Can you say Harry?'

'Hari.'

'Not Hari. *Har*-ree as in h-a-r-r-i-e-d.'

'Hay-ri.'

'Not *Hay*-ri. *Har*-ree.'

'Harr . . .'

That's it. *Harrr* . . . ree.'

'Harrr . . .'

'You are not getting the *r* right. Your tongue doesn't touch the roof of your mouth. It's very difficult, for us Italians too. Here.' George points an index finger into his mouth. He growls like a tiger. 'Harrrrrrr . . . Take the tongue midway. Now say it after me. Har-ree.'

'Ha-reee.'

'You have to emphasise the first syllable, not the last. *Har*-ree.'

In my confusion I say 'Hari.'

'That's your Indian name.'

'But you don't pronounce *your* name in the American way. You say Jee-orj. With two syllables.'

There is a moment of awkward silence.

'Sorry,' I say. '*Ha*-ree.'

George shrugs and purses his lips. Then he mumbles, in a practising tone: 'Jo-orj.'

'*Har*-ee.'

'That's better . . . *Har*-ree.'

'*Har*-ree.'

'That's it . . .'

'*Harry*!'

'You did it!' He face was brimming with joy. 'That was grrreat! That was *fantastic*! Now I want you to go up to that girl and introduce yourself.'

I take the challenge. I walk up the aisle to the girl's seat. 'Excuse me,' I say in my politest voice, 'I'm Harry.' She smiles and we chat.

I return to my seat and clasp George's outstretched hand. 'It's easy!'

'That's another thing: America is easy. The easiest country in the world!'

American Letter
by Hari Rana

I awake to find an empty seat beside me. The bus is accelerating.

I look around. George is nowhere in sight. I check the overhead luggage rack. His bag is gone. A piece of folded white paper is jutting from my jacket's breast pocket. It's a note from George and in it are two twenty dollar bills. The precise handwriting reads:

Dear 'Harry',
I would have said goodbye but I didn't want to disturb your sleep. I could tell by the smile on your face that you were dreaming about a new life in America. I am sure you will reach your destination, wherever and whatever it is. Just throw your great Indian rope into the American sky and start your climb.
With best wishes on your journey.
George

American Letter
by Hari Rana

"Got a cigarette, brother?'

I was lost in my thoughts and didn't notice a young black man, presumably one of the hundreds of Greyhound travellers loitering in the parking lot.

'Sorry, I don't smoke. But I have some tea.' I extend a paper cup in which I have brewed tea from the hot water in the bathroom. With just a little over 50 dollars left, I decided not to buy any tea at the rest stops.

'*Tea*?' The black man says the word like it's some disease. 'Are you from *India*?'

I nod.

He fluffs his fuzzy hair. 'My name is Jackson. What's your name, man?'

George's words ring through my head: *You can be what you want in America.* I am ready: I want to become a new person. But who? The first person I think of is the Bengali, my former colleague at UNI.

'I am Ashit. Ashit Chatterjee.' I tilt my head sideways, take a long sniff and give Jackson a wary look.

'A-*shit*?' Jackson buckles at the waist and convulses with laughter. 'You mean, like . . .' He squats and squeezes his eyelids painfully.

I try to look offended. 'Ashit is a Bengali word. Bengali langh-uage is bhery po-lite. Not like Enghlis.' I have made a convenient switch to a Bengali accent; if I'm going to become another person I might as well have some fun.

'What the *hell* is Ben-*gaali*?' Jackson places a foot on the bench and folds his arms disrespectfully.

'Bengali is the sweetest langh-uage in the whole bhorld.'

'I thought that was like French, man.'

'Phrench phor you.' I lower my shoulders, extend my neck forward and purse my lips in a I-couldn't-care-less gesture. 'Bengali phor me.'

'How many languages do you have over in India anyway?'

'Phipteen ophissally certified. Dialects are changhing ebhri twenty-phibe kilometres. India is a ghreat country.'

I am beginning to enjoy this.

'India is habing the bhorld's larghest pool of technically skilled mane-power, the second larghest populayson and the third larghest army whose tradison goes bhek to our first waar of indhependence which we phot against the Britis in 1857 ay-dhee . . .'

'Great!' Jackson gives me a thump on my back. 'Now I'll just be going on back . . .'

' . . . bephore 1857 we were reghularly enghazed in phytting the Mugalj, Turks, Afghans, Huns and other Islamic barbarianj. In Bhorld Bhar II our trupps saw axon in Ehuropp, Africa, Middil Ist, Southist Asia etcetera. We hab phot against China and ghiben the Pakistani dogs a bloody nose on three okasuns.'

'You an expert in military history or something?'

'Am bhijiting scholar in rejidence.'

'At the Pentagon?'

'At Harvard uni-bhersity. Going there now.'

'I got news for you, A-shit. Harvard's on the East coast. You, me and the dog are headed *West*.'

I can't think of a face-saving response. But I realise – thanks to the very same enthusiasm that got me into trouble – that I'm half grinning and half laughing. And there's no better way to buy time than with the half-grin-half-laugh trick – one of the Bengali's favourites.

'Bengalis' – I add a little more laugh – 'love trabhelling.'

Jackson gives me a thoughtful look. 'You do know about the plague in your country, don't you?'

'Of course, of course.' I shake my head. 'India is allowed

to hab plague. We are an anscent country . . . Plague is a legacy of the Bhritis colonijers, also that of Christophur Columbhus . . .'

'That's not what I meant, Mr Chatter . . .'

' . . . Jee.'

'I just hope you haven't brought the plague with you to *my* motherfucking country.'

On my way down the aisle to the toilet, I pass a lady sitting alone holding a newspaper. I scan the headlines on the front page with the practised ease that comes from long years of association with the printed word. My eyes focus on a headline: 'DOCTORS DESERT HOSPITALS AS DEATH TOLL IN INDIA PLAGUE TOUCHES 600.'

'Excuse me, madam.' I stand with my chest puffed, my voice like a drill sergeant. 'May I borrow that newspaper for a minute, please?'

The lady is taken aback.

'Sorry, madam, I didn't mean to startle you.' I bow slightly as I've seen military officers do. 'I just wanted to read about . . .'

'The plague?' She gives me a quick look. 'Are you from, you know, *India*?'

'That is an insult, madam.' I let out a snort. 'I am from Pakistan.'

'Oh!' She covers her lips with dainty fingers. 'Sorry.'

'Actually madam, I wanted to read about the squash championship.' I remember seeing something about squash in a newspaper I salvaged from a dustbin at an earlier stop. 'You see, Jahangir Khan is my cousin brother. Jolly good player. World champion.'

'I played squash in college.' She is middle-aged but handsome, with a full figure and large dreamy eyes. 'It's a great game. Would you like to sit?'

'My game is hockey, madam.'

'Please.'

I sit in an exaggeratedly erect posture.

'Ice hockey or field hockey?'

'Field.' I bring my wrists together and wriggle them.

'In America it's a woman's game.' She laughs. 'My daughter plays field hockey.'

'In Pakistan we don't allow our women to play.' I give her a stern look. 'It is against the Koran.'

'No games?'

I shake my head. 'Not even musical instruments. Even playing with friends when small is strictly prohibited. If you're a female. That's the law.'

'How about India? Do women there participate in sports?'

I feign a bitter expression. 'Indian women participate in everything. The men are lazy and only like to drink tea and smoke. In the night they consume alcohol and abuse their women.' I shake my head contemptuously. 'No wonder India has the plague.'

'Are you a Moslem?' She pronounces the word 'Mozlem'.

'Original and non-converted.'

'I have many Moslem friends. I stayed in Qatar for two years.' Her eyes have a wet, far away look. 'God, what a lovely time I had . . . wild parties straight out of the Arabian nights.' Her cheeks flush. 'I knew this man, the son of an oil sheikh. He was connected with the Saudi royal family. Lived in a grand palace with servants, guards, the works. Very fond of hunting. An enormous collection of guns.' Her face turns a little dark. She lowers her voice. 'He was constantly getting into trouble with guns but his father was influential.' She sighs. 'We would drive out into the desert on weekends and camp for the night. Deserts are gorgeous.' She shuts her eyes. 'In the day we would fly falcons. D'you do falcons?'

'I have falcons at home. At my country estate. Several.'

'Fascinating! How much do they cost in Pakistan?'

'Oh . . .' I wave a hand vaguely.

'They're so expensive in Qatar! Is Pakistan near Qatar?'

'It's quite far. But we are part of the same Islamic brotherhood.'

'You're an Arab,' she exclaims, fixing me with a penetrating gaze. 'I wouldn't have guessed.'

'Well, a Muslim. One-hundred per cent, full-blooded Muslim.'

'Wow!' Her eyes drop to my crotch.

The bus slows for a stop. I look out of the window. We are on the highway, not at a rest stop or bus station. A man in baggy shorts and a T-shirt is standing on the side of the road, alone, with a duffel bag. The driver gives two short blasts of the horn and pulls a lever on the dashboard. The hydraulic door of the bus swings open. The man climbs the steps and the door shuts behind him.

'Howdy Eric.' He thumps the driver's outstretched hand. 'How's the hammer hanging?' He smiles at the passengers and announces in a polite tone: 'Appreciate it folks. Mighty friendly of you. I'm not going far . . .'

'Oh God,' sighs a woman behind me. 'Not another excon.'

' . . . just an hour down the road.' He ambles down the aisle, dumps his bag in a window seat and sits across from me.

'Hi,' he says. 'I'm Bobby.'

'Hari.'

'How ya doing, Harry.'

I realise to my amazement that Bobby has taken me for something I'm not. I am 'Harry'. Somehow I feel upgraded.

'Where you from, Harry?'

'New Jersey.' My brain kicks into the 'change' mode. 'I'm American.'

Bobby appraises me.

'Naturalised.'

He smiles. 'How long have you been in America? And where are you from originally, Harry?'

A newspaper on the seat next to me is opened to a story on the plague. Airlines have started cancelling flights to India.

'Um, Qatar.'

'Qatar, Qatar,' he says, savouring the sound. 'Can't say I've ever been there. Not quite sure where it is, to tell you the truth, although I have the general idea. Lots of sand, right? And oil?'

'My father owns an oil company.'

'Good for him, Harry. He must have money coming out of his petunias.' He was in his early thirties, with a rugged and intelligent face.

'That's correct,' I replied. Then I realised how stupid it sounded. 'I myself had other interests so I migrated to the States. With my father's help, of course.'

'Well, good for you, Harry. What do you do?'

'I'm a journalist.'

'A journalist!' He sits up. 'Whereabouts?'

'At the UNI bureau in, um, New Jersey.'

'Fantastic!' Bobby's face is aglow. 'You cover the whole state?'

I nod.

'Maryland too?'

I keep nodding.

'Sometimes a business trip to Delaware? Take the Concorde?'

I can't tell whether I'm being mocked or not. I decide to act professional. 'Another reporter covers Delaware.'

'Well, Harry, the fact is I'm a journalist too. Not quite in your league: I never worked for one of those big wire services. But I've done my time, paid my dues, on quite a few newspapers and covered more town meetings than I care to recall. Had a column once, actually. I enjoyed that. I applied to AP years ago but . . .'

My amazement knows no bounds. An American looking up at me because of my UNI work! 'Actually,' I interrupt, 'I'm writing a series of columns on this trip.' I fish out my notebooks from my jacket and show them to Bobby.

'Well that'll be a scintillating series, Harry. Your trip across America – on the dog!'

'Where are you working now?'

'I'm in radio, Harry, the medium of . . .' He paused. ' . . . of the forties. I'm an old-fashioned kind of guy. Anyway, I've got a once-a-week slot on public radio. It's got its following, I guess. A couple of thousand of my closest friends. And I write fiction, Harry.'

'Fiction?'

'Yup. Written two novels.' He grins. 'Don't look for them in B. Dalton, though. I'm having a *little* trouble getting published. You should see them sometime. The problem . . .'

Someone taps me on my shoulder from behind. I turn around. A woman is holding a Walkman with a dangling headset.

'I just heard the news,' she says breathlessly. 'India's completely sealed. There's a ban on all flights going in or out.' She takes a deep breath. 'The U.S. Secretary of Health has announced that any visitor from India, or anyone who has been in India recently, should contact the local health authorities if they develop any symptoms of plague.'

I sneeze loudly.

'You're from India, aren't you?' asks the woman.

I give her a blank stare.

'Ma'am, Harry here's as American as apple pie.' Bobby winks at me. 'Isn't that so, Harry?'

The woman looks suspicious – and not without reason. Just a few hours ago I had introduced myself as a chemical engineer working for Union Carbide in Bhopal.

'But I thought . . .' She stands up and strides purposefully to the back of the bus. I see her talking to other passengers and pointing up the aisle at me.

Bobby, unaware of what is going on, resumes our conversation: 'I hope you're not writing a novel, Harry. You know why? Whenever I meet someone who's writing a book I say to them: "Hey – don't. *Please* don't." Because I just know *their* manuscripts are going to pile up like this' – he lowers his hand to the floor and raises it – 'on top of *my* manuscript. And by the time the publisher gets around to reading their pathetic attempts, he's so sick that he throws the whole pile in the trashcan and my . . .'

Out of the corner of my eye I see that my former neighbour has started talking to the Greyhound lady, who has hovered around the bus like a spirit of the roadways. They are pointing at me. I hear the Greyhound lady's whisky voice getting louder. She points beyond me.

Just then Bobby rises from his seat.

'This is my stop coming up, Harry.'

The Greyhound lady comes up the aisle. She skirts me with a suspicious look, leaving behind the smell of liquor. But she can't go any further because Bobby is blocking her way.

''Scuse me, ma'am. Have to talk to the driver.' Bobby walks up to the driver.

'Wicked young man!' The Greyhound lady wags a finger in my face. 'You could infect us all!'

Bobby returns down the aisle. 'It's not a scheduled stop but I'm a regular.' He extends his hand. 'Harry, it's been fine.' He squeezes his body against the side of a seat to make way for the Greyhound lady. 'You're welcome, ma'am.'

The Greyhound lady gets by Bobby, giving him a dirty look.

'Put her in your columns, Harry.' Bobby hoists his duffel bag on his shoulder. 'She's straight outta Dickens. Whooo – are you getting that smell?'

I feel the bus decelerating.

'Come and visit sometime,' says Bobby. 'Probably no stories for UNI – it's not *that* hot a town. Any time you're in the area.'

'What about now?'

'Why sure, Harry. Anything for a fellow hack.'

I grab my suitcase from the overhead shelf and quickly

follow Bobby up the aisle. Using his body for cover, I duck past the Greyhound lady. She looks enraged. The bus halts, the door opens. Bobby bids the driver farewell. I am already safely disembarked.

The door shuts. I hear the Greyhound lady shouting.

'I think they liked you, Harry.' Bobby adjusts his duffel bag. 'You were real popular on the dog, yup.'

'Yeah.'

'But who was that black guy calling to? Who was he calling ass shit?'

I watch as the bus disappears between two mountains.

'It's a bit of a hike, Harry. About a mile.' The day is fine, with bright sunshine. 'People don't walk much in New Jersey, I imagine – not without getting shot at anyway.' We trudge along the highway, talking, and then turn into a thick forest along a path.

'Where are you headed anyway, Harry?'

'Seattle.'

'What for?'

'To a university.'

'What happened? You flunked Spanish again?'

'I have a John Dewey fellowship at the University of Washington. I'll be philosopher in residence for three months.'

'Wow,' says Bobby sounding impressed. 'I feel honoured: I'm walking with Plato.' After a few minutes we come out of the woods. Bobby waves his arm and announces: 'There it is, Harry boy. That's my mansion.'

In front of us, about fifty metres from the edge of the forest, stands a solitary wagon-type structure on wheels. I learn in the course of my subsequent conversations with Bobby that it is called a trailer.

'And yonder.' Bobby points. 'My backyard.'

I am stunned: behind the trailer is a range of looming mountains. I feel I have been magically transported to the Himalayas. Everything, except the trailer, of course, is just the same as it would be in Almora or Kulu-Manali. I turn to Bobby. 'This is beautiful,' I say. 'Fantastic!'

'Welcome Harry,' he says, 'to my little piece of paradise.'

American Letter
by Hari Rana

'We haven't written jack shit, Ha-rry. And we've only got two days more!' Bobby sprinkled cheese on beans and ladled them onto a *chappati*-like pancake called a tortilla. 'What are we gonna do, Harry?'

I was Hari no longer. I wondered if I would ever respond to my own name again. I was 'Harry' – a name Bobby used at least twenty times an hour.

'It's all your fault, Harry. Because of you I've been sitting on my duff doing nothing.'

That was the baldest of lies. In the past three days we had taken hikes into the mountains, accompanied by Biscuits, Bobby's over-affectionate mutt; we had swum and canoed in an enormous blue lake; zoomed into a forest on cross-country bicycles; seen a baseball game and a jazz concert; spent evenings drinking beer in a dimly lit bar in the company of pretty girls who could send a man's blood pressure to dangerous levels. Friendly girls. Happy-go-lucky girls. Good old red-white-and-blue *American* girls.

'Harry . . . we're *waiting*.'

This was Bobby's way with me: he always used the first person plural – we were 'we' from the moment the Greyhound bus disappeared between the mountains – and a mock admonishing tone that suggested I was responsible for all that occurred, especially the negative things. When there was no milk in his refrigerator, it was: 'Harry. Have you drunk all the milk again?' When the car needed petrol, it was: 'Harry. Just look at this tank. This isn't Qatar, ya' know.' When it rained, or snowed, I was certain to be blamed, although the weather had been perfect.

We munched our beans and tortillas, which had been my staple diet in the trailer.

'I've got it!' Bobby snapped his fingers. He rose from the dining table, licking sauce off his fork. 'I've got the ideal subject for my broadcast, Harry.' He moved to his computer.

I cleared the breakfast dishes. 'Wonderful, Bobby.' I closed the door of the miniature refrigerator. 'What is it? What's your subject?'

He flicked the machine on. 'Harry, boy, I'm gonna make you a star.'

'Excuse me?'

'Shit.' He leaned over and pushed in a diskette. Then he faced me again. 'You. You're the subject of my broadcast. You – the star from Qatar!'

I didn't get it. I knew that Bobby was extravagant in his praise, the way people in India were not. But was I, Hari Rana, star material? Was it something to do with my habits? Bobby had said to me: 'Harry, you're the best house guest I've ever had.' He proceeded to explain. 'You're easy on food, Harry. You don't mind sleeping on the couch. You help with the dishes. You don't get bored. And Biscuits likes you.' He turned to Biscuits, who was lying on the floor. 'That's the most important thing. Isn't it, Biscuits?' The dog wagged its tail; it occurred to me that he spoke to the two of us in similar cadences. 'See, Harry?' announced Bobby. 'If Biscuits agrees I *must* be right!'

Bobby's was a quintessentially American style of living. It was light and unencumbered, making, by comparison, existence in India seem impossibly complex, tied down, burdensome and inert. His trailer, at the bottom of the magnificent Rockies, was a masterpiece of simplicity and mobility. It was not much larger than a railway bogie and furnished with only the essentials. A raised wooden platform with a few steps led to the door, which opened into the main living space.

A kitchen was on the left, consisting of a propane gas stove and a small refrigerator, whose door was plastered with pictures of American celebrities and politicians. Bobby called it, with rather heavy irony, the 'US Hall of Shame'. At the far end of the room, by an uncurtained window, was Bobby's 'study'. There was a chocolate-brown desk with a rusty swivel chair. Scrawled on the wall facing the desk were the words 'Zest' and 'Gusto'. (Bobby said they were the only ingredients necessary for good writing, an idea borrowed from one of his favourite authors, Ray Bradbury.) His laptop computer was perched atop two encyclopaedias and connected to a car battery on the floor. Surrounding it were books, sheaves of paper and a trio of fabric-wrapped balls the size of lemons. (At first I thought the balls were paper weights. Then I saw Bobby juggling them.)

In between was the living-room proper with its old couch, a floor mat made from some coarse material and, on the wall facing the couch, a canvas painting. It was the only decoration in the trailer. According to Bobby, it was a present from a former female friend. It showed a stream gushing past a gigantic vagina-shaped tree. Bobby called it 'The Cunt'. Adjacent to the living-room was a bathroom equipped with a sit-down toilet and a propane-powered shower. At the far end of the trailer was Bobby's bedroom.

Bobby, with Biscuits, had been living in this Spartan environment for four years. He came from the mountains of New York's Hudson River Valley. His brothers worked on Wall Street; each was a multi-millionaire with a million-dollar house. Of his two sisters, one was married to a top lawyer and the other to a wealthy businessman. Bobby was the only one in the family who, in his own words, 'lived poor' out of choice. ('Eating and drinking are my only vices, Harry,' he said, a plain exaggeration considering that his diet was heavy on beans and tortillas and pretty light on alcohol – he only drank beer.) He had lived in several cities in his thirty-three years. 'In the city I was swimming upstream,' he explained. 'It was hard work, Harry, and I wasn't learning a thing. Now . . . well, I don't work so much.' He made the point firmly, as if trying to convince both me and himself. 'I enjoy every second. And I learn. I learn a lot.' Bobby wasn't a dropout. It's just that Bobby didn't believe in acquiring. He worked three days a week in a bakery, kneading and baking bread, to cover expenses. The rest of his time he devoted to his weekly radio spot, for which he was paid a small retainer, and writing novels he hadn't yet been able to sell. 'Wall Street is about shuffling paper. Not paper – fucking pixels. You know pixels, Harry? On the computer screens? My brothers do pixels every day. Millions and millions of them. That's not something I can *do*.'

And Bobby had fun. He drove to the city on weekends, staying up late into the night with his friends over endless pitchers of tap beer. I was amazed by the cheerfulness and bonhomie of an American bar. Even a stranger like me is greeted like a resident. Pretty women smile at men, unafraid of being molested or pounced upon. Conversation and humour flow faster than the spirits. These scenes are so unlike the depressing atmosphere of Indian bars, aptly named 'watering holes' because men – you rarely see a woman – go there with the sole intention of pouring alcohol down their gullets. Everywhere we went, women snuggled up to Bobby. He treated them with casualness. He told me: 'Harry: I get sex when I need it. Or want it.' He winked. 'Otherwise, Biscuits is company enough for *me*.'

'Um, Bobby, I don't think that's a good idea.' I was talking about his proposal to turn me into a radio star on his next broadcast.

'Too bad, Harry.' Bobby swivelled in his chair. ''Cause you're all I've got. Let's get started.' He poised his fingers on the keyboard. 'Date of birth?' He typed. He turned his face. '*Ha*-rry?'

I told him. He typed again, biting his tongue. 'And, um, place.' He stopped typing and looked at me. 'Harry?'

'Yes, Bobby?'

He gave me a wide smile. 'Harry, let's make this *good*.'

And I thought to myself: *I'll make this good. Or I will blow the friendship of a lifetime.* So I succumbed. I decided to become Harry, the American immigrant from Qatar. *Why not?* George's words echoed in my brain: *You can become.* I imagined bringing George and Bobby together in a bar, where they would share pitchers of beer and swap philosophies. They would like each other, I was sure. I faced Bobby. 'Go ahead,' I said. 'Shoot.'

So started an extraordinary interrogation. For the next thirty-six hours Bobby asked me every question I could have conceived. 'Your mother tongue is Arabic, right? So how come your English is so good?' This was in the car on the way to town. Over lunch at the diner: 'You say you were always fascinated with America. Were there influences that shaped your impressions about America? Like movies?' He meticulously took down everything I said, circling back to confirm details. 'You were born in September 1958, so you couldn't have come to America at the age of twenty-five. That would be nine years ago and you said you've been here seven years . . .'

I was astonished by his professional skills. The questions were logical and relentless. I realised: Bobby was a fine journalist. Some questions were easier than others: it was simple to describe my family, my childhood, the universal things. But at times I was stumped: what is the life of a rich Muslim from Qatar anyway? I had to stretch my imagination. For I felt absolutely compelled to make Harry's life good. Bobby wanted it that way.

The questioning continued at all times, everywhere: in the forest during our daily walks; while biking and canoeing; in bars; over morning coffee, lunch and dinner. It was the most exhausting thirty-six hours of my life. Not because the questions were difficult but because I had to remember the answers so as not to get caught. Once, I called 'my country' – that is Qatar – poor. 'Poor?' Bobby exclaimed. 'With all that oil? Harry, who's ever heard of a poor sand nigger?'

My interrogation ended as abruptly as it began. It was dusk and we were returning from a walk in the mountains. I suppose I was under so much stress that I didn't notice Bobby's questions cease. All I remember is that we were descending a hill. I stopped to look at the setting sun. Bobby stopped, too. The wind was still and there was silence all around. Dusk always induces a sadness in me. In my village, it is invariably associated with the end of the day's activity and the beginning of a short, dull night. It's a time when light falls, men return home with sagging shoulders, women grow louder. And peacocks start to cry. They have a strong and strident call: stronger than their ordinary timorousness would suggest.

I said, 'It's beautiful.'

'Isn't it, Harry?'

'You're lucky to live here.'

He nodded.

'The only thing I miss is the peacock's call.'

'Is that right?'

'They call at sunset. In my home country.'

'Really.'

'When it's cloudy they call all day.'

'Why?'

'Because they think it'll bring rain.'

'You must miss home at times. Every once in a while.'

'I do.'

'Even after seven years.'

'Yeah.'

'Funny,' said Bobby, slapping his notebook shut. 'I wouldn't have thought of peacocks and rain in Qatar.'

Back at the trailer, Bobby spent more than an hour typing notes into the computer. He suddenly said: 'Harry.'

I turned.

He punched some concluding keys on the keyboard. He reached and flicked off the machine. The screen went black. 'I thought we weren't gonna make it, Harry.' He stood up. 'But this is fine. Just fine.'

I gulped.

And, Bobby announced, I was being given a reward. He had planned a dinner with some friends at one of his favourite restaurants in town.

'You don't have to do that, Bobby.'

'My pleasure, Harry. We're taking you to the Taj Mahal.'

'The Taj Mahal?'

'You don't like Indian food?'

I hesitated a second.

'You *don't* like it.'

'No, I like it. I like it very much.'

'Doesn't look like it.'

'I do.'

'I just assumed they'd have a lot of Indian restaurants in the Middle East.'

'Of course they do. Millions of them. Most of the restaurants are Indian. Employing thousands of workers from India, especially from Kerala, a southern state . . .'

'Maybe not so many in Qatar.'

'Bobby – I *love* Indian food.'

'We can tell them to cut the spices. Not too spicy: not for old Harry. The Star from Qatar!'

The Taj Mahal was a shabby, first-floor restaurant in the old section of town. A stereo blared sitar music into the lane. Steep steps led to a large, open room with brightly coloured wallpaper and a dozen round tables. At the far end was a counter and behind it, in public view, the kitchen. I gasped when I walked in: instead of the ubiquitous smell of French fries or pizza – the olfactory footprints of American restaurants – I caught the warm smell of burning onions, *naan* and, I think, an undercurrent of Dettol. I felt like I had stepped into a *dhaba* on G.T. Road.

Bobby's friends – two women and a man – were already seated when we arrived. Bobby introduced us. The first woman, Molly, was young, blonde, bespectacled, plump and big-breasted. She looked in her late twenties. Dianne, the other woman, was slim with reddish-brown hair, small breasts and a sophisticated air. She was in her late thirties. The man, whom Bobby referred to only as 'Big Guy', had a square, reddish face, a strong handshake and an eager expression.

'Bobby's told us about you,' said Molly. 'You're staying out at the trailer?'

I nodded.

'You almost look Indian yourself,' said Dianne.

'Harry an Indian?' said Bobby incredulously.

'He can't be Indian,' declared Big Guy. 'He doesn't smell like curry. All Indians smell like curry.'

'He will soon,' said Bobby. 'Who's ordering?'

No sooner had we sat down than a scruffy looking waiter walked up to our table and addressed me in Hindi: '*Aap Hindustan se aaye hain?*'

Without thinking, I blurted out: '*Haan.*'

'*Kahan ke rehne wale hain aap?*'

'He speaks your language?' asked Dianne.

My brain whirled. 'He must have worked in the Middle East. There are a lot of Indians there.'

I turned to the waiter. '*Angrezi jante ho?*'

'*Bas, do-chaar luvz.*' He grinned shyly.

'In Saudi Arabia,' I said to Bobby. 'He learned Arabic there.'

'Harry finds friends everywhere he goes,' declared Bobby with a wave of his hand.

'Tourist visa *pe aaya tha. Fill haal* illegal *hoon.*' The waiter motioned towards the kitchen. '*Yahan sab* illegal *hain.*' He whispered in my ear: '*Zada tar* Pakistani *hain yahan.*'

I nodded.

'*Aap ka shubh naam?*'

'Hari Rana.'

'*Aap kahan ke rehne valey hain?*'

'*Dilli.*'

'*Mera saadu Dilli mein rehta hai. Vaisey kahan ke rehney vale hain?*'

'*Vaisey matlab?*'

'*Matlab kaon sa* state?'

'What's he saying?' asked Dianne.

'He's recommending the . . . curry.'

'That's a disappointment, Harry,' said Bobby. 'I was going to order the Chateaubriand. Can we have two pitchers of Bud Lite please.'

The waiter scurried away and returned with two jugs of beer and five mugs. He distributed menus and then stood by me.

'Actually, the chicken curry is delicious,' announced Molly. 'Harry, do you like chicken?'

I felt a lump in my throat. I was a vegetarian. But whoever heard of a vegetarian Arab? 'Depends.'

'On what?'

'How it's cooked.'

'Arabs like red meat.' Bobby ran a finger down the menu. 'Beef Vindaloo. "Made from the choicest red tenderloin," it says.'

The waiter edged closer to me. '*Aap* Rajput *hain?*'

'*Kya?*'

'*Matlab aap* Rajput *hain ya . . .?*' (You are a Rajput or . . .?)

I felt like I was in an Indian village. I tried to turn my attention to Bobby and his friends. But the waiter was implacable.

'*Aap kaam kya karte hain?*' (What do you do?)

'*Patrakaar.*' (Journalist.)

He took a step back.

'Harry,' said Bobby. 'I'm glad you've found a friend. But are we ready to order?'

The limpet, as Rajiv Gandhi would have called him, detached himself and scampered towards Bobby, who began dictating the order. As soon as he left, Bobby lifted his beer mug.

'I'd like to propose a toast,' he said, 'in honour of my friend Harry who, as you know, has come to our country by way of his native land of Qatar.'

Bobby's friends erupted into cheers.

'Like all of us here in the United States, I thought Qatar was a brand of colour television. But it is not. It is a proud country, like all countries, with wonderful men and big-hearted women and peacocks who cry in the hope of rain.'

'Do they?' said Molly. 'That sounds so beautiful.'

'Quasar!' cried Big Guy. 'Not Qatar, asshole!'

'Also, I'd like to announce that our new friend Harry happens to have been awarded an honour he'd be unlikely to receive anywhere else in the world. He has been chosen as the subject of my radio spot this week.'

Big Guy thumped the table. Molly clapped. Dianne gave a sweet smile, exposing an inwardly bent canine that made her look very cute. Suddenly I couldn't decide whom I preferred: Molly or her.

'So Harry.' Big Guy took a swig of beer. 'What's Qatar like?'

This Qatar business had gone on far too long. Luckily the waiter didn't know English. Otherwise my secret would have been blown to smithereens.

'You know how it is with the Arabs,' I said. 'Always fighting with each other.' I was hoping that a negative comment would steer the conversation to some other topic.

'Oh, that's too bad,' said Molly.

'I think it's good,' said Big Guy nodding his big head. 'Violence is one of the hallmarks of a free society.'

'Come on,' said Dianne, 'that's ridiculous.'

'Take the Russians,' declared Big Guy. 'They pulled their punches for seventy years. As soon as communism collapses . . . boom! Everybody starts expressing themselves. They're free!'

'Big Guy likes a fight.' Bobby slapped Big Guy on the shoulder. 'That's something you've got to know about Big

Guy from the start, Harry. He likes his fights, don't you, Big Guy?'

'I'm Irish,' said Big Guy.

'Too much testosterone,' said Bobby.

'What do Arabs fight over, Harry?' Dianne smiled, fluttering her long eyelashes. 'Other than Israel and all that.'

'Not women, if that's what you're thinking.' Big Guy looked at me and raised an eyebrow. 'Isn't heterosexuality banned in the Arab world, Harry?'

'It's part of our population control programme.' The laughter was quick and loud: I think everyone was relieved I hadn't taken offence. I turned to Dianne. 'There's an old joke: a trumpeter is standing outside the headquarters of the Arab League in Cairo. Someone stops and says to him: "What are you doing with that trumpet in your hand?" He says: "I've been told to blow this trumpet when Arab unity comes along."

'The man says: "How much are you paid?"

'"Fifteen pounds a year," says the trumpeter.

'"Fifteen pounds? That's nothing!"

'"I know," says the trumpeter, "but it's a lifetime job."'

Everyone laughed.

'The Arabs are lunatics,' said Big Guy. 'I knew a guy who worked in the Gulf and I'll never forget a story he told me.' Big Guy gave his big head a slow shake. 'He worked with this guy who was living alone, right? His wife was away in Germany or something. He was taking care of their year-old child. One weekend, he locks his house and drives downtown to get some milk. On the way he has an accident – knocks down some asshole or something. The cops lock him up and tell him he's gonna stay there till Monday because the courts are closed. The guy says: "I have this baby. Lying alone in the house." The cops say: "So fucking what?" He begs them to send someone to feed the baby. The cops read him their Moslem law that says he knocked down a guy, a Moslem guy, and he's going to stay in jail until court convenes on Monday. This guy says,

"You don't understand. My baby's gonna *die*." The cops say tough luck, that's the law.'

Big Guy took a deep breath. 'On Monday, he pays a huge fine, gets back to his house and finds his baby dead.'

There was stunned silence at the table.

'Dehydration.' Big Guy drained his beer mug.

'I can't *believe* this is true.' Dianne turned to me with outrage.

All I could think of was to bow my head and shake it.

'Would an Arab have been treated the same way?'

'No,' I said in a shamed tone. 'He wouldn't.'

'That's terrible,' said Molly.

'Things like this happen in my country. We are very backward. Islam is a very tolerant religion but . . .' I lifted my hands as if requesting forbearance.

'What a *rotten* country,' said Dianne.

'I give Harry credit,' said Big Guy. 'He admits his country's faults. Which can be hard to do.'

I looked up and smiled.

'Harry,' said Molly. 'Are you married? Back in your country?'

'Actually, I'm American now. I've been naturalised for seven years.'

'Of course,' said Molly. 'I'm sorry.'

'No problem.'

'Then are you married here?'

'Tell 'em, Harry,' said Bobby.

'Well, sort of.'

'You're divorced?' asked Molly.

'Harry was married very young,' said Bobby. 'Isn't that right, Harry?'

'Um, yeah.'

'To a child bride,' Bobby said.

Molly and Dianne stiffened. Big Guy gave me a wary look.

There was silence at the table. 'A child bride?' asked Dianne.

I nodded.

'How . . . unusual,' said Molly.

'I tell you, gang,' said Bobby. 'This is going to be one hell of a broadcast.'

'How old were you,' continued Dianne, 'when you married your child bride?'

'Nineteen.'

'That's not so bad,' said Molly positively.

'How old,' interrupted Dianne, 'was the bride?'

'Young.'

'*How* young?'

'She was a girl.'

'A girl?'

'A young girl.'

'She was twelve,' said Bobby.

'*Twelve?*' Dianne craned her neck forward like a camel.

'Twelve years old, folks. Not even a woman yet. That's how Harry describes it. Isn't that right, Harry?'

'You mean she hadn't even . . . ?' Molly sucked in her breath, her large eyelashes fluttering. 'And they made her get . . .'

'She was from India,' I said.

'*India?*' asked Dianne.

'This is common in my country. Very common. We are always importing young Indian girls for marriage.'

'Did she smell like curry?' asked Big Guy.

'Big Guy!' scolded Bobby.

'I'm sure they smell like curry even at twelve.'

'Have some consideration for the waiter,' said Bobby. 'Or maybe we'll have to tip him.'

'She smelt beautiful, actually,' I said. 'She was very beautiful. In my country, we believe that Indian women are beautiful. Maybe the most beautiful in the world.'

There was silence. My eyes met Molly's for a second, but she broke contact. Then Dianne spoke in a low tone. 'So you married this twelve-year-old for her beauty.'

'No,' I said. 'It is custom. I didn't want to marry anyone. Honestly.'

'Uh huh.' Dianne folded her hands across her chest. I noticed that everyone had severe expressions except for Bobby, who was grinning widely.

'We didn't even live together like a couple.' My mind raced. 'We never even really . . .'

Their expressions softened. I was on the right track.

'In fact, she became more of a servant than a wife.'

'You brought a *twelve*-year-old girl from India and made her your *servant*?' Molly had tears in her eyes.

'Now that's *really* horrible,' said Dianne.

'Good help is hard to find,' crowed Big Guy. 'In Qatar.'

'Poor little girl,' cried Molly.

'A lot of Indian girls do that,' I added hastily. 'My father . . .'

'And *you* didn't mind that your wife was working like a servant?' asked Dianne.

'I was completely against it,' I said indignantly. 'You have to believe me.'

Molly looked at me hopefully.

'And that's why . . . that's why I decided to send her back to India!'

Dianne and Molly looked at each other with befuddled expressions.

'This is news to me,' said Bobby. 'Harry – what's going on?'

'Good guy, Harry,' said Big Guy. 'First you say she'll be your wife. Then you make her your servant. And then you send her *back* – to fucking India. Land of the plague.'

An embarrassing silence followed. All eyes focused on me, except Bobby's. He was scribbling in the notebook he had pulled from his back pocket.

'It's not that bad a place,' I said lamely. Then the waiter came along with the food. He announced the names of the dishes, placed them on the table and departed.

'It must have been tough living in a country like that.' Big

Guy bit hungrily into a piece of tandoori chicken. 'Fucking Qatar.'

'It's no wonder Harry got into drugs,' said Bobby.

'Drugs?' said Big Guy. 'Which ones?'

'Smack,' said Bobby. 'Harry was addicted to heroin for a while.'

I tried my best to appear cool and unruffled.

'*Gawd*,' said Molly. 'I've never known anyone who took heroin.'

'You don't *look* like you've been on drugs, Harry,' said Dianne.

'A bit,' I said. 'For a while.'

'I'm *shocked*,' said Big Guy in a joking tone.

'The beef is great.' Bobby eyed my plate, which was still full. 'You're not eating, Harry. Something the matter?'

'Not at all.'

'You gotta eat, Harry,' said Bobby. 'Or you'll starve.'

I put a piece of meat in my mouth and pretended to chew it. Then I shut my eyes and swallowed. I felt as if I had swallowed a snake. My stomach cramped up, shooting electrical impulses throughout my body. It took all my will-power to stop myself from throwing up. When I opened my eyes the waiter was standing by my side.

'*Badbu aa rahi hai na gosht mein?*' he said. (The meat is stinking?)

I nodded, smiling at him. '*Lagta hai.*' (I think so.)

'*Gore bahut* like *karte hain ye khana.*' He giggled. (The white people like it a lot.) '*Kuch bhi de do inhen – kuccha, pukka, sada – sab kha jate hain.*' (Give them anything, they eat it all.)

'What's he saying?' asked Big Guy.

'He's asking how the food is.'

Big Guy raised a thumb at the waiter. 'Very nice. Thank you.' He scooped a chunk of meat from his plate and shovelled it in his mouth.

'*Dekho sale ko.*' The waiter grinned. (Look at the bastard.)

'*Khae chale ja raha hai gadhey ke maafik.*' (He is going on eating like a donkey.)

'This is my favourite.' Big Guy licked his lips and beckoned to the waiter. 'How do you make this lamb?' He looked at me. 'Harry, interpret his Arabic, would you? How do they get this great taste?'

'*Kya keh raha hai?*' the waiter asked.

I explained the request.

'What's he saying, Harry?' asked Big Guy. 'Sounds like a lot of work.'

'Do you really want to hear?'

'Every word.'

'All right.' I took a deep breath. 'First they take four kilos of onions . . .'

'Hold on,' Big Guy interrupted. 'How many pounds is that?'

'Nine pounds.'

'Nine pounds!' Big Guy rubbed his head. 'Holy guacamole!'

'They peel the onions and push them through a cabbage slicing machine. Then they stir them in a pot over a high flame for two hours. I paused. 'Do you really want to hear this?'

'Go on, Harry.' Bobby whipped out his notebook. 'You've just given me an idea for my next spot.'

'After conquering the onions, they add oil, canned tomatoes, canned ginger, canned garlic. Then comes more grunting and squashing and pulping until everything is reduced to a mushy brown mixture. Then they add raw lamb and boil it with the onion mixture for half an hour.' I exhaled deeply. 'The lamb curry is ready.'

'That's *it?*' Bobby waved his pen.

'That's it.'

'You're sure you haven't missed a few steps?'

'Nope.'

Bobby scribbled in his notebook.

'There's one more thing.'

Bobby raised his eyebrows expectantly.

'All the dishes are cooked in the same way. For chicken

curry, they add raw chicken to the onion mixture. *Keema* curry: minced meat with the onion mixture. Eggplant curry: chopped eggplant . . .'

'That's enough, Harry.' Molly got up. 'I think I'm going to throw up.' She headed for the exit door.

'That's the most *disgusting* way to cook food I've ever heard in my life.' Bobby thumped me on my back. 'I *love* it, Harry, love it.' He did an imitation of me: '*Grunting, squashing, pulping*. What juicy words. Now I know why the waiters here are always laughing. It's not their sense of humour.' Bobby waved his notebook in the air. 'They're laughing at us assholes who eat this crap.'

Everybody rose to leave. We caught up with Molly at the door. She gave me a sheepish smile and linked her arm in mine.

Just inside the restaurant door, the waiter stopped me.

'*Meri khansama se shart lagi hai*,' he gushed. (I have laid a bet with the cook.) '*Mein kehta hoon aap Rajput hain, vo kehta hai Jat.*' (I say you are a Rajput. He says you are a Jat.)

'*Na* Jat *na* Rajput.' (I am neither.)

'*Phir kya caste hai aapki?*' (Then what is your caste?)

'*Amereekan.*' (American.)

As we walked in the cool breeze outside I reflected on the events in the restaurant. I was struck by how open Bobby and his friends were – how genuinely interested and accepting of me. And I thought to myself: This is the wonder of American society: everyone sinks or swims on the basis of personality – and nothing else. No one cares whether I'm an Arab from Qatar, an aborigine from the Andamans or an Eskimo from Greenland. All that matters is my ability to communicate. To be who I am without fear of being disliked or rejected: what a liberation! And what a contrast from that Indian waiter who, though his feet were on American soil, couldn't get his head out of that slimy Indian sludge-pit of caste, region, family connections, language – all the Indian evils.

I said to Molly: 'Not all Indian food is like *that*.'

*

After saying goodbye, Bobby and I went out to a bar. I hoped a couple of beers would soothe my meat-queasy stomach. We sat at the far end of the bar and I ordered my usual Bud Lite. It hadn't taken long: I already had a favourite drink.

'Well, Harry.' Bobby wiped froth from his lips. 'The one thing we haven't talked about is your philosophy. I mean, you've been invited to a university as a philosopher. What is your philosophy, anyway?'

My mind was so occupied with my new persona as an Arab that I had almost forgotten I was Hari Rana, philosopher-to-be at the University of Washington.

'*My* philosophy?'

'Yes, your philosophy.'

'Er . . . I don't know.'

'But Harry. You're the philosopher-in-residence.'

I was on the spot. I didn't know what to say. But I didn't want to let Bobby down. I pondered for a while.

'I don't know how much I can say about life, Bobby. But I do know one thing . . .'

I hoped that what I said wasn't ridiculous. It was sincere. But was it profound? I wasn't sure. All I could tell was that Bobby shut his notebook and seemed satisfied.

The next day Bobby sat glued to his computer. His radio piece was to be broadcast that night and he spent the entire morning and afternoon working on the script. It was a hot day but he didn't notice it. He was like a *sadhu* in active meditation: he didn't utter a word and didn't seem to hear a thing. Nothing distracted him: not the flies buzzing around the trailer, not the cawing of a pair of hungry crows on the kitchen window, not Biscuits' barking at the birds. It wasn't a placid or pleasant sight. I was amazed at the torture he went through, something I had never witnessed at UNI. He flipped through the pages of his notebook, circling and underlining his notes with a savage red pen. He would gaze out of the window and swear.

Then he would start typing with renewed vigour, his long fingers moving on the keyboard like a spider doing a tap dance. Every now and then he would jump up from his desk and stride to the kitchen to refill his coffee mug. On the way he would say to me: 'If it wasn't for you, Ha-rry, I wouldn't have to go through all this.' (This was ridiculous: if I wasn't the subject of the piece something else would have been.) But he'd fail to make eye contact with me. And then he would get a far-away look, trot back to the computer and start typing anew.

Finally, at 5 p.m., Bobby stopped typing. He rose from his chair, fed a roll of paper into his printer and pressed a key. A screechy, metallic sound filled the trailer.

I examined the dot-matrix printer. 'I think you need a new ribbon, Bobby. And a good cleaning.'

'We don't have time, Harry,' he yelled. 'I have to shower. Can you feed Biscuits?'

Fifteen minutes later we were in Bobby's car, headed for the radio station. There was very little traffic on the highway. Bobby cruised along the extreme right lane, holding his script against the steering wheel and making scribbled changes all along the way.

The radio station was located in a building on a quiet tree-lined street. I followed Bobby into a room with a large glass window. Beyond it was a recording booth with a chair, a microphone and a counter with an array of electronic gadgets.

'That's where I do the recording, Harry.' Bobby pointed through the glass window. 'You can hear me through those.' He pointed to a set of speakers mounted on either side of the window.

A woman in a brown skirt and jacket was sitting behind a desk next to the glass window; several people sat on couches at the far end of the room. Bobby walked through a door and appeared on the other side of the window. He sat and adjusted the microphone, script in hand. I took a chair. A few seconds later the woman nodded. Bobby moved towards the microphone and said: 'Ready?'

'Level,' said the woman.

'Harry,' said Bobby. 'Harry, Harry, Harry.'

'Okay,' said the woman.

'Ready?'

'Ready.'

Bobby's head was lowered. The woman pressed an illuminated button on a box before her. A voice started speaking, sounding like Bobby's, only slow and oddly emphatic. It said: 'Welcome to My Life. Jottings of a Confirmed Itinerant. By *Robert Spooner*. This week . . .'

Suddenly Bobby looked up. He leaned towards the microphone and said: 'The . . . Secret . . . V.I.P.' He turned to me and winked. He sat back and some music was played. When it trailed off, the woman gave him a hand signal and he leaned forward again.

'Good Evening, folks. I'm Robert Spooner. I was travelling recently. On the Dog – Greyhound – Leave the Driving to Us. I happened to meet an interesting fellow. Someone who had come a long way. In fact, he had been on the bus for seventy-one hours. Seventy-one hours worth of Cheez Doodles and Good-N-Plenty had reduced him to a pretty sorry state. I didn't feel I had any choice as a Christian. So I scraped him out of his reclining seat and hauled him back to Chez Spooner, the Trailer That's Goin' Nowhere, also known as The Old Dump. AKA – *home*. A little American hospitality. Hasn't killed anyone yet, as far as *I* know.

'All I knew was the guy's name: Harry. I discerned a certain difference in Harry. He didn't look like a Harry. He had dark skin and a suitcase that must have come through a time warp from World War I. He had a funny way of talking. At first I thought it was all those Cheez Doodles. But Harry's way of talking was an accent. I would have guessed he was from India or Pakistan or somewhere. But I knew in an instant that wasn't so. Big Guy, whom chronic listeners will remember from my Super Bowl broadcast, says that all Indians smell like curry. I leaned over and took a sniff. Harry smelled sweet: maybe it was all those Good-N-Plentys.

'Turns out Harry was an A-rab. From a little country called Qatar. First chance I got I took out my map and looked it up. Could barely find it. Itty bitty little place. But if you press your finger on the map, remove it and then sniff, you get a distinct whiff of petroleum. Black Gold. Texas Tea. Qatar is an oil state, friends. And my new friend Harry was a rich A-rab who grew up with oil under his sandbox.

'Now, I knew nothing about A-rabs. Yet here I was suddenly, shacked up with a real live Sand Nigger – that's what we called them back in Hicksville – and living cheek to jowl, which is the only way in Chez Spooner, considering Biscuits and all.'

Through the window, Booby winked again.

'For all of you Biscuits fans, I should mention that the mutt took an instant liking to Harry. I thought she liked the smell of his greasy bell-bottoms. But I have to admit it must be something more. Every night, Biscuits leaves my bedroom and curls up next to Harry on the living-room couch. She's never done that before.

'Anyway, what did I know about A-rabs? I thought they liked to blow up discotheques, especially when American soldiers were inside. But Harry likes dancing at them, and drinking at bars, which was another thing I thought A-rabs didn't do. I thought A-rabs were always wrapped up in white robes with nothing on underneath. But Harry wears regular clothes and standard underwear – I discovered this at the laundromat – bearing an impressive label reading VIP.

'I was to learn much about Harry, and life in Qatar, over the next few days. I asked why his English was so good. He gave credit to his mother, who showered him with affection only when he spoke in English.' Bobby turned a page of his script. 'When he spoke Arabic, she locked him in a bat-infested room.'

Suddenly I wondered if they had bats on the Arabian peninsula.

'What a life Harry's had! His father was a bigwig in the government until the 1973 war. In America we tend to think of that war from the Israeli point of view. We forget that when the Arabs were creamed, they lost good men. Including Harry's father.'

I bowed my head.

'His uncle Irfan was killed in Beirut in the early 1980s. Two cousins, Mohammed and Fatima, died in Baghdad in 1991. According to Harry, they were hit by smart bombs.'

I hoped no one would try to draw this family tree.

'And Harry's best friend from childhood, Fukruddin, died in Afghanistan fighting with the Mujahedin. He was only twenty years old.'

Everybody in the room was looking at me with long faces.

'In Harry's words: "Robert: It isn't easy being an Arab."'

The truest words 'Harry' ever spoke.

'But Harry's life hasn't been all bad. He married early, true.' Bobby's voice dropped. 'And when they say early in Qatar, they mean early. He's had problems with substance abuse, and I don't mean petroleum.'

I looked at Bobby and grimaced.

'But Harry bounced back. He's had a dynamic career as a journalist. In the spare time, he did a little writing, nothing heavy, mind you, just a little treatise on metaphysics. Folks: Harry is headed for the University of Washington in Seattle. Not because he flunked Spanish.' Bobby turned and widened his eyes at me. 'Harry has been invited as philosopher . . . in . . . residence. Not bad for an A-rab from Qatar.

'I happen to think he deserves it. Because of something he said to me this week. He said, "Robert: some people believe in reincarnation. Some believe in prayer five times a day. Some believe in holy bread and wine. These things do nothing but separate people in this life. Because these days, Robert, I can't understand a simple fact: if I really am going someplace after I die, if my spirit really does move on – what could keep it

from coming back? To my family – to friends like you? Nothing
– nothing could keep *me* back." '

It sounded so good: I could barely believe it came from me.

'And, friends, we all know how Harry would get back: on
the Dog, of course.'

Our eyes met and I laughed, with happy tears in my eyes.

'Harry wasn't born a Harry; his real name is Hanif. But
folks, he's Harry now. Harry is an American: he was naturalised seven years ago. So if you're ever on the Dog and you
spot a guy with a kinda funny way of talking, with Willie
Loman's old suitcase and, whether you realise it or not, VIP
underwear on underneath, don't give him the brush. My
recommendation – and Biscuits' – is to give him a good sniff.
If you don't smell curry, he may be Harry. Or some other
good American citizen.'

Music filled the room and Bobby started gathering together
papers. The woman said: 'Clear the studio, please.' I walked
out into the hall. After a few minutes, the door opened and
Bobby emerged smiling.

'How'd I do, Ha-rry?'

'I thought it was wonderful.'

'I told you we had to make it good. Was it good?'

'It was good.'

He pulled on a sweater. 'I think so too, Harry. But we won't
know for sure until nine' – he looked at his watch – 'when the
fans make their judgement.'

The fans were gathered at Bobby's favourite bar, a place
called Dead-Eye Dick's, at the edge of a large lake. It was a
Saturday night and the bar was packed with young men and
women. A juke box at the far end blared deafening music.
The crowd was forced to talk and laugh at the top of their
voices. I stuck close to Bobby as he manoeuvred through the
crowd, shouting greetings left and right. A breeze blew through
large windows; the lake was choppy, glints of moonlight
catching on its surface.

My eye caught a blonde girl in a filmy white dress standing

by the windows. She was waving in our direction. 'It's Molly,' I said, jabbing Bobby in the ribs. 'Over there – Molly!' I waved at her madly like a long lost friend. We bought beer from the bar and joined her.

Molly gave me a peck on my cheek and rubbed my back. 'It's so good to see you.'

Her kiss almost sent me swooning.

'How did the recording go?'

'Super.'

Bobby looked at his wrist-watch. 'Half an hour.'

'I can't wait to hear it,' she said. 'Are you excited, Harry?'

'Oh yes.' I was looking at her hair, which cascaded over her impressive breasts.

At 9 p.m., the bartender shut off the juke box and turned on a radio. The crescendo of voices subsided to a murmur. A car commercial came on the radio, followed by another for a pizza chain. Then Bobby's voice, sounding mechanical and artificial, echoed across the room.

'Welcome to My Life . . .'

The crowd went completely quiet. For a brief moment, virtually every head in the bar turned towards Bobby.

Bobby stood. 'That's my cue.' He turned and walked to the darkened jukebox.

'He always does this,' said Molly. 'I think he has to concentrate. Or maybe he's embarrassed.'

Bobby grabbed the sides of the jukebox as if for support. His face was now in profile: he had an intense expression, similar to the one when he worked on the computer.

' . . . Jottings of a Confirmed Itinerant. By Robert Spooner . . .'

I stood with a hand in my pocket, gripping my mug of beer as tightly as I could without breaking it. I was nervous but my brain had never been more alert in my life. Every word that Bobby spoke was like a word from heaven.

The crowd laughed about the Cheez Doodles and Good-N-Plenty. When Bobby reached the section in which my name was introduced, Molly raised her arm and pointed downward over my head. I grabbed her hand.

'Later,' I said. 'Let them listen.'

The laughs and wisecracks fell off when Bobby got to the serious part. I felt an indescribable thrill when he mentioned my philosophy: 'Nothing could keep *me* back.' Molly was beaming at me as if I were a genius. I think it was the happiest moment of my life.

The broadcast ended to thunderous applause. Molly gave me a kiss on both cheeks. Then she hooked her arm in mine and we marched to the bar, where Bobby was ordering a beer.

'It was okay.' Bobby looked over-serious. 'But the curry line in the end didn't work.'

'What do you mean?' I asked.

'The logic broke down.'

'How?'

'A person who smells like curry could still be an American. He may be an Indian immigrant.'

I nodded.

'Forget it,' said Molly. 'It was wonderful. I'm proud of the both of you.' She embraced the two of us simultaneously.

'Couldn't have done it without Ha-rry!' Bobby put his arm around my shoulder and gave a tight squeeze.

A tall girl in shorts joined us at the bar. She had the most muscular pair of legs I had ever seen on a woman. Bobby and she kissed – and not on the cheeks. Bobby introduced her as Heather, which I mistook to be 'Feather'. I called her Feather several times before being corrected. We drank pitcher after pitcher of beer and ate popcorn and French fries. We left the bar at 2 a.m. and drove back to the trailer. Bobby and his girlfriend were in one car and Molly and me in another. Biscuits, who was on a long leash outside the trailer, gave us her customary welcome of barks, jumps and licks. We sat for a while in the living-room and heard a hair-raising tale of Heather's latest rock-climbing exploit in the Rockies. Then the party split in two. Heather disappeared, followed by Bobby.

Molly said she had to use the bathroom. I went around the living-room turning off lights. Soon I was hearing noises from Bobby's bedroom. Molly returned. She came to me on the couch and kneeled in front of me, grasping my hands. We kissed.

We spent the night making love, as did Bobby and Heather.

I woke to the sound of crows the next morning. Out of the window, the first rays of dawn were creeping up behind the mountains. I turned to cuddle Molly but she wasn't there. I shut my eyes. Vivid images of our hugging and caressing flashed through my mind. I had never felt so invigorated in my life. I swung my legs off the couch and was just about to get up when I noticed a piece of paper lying beside the pillow. It had neat handwriting.

Harry Dear,
Sorry but my parents are coming to visit and my house is
a mess. How about getting together at Dead-Eye Dick's
tonight? Heather and I will be there at 8. I hope you guys
can make it.
Much love,
Molly
P.S. Great kisser! Do they communicate with tongues in
Qatar?

I was amazed at how wilful and independent American girls were. They drove cars, had their own houses, invited men out to bars and complimented them on their love-making. I put the coffee pot on the stove. Then, as I did every morning, I switched on the small radio lying on the kitchen counter. A deep male voice cut through the silence all around:

'A symbol of America's pioneer past, the Rockies are unsurpassed in their grandeur and massiveness . . .'

I opened the door and took in their majestic sweep. To

behold such a splendid sight while sipping morning coffee had to be one of the great pleasures of life.

The voice on the radio went on: 'The history of America is a history of the Rockies and its pull on a new nation: a nation of people being drawn westward to find land, to find gold, to find themselves.'

I pondered the words. It was what set our races apart. For the white man, travel was education, expansion, an exercise in self-discovery; for the average Indian, it was nothing but a dilution of his essential. Travelling across the waters was proscribed for the Hindus by the very Vedas. No wonder India was such a failure.

Bobby emerged from his bedroom yawning.

'Morning, Harry.' He held his head. 'We must have drunk enough last night to sink a battleship.'

'A whale.'

'So did you have a good time last night, Harry, or what?'

'It was heavenly.'

'The couch wasn't too uncomfortable?'

'It was perfect.'

'Attaboy, Harry. Be with you in a minute.' Bobby staggered to the bathroom, coughing. I heard him run the water. After a while, he joined me by the door of the trailer, face still damp and hair pulled fully back from his face.

'Lovely morning.'

'It's beautiful, isn't it?' I turned to face him. 'Bobby, I was just thinking. I'm enjoying myself so much here. With you. With Molly.'

Bobby gave me a puzzled look. 'What, Harry?'

'My programme is beginning soon.'

'Just when we were getting to know Harry the man, we lose Harry the philosopher.'

'I wish I could stay forever.'

'You're welcome, Harry. Any time.'

I wondered if the university authorities were anxious about me. Perhaps they had already informed the police that I was missing. 'I have a small problem. I wonder if my bus ticket is valid.'

'Why?'

'I don't think I was allowed to get off.'

'It was a non-stop fare?'

I nodded.

'Well, Harry, you may just have a problem.' Bobby walked to the telephone. 'Where's your ticket, Harry? It should have the number for Greyhound.'

I got a plastic packet from my suitcase in which I kept my ticket, documents and an assortment of newspaper clippings. I took out the ticket but there was no telephone number on it.

'Look on the folder,' he said.

I spread the contents of the packet on the dining table and searched for the ticket folder. I found it and read out the number to Bobby.

Billy dialled the number and then hung up. 'It's busy.'

'Would you mind if I went for a walk?'

'Not at all, Harry.' Bobby poured himself a cup of coffee. 'Enjoy the mountains while you can.'

'I won't take long.'

I picked a trail I knew from previous walks. It wound past boulders, bushes and stunted trees with twisted branches. Birds flew overhead and the odd butterfly hung in the air. I moved up the path with surprisingly little effort. It was as if the night had bestowed on me an inexhaustible supply of energy. I soon reached the summit and looked down. Bobby's trailer below appeared no larger than a matchbox.

A cool breeze caressed my face. The sun, looking like a half-cut orange, peeped over two cliffs in the distance. This was life, I told myself. I had never appreciated nature back home. Somehow, only here, in a foreign land, did it seem significant. I wondered if there was a reason: had something been opened up to me? Looking down, I realised a small sadness was part of my euphoria: I would have to leave soon. I watched Bobby's trailer, motionless, and vowed I would return as often as I could to this site of my American awakening.

As I raced back to the trailer the sun was rising in the sky. I wondered if Bobby had got through to Greyhound and if my ticket was still valid. If not, I might be able to borrow from him and return the money by post from Seattle. I knew Bobby wouldn't mind. He certainly trusted me by now. If the situation was reversed, I'd lend him any amount of money he requested, even if I had to steal or go to jail! And I hardly wanted to ask the money of the university people who appeared to me, in contrast to Bobby, towering figures of immense distance and foreignness.

When I was several hundred metres from the trailer I saw the figure of a man standing in the trailer doorway. He was erect and motionless and he held his hands behind him like a soldier. I was reminded of my wrestling coach at school who would plant his feet firmly apart and challenge any student to budge him. It wasn't Bobby, I knew, because Bobby never stood with feet wide apart like John Wayne. Who could it be? Molly's father? Her brother?

As I got closer, I realised my mistake. It was Bobby, but not the Bobby I had known. His eyebrows were bunched together in knots. His forehead was a bed of wrinkles. His mouth was clamped, which was extremely unusual: Bobby always kept his mouth a little open as if in perpetual wonderment at the world.

My pace slackened. Perhaps Bobby was doing an imitation of someone. He had a penchant for mimicry. Who was he imitating? Muhammed Ali? Rambo?

I walked forward. A dark object caught my eye. It was my suitcase, resting on one of the steps leading to the trailer.

I looked up at Bobby's frightening face. 'What happened?'
Bobby looked over my head.
'Bobby,' I stammered. 'What's going on?'
He lowered his gaze slowly.
'What?' I pleaded. I could feel my heart pound.

He stared at me for a milli-second. Then, uttering each word slowly and deliberately, he said: 'You know.'

I looked at him.

'You know . . . *Hah*-ri.'

My chin started to tremble.

I saw Bobby's right hand move from behind his back. Between his thumb and index finger was a blue-coloured booklet. It was my passport. I stared timorously at the three lions of the Ashoka pillar.

'I'm sorry, Bobby.'

'You're not from Qatar.'

'No, I'm not. I'm sorry.'

'You're not a sheikh's son.' Bobby spoke through clenched teeth. 'You're not anything you said you were. You're not even a fucking American.'

I wanted to say something but couldn't.

'You're a fucking Indian.'

I bowed my head.

'You're a – a towel head. A guy from the land of the plague! Living in my trailer. Drinking from my glasses. Fucking *my* friends.' He raised the hand holding the passport. 'Fucking me over completely.'

I felt dizzy.

'You're a *liar*,' he shouted. 'Hari Fucking Rana. I can hardly believe it: you're an Indian!'

Bobby's voice jolted me back to my senses. 'What was all that bullshit? About Fatima and Mohammed and peacocks crying for rain. I should've known: it doesn't rain in Arabia.'

Tears welled in my eyes. 'The peacocks were real. They're in India.'

'Great.'

'My lips quivered. 'I did it for you, Bobby.'

He made a gesture of violent impatience.

'It was you . . . you asked me to make it good.'

'You call that good?'

'For your programme.'

'*Good?*' Bobby thrust his head forward. 'You made a fool of me.'

I looked at him.

'That's *my* broadcast. You may think it's something stupid, something silly, like my family does – but my ass is on the line every week. That's *me* every week. That's what I *am.*' He punched his chest with a fist. 'Thousands of people listen to that broadcast. They know Robert Spooner for what he tells them every Saturday night at nine. You made me lie on air. And that's something Robert Spooner doesn't *do*. I don't know how to handle this. I guess I'll have to do another programme, next week, saying I was hoodwinked. Maybe that's the best I can do. By some guy off the Greyhound bus . . . a stranger . . . I don't know.'

I was looking at my feet. Suddenly I saw Bobby's shoes. I saw his hand, his arm, as he leaned down and picked up the passport in the mud. He wiped it on a blue-jeaned thigh. 'Here.' Bobby held out my passport.

I shook my head.

'Take it. It's yours. You're the Indian.'

We were on the same level now. I looked at him. He seemed softer.

'Go on.'

I accepted the passport.

'You better go.' He pointed to my suitcase.

'My bus ticket . . . ?'

'It's invalid.'

'I have no money.'

'I paid for a new one. I charged it. You just go to the ticket counter and tell them your name. Your real name.'

'How do I get to the station?'

'Cut through the forest and hitch a ride from the road.'

I swallowed. I picked up my suitcase. Bobby turned and walked up the steps.

I had barely gone fifty feet when I heard a noise. It was

Biscuits. She had slipped through Bobby's legs and was running towards me.

'Biscuits!' yelled Bobby. 'Get inside.'

Biscuits lowered her tail and scampered back into the trailer. I walked on.

'Ha-rry,' shouted Bobby.

I stopped and, reluctantly, looked back.

'Give 'em hell, Harry. Back in India.'

The words hit like a bullet in the heart.

American Letter
by Hari Rana

The plague has reached a horrible peak. There are headlines in *The New York Times, USA Today* and *The Wall Street Journal* about thousands of victims, disruption of essential services and widespread panic. The cover of *Time* shows a team of doctors wearing masks surrounding a bed-ridden man, scrawny, with swollen armpits and a look of terror on his face. The caption: 'The Terrifying Face of Plague'.

I am on the bus, midway between Bobby's place and Seattle, eating a doughnut with chocolate sprinkles and reading discarded newspapers and magazines. Everything is as it was. Indeed, I might never have left the bus. The people seem the same, in their stretchlon jeans and slogan-scrawled T-shirts. The driver is identical: a nondescript fatty in a uniform and peaked cap leaking rusty jokes. The bus might be the very vehicle, with its broken recliners and chemical toilet smell. Everything is as it was a week before, except for the old lady with her flask and she is hardly missed.

We drive by mile after mile of mountains interspersed with identical-looking towns bearing similar-sounding names. Neon signs, full of cheer, advertise the rest stops but they are filled with morose travellers. Hoardings urge the traveller to tune in to the local radio station for the latest weather forecast, as if the weather could have any effect on his sagging spirits.

We stop at an underground bus station with rows of dusty buses. The air has a dank, pungent odour reminiscent of bat or vulture droppings. I use the toilet. Men lurk around furtively, waiting, not even bothering to wash their hands or make other pretences.

Outside, a man in tattered clothes accosts me. 'Got some change?'

I walk past two white women smoking. 'I don't know about you,' says one. 'But I'm going to get myself a man at the next stop.'

And give him AIDS, I think.

Later, as the bus pulls away from the station. A woman across the aisle says to me: 'And where are you from?'

I shrug.

'I thought you may be from . . .'

'I'm sorry.' I look at her: her eyes, which are milky blue, her curly brown hair, her pendant pointing towards a crack of white flesh. She squints kindly, trying to understand what I am trying to convey. The smile exposes fine wrinkles at the corners of her eyes. I am forced to look away.

'Maybe you just want to be left . . .'

'I'm sorry. It's not you.' I stand, grab my suitcase and move up the aisle to another seat. I can't look at the woman: I don't know how she takes it. I don't speak to another soul for the rest of the journey.

The Times of India
'Land of Satan'

Sir:

It is said that America was discovered by a sailor (who was really looking for India). Within that statement one can find the kernel of all the conceit that Americans suffer from. How absurd and arrogant for (white) Americans to claim that their ancestors 'discovered' the country. How could that be when America was already there! It had existed as the homeland of native Indians for thousands of years before Columbus swept up on its shores. Still, the white man has made the world believe that it was he who 'discovered' America.

Pandit Nehru, perhaps the most deracinated Indian public figure to date, took a leaf out of the white man's book when he wrote *Discovery of India*. In his Independence Day speech, Nehru went so far as to speak of the 'birth' of India as a unified, independent nation. Ha! Like America, India existed as a civilizational unit long before it became a so-called nation state. Whatever the illusions of Nehru and his colonial mentors, India was neither a creation nor an invention of the British.

In fact, it is the idea of the nation state – Europe's gift to the rest of the world – that is the root of all our problems. Before the nation state came into being, smaller kingdoms paid bigger ones some sort of token obeisance and were left alone in return. Thus China and Tibet lived in peace for centuries – until the British came along and told the Chinese where their boundaries ended. The result: China invaded Tibet.

Today, the role of global troublemaker has been assumed by the United States of America. This 'Land of Satan', as Ayatollah Khomeni aptly named it, follows a simple strategy to ensure its enduring prosperity: First, it creates friction among the smaller nations of the so-called Third World (just like the British created hostility between

Hindus and Muslims to divide India). Then it sells them weapons of war. As long as the wretched of the earth keep at each other's throats, American GNP can never go down.

I recently undertook a trip to America. I had no desire to discover it anyway – it was a chance scholarship in philosophy to an American university that took me there. I went with the hope of learning something from Americans and perhaps teaching them something about India in return. But they wished to learn nothing from me. For Americans think they own the world. They appear to be friendly and down to earth, but are in fact the most arrogant and selfish people. There are some Americans who like Indians (and presumably other Asians) but that's only because they find Asians exotic. The fascination soons wears off, giving way to naked hatred and contempt. To cut a long story short, I returned home without going to the American university for even a single day.

God's chosen land, as Americans like to call their country, is in fact a living Hell: it is the most violent, immoral, soulless place on earth. A country where:
– One out of six adults has suffered child abuse.
– Almost a third of the population commits adultery.
– 54 per cent people privately admit to holding racist views.
– Fully 91 per cent regularly tell lies.

Someone once said that America is the only nation in history that has miraculously gone directly from barbarism (presumably after its 'discovery') to degeneration without the usual interval of civilization. On the day that I left the country, I bought a book at the airport. Entitled *The Day America Told the Truth*, it is the most comprehensive survey of private morals ever conducted in that nation. There is a chilling confession in the book that I will never forget. A murderer recounts how he severed the jugular vein of a sleeping woman and then 'counted her heartbeats out of curiosity to see how long it'd take her to die'. The confession ends with these words: 'I knew exactly what I was doing . . . I knew it was against the law . . . I felt powerful, invincible, sort of, you know?'

Readers be warned. That man was sort of like America.
Hari Rana
New Delhi

December 10, 1992

Ashit Chatterjee,
News Editor,
Union News International,
Claridges Hotel
New Delhi 110 003

Colonel Narendra Pai
Lancer's Lodge
P.O. Urulikanchan
Dist. Pune 412 202

Dear Colonel Pai:

This letter is on behalf of my ex-colleague, Hari Rana, who has requested me to forward a letter to you. As you can see from the letter-head above, I am the News Editor at the UNI bureau in New Delhi. As such, I am the man who guides with tender but firm hand all the coverage of the bureau, ordering reporters impulsively here and there, mediating with governments, shouting down the lines to parts hither and thither and guiding stories from first capital to final full stop by way of correcting its grammer, fixing spelings and generally sproocing up myriad finishing touches. So next time you see a UNI story from India, Nepal, Bangladesh, Sri Lanka or Bhutan, you can be sure that Ashit Chatterjee had his hands in it, even if it bears some other ostensible byeline. Maldives too.

Hari undoubtedly told you about me in his letters, Colonel Sir, which I imagine were full of tales about me. We shared exciting times, Hari and me (and some less distinguishable others) and he liked putting them all down on paper. 'He liked to write' – that's how he's fondly remembered by our bureau chief, Damon Hatcher, the latest in our line of *firangi* nagas, our collective recompense for horrible sins in our past lives.

We must have been *kutta*-fuckers, Colonel Sir, to deserve such fates. I could go on at length. But this letter is about Hari.

It should be pointed out at this point that Hari's departure was, in fact, a major blow to me personally and a setback to my life-long goal of levelling the racial playing field at the bureau, even at the expense of killing off the other team. He resigned from UNI, Colonel Sir, mere minutes after I was appointed News Editor. The timing may have been complete coincidence. Nonetheless, it was the most bitter-sweet day of my life. Sweet because I had triumphed as no Indian had triumphed before: I had become News Editor! An Indian had felt the sweet smack of flesh against the News Editor's saddle, heretofore monopolised by the broad arse of the Whiteman, and he did so not because of seniority or professional ability but because he was more cunning. What a feeling! My next goal was to take our long-running cloak-and-dagger struggle with the *firangis* to a higher plane. I was ready to ride into open battle: the dagger was poised inches from Damon Hatcher's chest! I wanted Hari with me. He had been invaluable support in the bureau's wrenching, back-stabbing political strifes, many of them due to my efforts. Then he resigned. He abandoned the battlefield for a trip abroad and the Indian staff has never managed to reunite. We are back to our guerrilla wars, Colonel Sir, although I still have hope. I know your good wishes are with me.

Despite all this, Hari was like the younger brother I never had. (Although, in fact, I have quite a few younger brothers, all jobless parasites.) And as you seem to have meant quite a lot to Hari, I have taken this liberty to write a few lines to you myself, since he has lost your address and asked that the enclosed letter be sent on to you knowing, as he did, that your address was in his address book in his desk next to the telex machine.

This might immediately set off alarm bells in your brain and, to be frank Colonel Sir, I have to admit from the start that our mutual friend Hari Rana is, in fact, missing. We have been visited by officers of the CBI and CID on a regular basis, so regular that we are thinking of inaugurating an interrogation room next to the newsroom. I have suggested the bureau chief's office – then we can send the Whiteman home where he belongs! This is just a joke.

Back to Hari. His is a most unusual story and you will be both concerned and intrigued by it, and possibly horrified. Details are forthwith and please don't let the mention of CBI concern you. They have been most courteous and although they have taken down your name and address, I am sure that being ex-Army you will not be harassed or subjected to prolonged third degree, although your neighbours will probably wag their tongues behind your back and revel in your misfortune. I, of course, as Hari's most trusted friend in all of north India – not counting Kashmir and Pakistan! – am concerned about him and his fate. Even at a time when one should be protecting one's own *chamdi*, or 'looking out for number one' (an American phrase that, I suspect, refers to an entirely different part of the anatomy), I am sticking my neck out for Hari. By writing this letter.

You are probably aware that Hari recently returned from a trip to the United States. It was his first visit to a foreign country and many were envying of him around the bureau. They were shown up good and proper, as the Americans would say. To cut what surely must have been a long story short, Hari showed up at the bureau a mere two weeks after he left, asking for work. At first I thought he had missed the plane and had been malingering around Indira Gandhi International Airport. But he told me quite plainly: 'Dada,' he said. 'I have come home.'

He looked very sad and withdrawn, as if something tragic had happened to him in America. I pressed him to tell me what was the matter, as a friend and confidante and most importantly as News Editor of the UNI bureau. All day long I was pressing him, Colonel Sir, in serious ways and joking ways and sometimes even in ways that turned angry when he would act in a manner that could only be considered disrespectful, especially to one who claimed often, or whenever convenient, to be like an elder brother to him. But Hari being Hari – he was also a very surprisingly stubborn person – didn't say a word.

When Damon Hatcher saw the look on Hari's face he immediately suspected him to be a plague carrier. Damon Hatcher, whom I have aptly nicknamed 'Danger' Hatcher, insisted that Hari be sent to the Infectious Diseases Hospital for a check-up, or else he would not be allowed to even step inside the bureau. Poor Hari had to comply, riding 20 kilometres in a bus to the hospital. He came back the next day with a report that acquitted him of plague. But in his absence, P.K., the office accountant, who is always licking 'Danger' Hatcher's arse instead of keeping clean the office books, planted the idea in his head that the Infectious Diseases Hospital (which is government-run) was a hot bed of plague germs and that anybody who visited it was bound to pick up the infection. So 'Danger' Hatcher immediately demanded that Hari be barred from the bureau.

'Barred?' I said. 'On what grounds?'

'He may be carrying the plague.'

'And where might he have picked it up?'

'At the Infectious Diseases Hospital.'

'And who sent Hari Rana to the Infectious Diseases Hospital?'

'I did.'

'Why?'

'Because I thought he might be carrying the plague.'

This is how things work at UNI, Colonel Sir.

In any case, none of us wanted to catch the plague and certain staffers had started wearing masks. P.K. wore three masks simultaneously, lined with naphthalene balls. So we jointly decided that Hari was indeed a risk and had to be gotten rid of so we sent him on the bureau budget to spend some time at the East West Medical Center, favoured by foreigners, figuring that he could at least do the country some good by passing along any infection he carried to them. He spent two nights there. Then, when P.K. got word of the expensive meals he was fed, the decision was hastily made to have him discharged.

Hari may have expected to return to his previous job in the bureau, which was chief of communications. Unfortunately this was impossible because after Hari resigned, his erstwhile assistant, Matthew, a converted Christian from Kerala, had been given his job. 'Danger' Hatcher took pity on Hari and offered him Matthew's old job as telex puncher, which luckily had not been filled yet. So Hari went to work in a dark corner of the communications room, like a character in a Premchand novel, next to an ancient machine that few bothered to use anymore. Matthew sat at a big desk managing our new computers. You can well imagine what this can do to any self-respecting man, Colonel Sir. And I don't know a more self-respecting man than Hari Rana.

Once he started sitting at the telex machine, the life-line of our business now old and stilled, Hari seemed to sink into a quicksand of despondency and self-defeat. We thought it was the bureau, the job, his tumble in station. But one day Hari indicated this wasn't so. He said: 'I'm happy to be back in the bureau with you guys, to be back here. Really.' Something had plainly gone wrong with Hari not in India but during his brief, terrible, trip abroad. He had intimated as much to me, Colonel Sir. When I asked why he had come back so soon, he merely shook his head. Why, I asked, didn't he wait until the plague had settled, until the rats had returned to their burrows, to come home? And he said, with some heat: 'They wanted me to wait. So many flights to India were cancelled. I had to change my ticket to another airline – to get back *sooner*.' Perhaps our forefathers were right about not going over the seas, Colonel Sir, the evil *kala pani*. I am against trips abroad, unless they are for necessary news trips paying considerable per diems. Recently I have spent much time in Iraq reporting the post-Gulf War situation. Fortunately too there have been two recent air crashes in Nepal.

But back to Hari. I watched with excruciating pains as he diminished day by day. I tried every tactic to get him to speak about his problem but he simply sat there in front of the telex machine virtually workless. He hardly spoke, except to our driver Omi Chand, once our peon-cum-sweeper, who insisted on being allowed to bring Hari his tea three times a day, with snacks, and wouldn't allow anyone else to perform the duty. Hari didn't join us for lunch. I was puzzled, mystified and frustrated. How, I asked myself, could a man with a mind as clear as a mirror suddenly become so inscrutable?

But Ashit Chatterjee is not someone to be defeated so easily. I took it as a personal challenge to solve the riddle of Hari Rana. I told myself, 'Ashit, what is the use of all your St Xavier's College education and traditional Bengali wisdom if you cannot figure out a simple Jat from the grimy dustbowls of Haryana? Are you a Bengali, man, or what?'

That day, I took my wife's lipstick and wrote 'HARI' on my bathroom mirror. My wife, who has an M.A. in Abnormal Psychology, suggested I read books on American Psychology. I said: 'Where is the need to study American Psychology? Since the whole world is finally veering around to the principles of ancient Indian Psychology? With its Vedic stress on detachment and also family life?' My wife and I had an ugly argument, which ended with the usual flinging of spoons and slippers and savage bumping of nether parts in the conjugal bed later on.

The next day I decided that since it was futile to try and understand Hari's problem, perhaps I should try to find a treatment for it. I decided to give him a break from his living tomb of a job. I went into 'Danger' Hatcher's office and said: 'Tomorrow is the consecration ceremony at Ayodhya.'

'Danger' Hatcher was typing something at his computer. He said without looking up at me: 'What's the story?'

'Nothing is expected to happen but we better be there.'

He looked at me and raised an eyebrow.

'In case something *does* happen.'

'But you just said . . .' (I won't bore you with the rest of this conversation, Colonel Sir, one of many we endure working for the Whiteman day in and day out.)

I'm sure you know the background to the Ayodhya story, but the Indian press has made such a hotchpotch of it I feel personally and professionally obliged to clarify it, especially for subscribers in far off parts such as the South. As you know, the whole controversy revolves around an ugly little dump of a building sitting on a dusty hill in Ayodhya. Hindus say the structure was originally a temple in honour of their god, Ram, and that Muslim invaders demolished it in the 16th century and converted it into a mosque; Muslims concede it might have been a temple at one point in time but now it is the Babri Mosque. And once a place becomes a mosque it remains a mosque and nothing but a mosque. Nothing surprising about that: Muslim fanaticism is well known to everybody. And nothing surprising, either, about the Hindu threat to tear down the mosque and build a Ram Temple: after all, they have suffered this humiliation for 464 years, their patience is running out and the building is a mildewy piece of crud that anyone with the least bit of taste would approve of tearing down, especially if it is a mosque.

But taste is not the point. In the ultimate analysis this is all bloody propaganda that harms nobody but the nation. Recently the Buddhists jumped into the fray, saying the disputed structure is neither a temple or a mosque but a Buddhist shrine! Next thing you know the Jews will be saying it is a synagogue and the Sikhs will be saying it is a bloody Gurudwara so that they can make it a militants' *adda*. And who knows? Even the Christians might join in and start holding masses in Ayodhya to aid in the converting of the masses. That leaves the Jains, but I don't think they would like to antagonise their Hindu brothers in view of what could happen to the millions of insects in case of mass gatherings, riots, etc., and maybe the earthworms too.

All of which brings us to the BJP. These scoundrels have invaded Parliament by exploiting the Ayodhya issue. (I have no personal animus against BJP or RSS, Colonel Sir. My only objection is that who the hell made this bunch of knicker-wallahs the self-appointed leaders of Hindus when the battle-field of the Hindu reform movement has historically been in Bengal!) Two years ago, these BJP-RSS crooks instigated brainless youths to attack the disputed structure in Ayodhya, which led to riots all over India in which about 1,000 people were killed. And now these rabid, blood-thirsty mongrels, who have given Hinduism and India enough of a bad name, are marching to Ayodhya once more with promises of building a new Ram Temple on the exact spot where the Babri Mosque stands. If Mrs Gandhi was alive she would have had them shot or at least knee-capped. But alas, India is rudder-less today.

'And,' I said to 'Danger' Hatcher. 'I'd like to take along Hari.'

'Hari?'

'There might be problems in filing the story. The nearest telex office is seven kilometres away.'

'So?'

'So I could waste time getting to and from the telex office. Hari can do it. He's done it before. He's not doing anything here anyway.'

'Take him.'

I went to the communications room. Hari was sitting in front of the telex machine.

'Hari.'

'Yes, Dada.'

'I want you to come with me on a reporting trip.'

He sighed and looked away.

'Hari. We're leaving early tomorrow morning. The Lucknow flight. We're going to Ayodhya.'

He didn't react.

'Hari,' I called. 'Shape up, man!'

'I'm fine.'

'No you're not, Hari. I know you've had a hard time. But bloody hell, man – are you listening? – bloody hell, stand up for something!'

He nodded wanly.

We flew to Lucknow, then hired a car to Ayodhya. The drive was two hours on difficult roads; Hari didn't say a word. When we reached the town it was swarming with people. We traversed narrow streets, passing countless little temples painted in bright primary colours, until we got to the Babri Mosque: a squat, ancient-looking edifice with three domes, the middle being the largest, standing all by itself atop a small hill. It was protected on all sides by three concentric rings of barbed-wire fencing. Below the hill were rolling grounds where thousands of people were moving about like a colony of ants. The great majority were the *kar sevaks*, a motley crowd of villagers and townsfolk for whom a free trip to Ayodhya was as much an outing as a demonstration of religious faith. They cheered lustily and listened with rapt attention to the amplified speeches of politicians and ash-smeared ascetics.

The first thing Hari and I saw was a mob of *kar sevaks*, barely 20 metres ahead, trampling the outermost ring of fencing. Inside the fence was the middle ring and then the first: within that were khaki-clad troops pointing their sub-machine-guns at the busy devotees.

We shoved our way through the crowds until we joined a group of foreign correspondents.

'What's going on?'

A German photographer armed with an array of cameras, said: 'The bastards have torn down the fence. They're going in.'

I saw a dozen wiry young men with shaved heads and saffron headbands climbing the second barbed-wire barricade. They moved with the nimbleness of monkeys. The crowd around them was shouting '*Ram Lalla hum ayen hain, mandir yahin banayen ge.*'

'Hari,' I shouted. 'Get some quotes. From them.' I pointed at the *kar sevaks*. 'I'll talk to the cops.'

I ran towards a brick building that served as the police barracks, 30 metres from the mosque. An officer with a pistol strapped to his waist was standing with a group of policemen. They were silently watching the spectacle. I strode up to the officer.

'Why aren't you doing anything?' I demanded. 'The mosque is being attacked.'

'We have asked the RAF to come in.' That is the Rapid Action Force, Colonel Sir, recently created especially for riot situations.

'The RAF is 20 kilometres away.'

'They have helicopters.'

'What about you?'

'We don't have orders to shoot.'

I ran back, pushing my way through the crowd. The second fence came tumbling down like a set of nine pins.

Hari was talking to a group of devotees. I pulled him by the arm.

'Did you get any good quotes?'

He gave me a distracted look.

'Hari,' I said, shaking both his arms. 'Are you all right?'

'Do you believe in personal change, Dada?' he asked.

The crowd was getting restive, kicking up plumes of dust. The cheering grew louder. 'What are you talking about?' I had to yell to be heard above the din.

Hari yelled back: 'Who are you, Dada?'

'You, Hari Rana, are asking me who am I? Don't you know? I am Ashit Chatterjee. From Bengal. Nothing can change *me*.'

The *kar sevaks* pushed us from behind. I felt a hand on my shoulder. It was the German photographer. 'What do you think?' he said, his face bathed in sweat. 'Surely no one will get past the last fence . . .'

'The RAF should be here any minute,' I said.

'Look!' said the photographer.

He pointed beyond the last remaining barbed-wire fence. The soldiers, who just minutes before had their sub-machine-guns trained at the riotous crowd, were departing from the mosque. They marched in single file, heads bent low as if in shame, to the police barracks. The crowds jeered and taunted.

'Bloody cowards!' I swore. 'Deserters!'

The German photographer started laughing. He bent over, holding his knees. 'I told you,' he said. 'Anything is possible in India.'

I called to the soldiers: 'You'll be reported! We're getting this all down on film! Your cowardice will be broadcast world-wide!' But my voice was drowned in the noise.

Just then the final fence crashed to the ground. There was a stampede. The *kar sevaks* swept up the hill like a giant pack of rats.

One of the correspondents said: 'They've got ropes. And axes.'

Suddenly, as if by some magic trick, an array of menacing iron implements appeared in the hands of the *kar sevaks*. There were crowbars, pickaxes, huge hammers. But the worst was yet to come: for why would they need that heavy equipment if not to demolish the mosque? Why would they need shovels if not to clear the debris?

A group of lithe young men scaled the outer wall of the mosque and disappeared inside.

I looked around. 'Where's Hari? Anyone seen Hari?' The correspondents were in a frenzy, shooting photos and moving up the hill towards the mosque.

The German photographer pointed at the mosque. A lone figure was standing on the central dome, waving a red triangle-shaped flag. 'Isn't that Hari?'

I couldn't believe my eyes. Hari Rana was standing on the highest dome, waving the flag with a frightful intensity. The bellowing of a quarter million *kar sevaks* rent the air like cracks of thunder from the sky.

'Hari!' I waved my arms at him. 'What are you doing up there, Hari?'

Hari saw me. He cupped his hands before him. I heard his reply: 'I belong here.'

A group of devotees appeared at the base of the central dome. They cast grappling hooks upward and soon were standing beside Hari. One gave Hari a pickaxe. He raised it over his head and swung it downwards, burying it into the dome. Pieces of mortar flew into the air. The *kar sevaks* started chipping away at the dome with hammers and crowbars. Below, a crowd of thousands rushed forward and soon everyone was hammering the mosque with rods and implements and sticks.

Hari bent forward like a soldier about to order a charge. He had an axe over his shoulder; his face was that of a man in a great rage. He pointed, looking around to his new friends and supporters. I wondered what he was doing. Then I realised that he was pointing at the foreign correspondents. I heard him scream: '*Vo rahe sale firangi! Hamen badnam karne vale! Maro saalon ko! Khatam kar do.*' He did his own translation: 'There they are! There are our humiliators! Bash them! Finish them off!'

Immediately, a mob of *kar sevaks* started running in our direction. I shouted at the top of my voice: 'Run, everybody, *run!*'

But it was too late. A brick hit the Voice of America correspondent. He toppled, clutching his head. A group of *kar sevaks* set upon another correspondent with sticks. He fell to the ground. The mob started kicking him.

I took to my heels. As I turned onto the narrow road leading to town, I stopped for a split second and looked back. Hari, his body convulsed forward, was still stabbing his finger at the Whitemen.

And that, Colonel Sir, is the last anyone saw of Hari Rana.

Dear Col. Pai,

I wanted you to know that I have come to the end of my lengthy journey. I lost my way and endured many hardships. But now I am home. I would like to write more – the empty page cries out to me and I have so many wonderful new tales I could tell! – but I now believe this to have been one of the false trails I followed. So I will put down my pen now, Col. Pai, and Hari Rana, writer, will take his final leave. Please know that he has discovered who he is.

I have found peace.

Your former pen-friend but eternal *Hindu bhai*,
Hari Rana